# THE EPICUREAN

## A TALE.

AND

# ALCIPHRON:

## A POEM.

*The Garden*

# THE EPICUREAN

A Tale.

AND

# ALCIPHRON: A Poem.

By THOMAS MOORE.

WITH VIGNETTE ILLUSTRATIONS
By J. M. W. TURNER, R.A.

**University Press of the Pacific**
**Honolulu, Hawaii**

The Epicurean: A Tale
and Alciphron: A Poem


by
Thomas Moore

ISBN: 1-4102-0808-7

Reprinted from the 1877 edition

University Press of the Pacific
Honolulu, Hawaii
http://www.universitypressofthepacific.com

In order to make original editions of historical works
available to scholars at an economical price, this
facsimile of the original edition of 1877 is
reproduced from the best available copy and has
been digitally enhanced to improve legibility, but the
text remains unaltered to retain historical
authenticity.

# PRELIMINARY NOTICE.

To introduce thus, by a new preface, to my readers, a work which has been for so many years before the public, and which, however undeserving of such notice, has been translated into most of the languages of Europe,* may be regarded as rather an unnecessary ceremony. Some circumstances, however, connected with this new edition, as well as with the Poems subjoined to the narrative, seem to require from me a few prefatory words. The idea of calling in the magic pencil of Mr. Turner, to illustrate some of the scenes of the following story, was first suggested by the late Mr. Macrone,—to whose general talents and enterprising spirit all who knew him will bear ready and

---

* Among the translations which have reached me are two in French, one in Italian (Milan, 1836, 24mo,—Venice, 1835), one in German (Inspruc, 1828), and one in Dutch, by Mr. Herman van Loghem (Deventer, 1829).

cordial testimony.   His original wish had been that
I should undertake for him some new poem, or story,
to be thus embellished by the artist.   But other tasks
and ties having rendered my compliance with this
wish impracticable, he proposed to purchase of me
the copyright of the Epicurean, for a single "illustrated" edition ; and hence the appearance of the
work under its present new auspices and form.

A few more words remain to be said, respecting
the Poems which occupy a portion of this volume ;
and which, with the exception of a few fragments of
them found scattered through the prose narrative, are
here, for the first time, published.   My original plan,
in commencing the story of the Epicurean, was to
write it all in verse, and in the form, as will be seen,
of letters from the different personages.   But the
great difficulty of managing, in rhyme, the minor details of a story, so as to be clear without becoming
prosaic, and, still more, the diffuse length to which
I saw narration in verse would be likely to run, de-
terred me from pursuing this plan any further ; and
I then commenced the tale anew, in its present shape.
Whether I was wrong or right in this change, my
readers have now an opportunity of judging for themselves.

In the Letters of Alciphron will be found,—heightened only by a freer use of poetic colouring,—nearly the same details of events, feelings, and scenery which occupy the earlier part of the prose narrative. But the Letter of the hypocritical High Priest, whatever else may be its claim to attention, will be found, both in matter and form, new to the reader.

THOMAS MOORE.

# A LETTER TO THE TRANSLATOR

FROM

———, Esq.

Cairo, June 19, 1800.

My dear Sir,

In a visit lately paid by me to the monastery of St. Macarius,—which is situated, as you know, in the Valley of the Lakes of Natron,—I was lucky enough to obtain possession of a curious Greek manuscript, which, in the hope that you may be induced to translate it, I herewith transmit to you. Observing one of the monks very busily occupied in tearing up into a variety of fantastic shapes some papers which had the appearance of being the leaves of old books, I inquired of him the meaning of his task, and received the following explanation :—

The Arabs, it seems, who are as fond of pigeons as the ancient Egyptians, have a superstitious notion that, if they place in their pigeon-houses small scraps of paper, written over with learned characters, the birds are always sure to thrive the better for the charm ; and the monks, who are never slow in profiting by superstition, have, at all times, a supply of such amulets for purchasers.

In general, the fathers of the monastery have been in the habit of scribbling these fragments themselves ; but a discovery lately made by them, saves all this trouble. Having dug up (as my informant stated) a chest of old manuscripts, which, being chiefly on the subject of alchemy, must have been buried in the time of Diocletian, "we thought," added the monk, "that we could not employ such rubbish more properly than in tearing it up, as you see, for the pigeon-houses of the Arabs."

On my expressing a wish to rescue some part of these treasures from the fate to which his indolent fraternity had consigned them, he produced the manuscript which I have now the pleasure of sending you,—the only one, he said, remaining entire,—and I very readily paid the price which he demanded for it.

You will find the story, I think, not altogether uninteresting ; and the coincidence, in many respects, of the curious details in chap. vi. with the description

of the same ceremonies in the Romance of *Sethos*, *
will, I have no doubt, strike you.   Hoping that you
may be induced to give a translation of this Tale to
the world,

I am, my dear Sir,

Very truly yours,

---

* The description here alluded to may also be found, copied
*verbatim* from Sethos, in the "Voyages d'Anténor."—"In that phi-
losophical romance, called 'La Vie de Sethos,'" says Warburton,
"we find a much juster account of old Egyptian wisdom, than in all
the pretended 'Histoire du Ciel.'"   *Div. Leg.* book iv. sect. 14.

# THE EPICUREAN.

## CHAPTER I.

IT was in the fourth year of the reign of the late
Emperor Valerian, that the followers of Epicurus,
who were at that time numerous in Athens, proceeded
to the election of a person to fill the vacant chair
of their sect;—and, by the unanimous voice of the
School, I was the individual chosen for their Chief.
I was just then entering on my twenty-fourth year,
and no instance had ever before occurred, of a person
so young being selected for that office. Youth, however, and the personal advantages that adorn it, were
not, it may be supposed, among the least valid recom-
mendations to a sect that included within its circle all
the beauty as well as the wit of Athens, and which,
though dignifying its pursuits with the name of
philosophy, was little else than a pretext for the
more refined cultivation of pleasure.

The character of the sect had, indeed, much changed,

B

since the time of its wise and virtuous founder, who, while he asserted that Pleasure is the only Good, inculcated also that Good is the only source of Pleasure. The purer part of this doctrine had long evaporated; and the temperate Epicurus would have as little recognised his own sect in the assemblage of refined voluptuaries who now usurped its name, as he would have known his own quiet Garden in the luxurious groves and bowers among which the meetings of the School were now held.

Many causes concurred, at this period, besides the attractiveness of its doctrines, to render our school by far the most popular of any that still survived the glory of Greece. It may generally be observed, that the prevalence, in one half of the community, of very rigid notions on the subject of religion, produces the opposite extreme of laxity and infidelity in the other ; and this kind of reaction it was that now mainly contributed to render the doctrines of the Garden the most fashionable philosophy of the day. The rapid progress of the Christian faith had alarmed all those who, either from piety or worldliness, were interested in the continuance of the old-established creed—all who believed in the Deities of Olympus, and all who lived by them. The consequence was, a considerable increase of zeal and activity throughout the constituted authorities and priesthood of the whole Heathen world. What was wanting in sincerity of belief was made up in rigour ;—the weakest parts of the Mythology were those, of course, most angrily defended, and any reflections, tending to bring Saturn, or his wife Ops, into contempt, were punished with the utmost severity of the law.

In this state of affairs, between the alarmed bigotry of the declining Faith, and the simple, sublime austerity of her rival, it was not wonderful that those lovers of ease and pleasure, who had no interest, reversionary or otherwise, in the old religion, and were too indolent to inquire into the sanctions of the new, should take refuge from the severities of both in the arms of a luxurious philosophy, which, leaving to others the task of disputing about the future, centred all its wisdom in the full enjoyment of the present.

The sectaries of the Garden had, ever since the death of their founder, been accustomed to dedicate to his memory the twentieth day of every month. To these monthly rites had, for some time, been added a grand annual Festival, in commemoration of his birth. The feasts given on this occasion by my predecessors in the Chair, had been invariably distinguished for their taste and splendour ; and it was my ambition, not merely to imitate this example, but even to render the anniversary now celebrated under my auspices so brilliant, as to efface the recollection of all that had preceded it.

Seldom, indeed, had Athens witnessed so bright a scene. The grounds that formed the original site of the Garden had received, from time to time, considerable additions; and the whole extent was now laid out with that perfect taste which understands how to wed Nature with Art, without sacrificing any of her simplicity to the alliance.    Walks, leading through wildernesses of shade and fragrance—glades, opening, as if to afford a playground for the sunshine—temples, rising on the very spots where Imagination herself would have called them up, and fountains and lakes, in alternate motion and repose, either wantonly courting the verdure, or calmly sleeping in its embrace,—such was the variety of feature that diversified these fair gardens; and, animated as they were on this occasion by all the living wit and loveliness of Athens, it afforded a scene such as my own youthful fancy, rich as it was then in images of luxury and beauty, could hardly have anticipated.

The ceremonies of the day began with the very dawn, when, according to the form of simpler and better times, those among the disciples who had apartments within the Garden, bore the image of our Founder in procession from chamber to chamber, chanting verses in praise of what had long ceased to be objects of our imitation—his frugality and temperance.

Round a beautiful lake, in the centre of the Garden, stood four white Doric temples, in one of which was collected a library containing all the flowers of Grecian literature; while, in the remaining three, Conversation, the Song, and the Dance, held, uninterrupted by each other, their respective rites. In the Library stood busts of all the most illustrious Epicureans, both of Rome and Greece—Horace, Atticus, Pliny the elder, the poet Lucretius, Lucian, and the lamented biographer of the Philosophers, lately lost to us, Diogenes Laertius. There were also the portraits, in marble, of all the eminent female votaries of the school—Leontium and her fair daughter Danae, Themista, Philænis, and others.

It was here that, in my capacity of Heresiarch, on the morning of the Festival, I received the felicitations of the day from some of the fairest lips of Athens ; and, in pronouncing the customary oration to the memory of our Master (in which it was usual to dwell upon the doctrines he had inculcated), endeavoured to attain that art, so useful before such an audience, of lending to the gravest subjects a charm, which secures them listeners even among the simplest and most volatile.

Though study, as may be supposed, engrossed but little the nights or mornings of the Garden, yet all the lighter parts of learning—that portion of its attic honey, for which the bee is not compelled to go very deep into the flower—was rather zealously cultivated by us. Even here, however, the young student had to encounter that kind of distraction, which is, of all others, the least favourable to composure of thought ; and, with more than one of my fair disciples, there used to occur such scenes as the following, which a poet of the Garden, taking his picture from the life, thus described :—

> " As o'er the lake, in evening's glow,
>   That temple threw its lengthening shade,
> Upon the marble steps below
>   There sat a fair Corinthian maid,
> Gracefully o'er some volume bending ;
>   While, by her side, the youthful Sage
> Held back her ringlets, lest, descending,
>   They should o'ershadow all the page."

But it was for the evening of that day that the richest of our luxuries were reserved. Every part of the Garden was illuminated, with the most skilful variety of lustre ; while over the lake of the Temples were scattered wreaths of flowers, through which boats, filled with beautiful children, floated, as through a liquid parterre.

Between two of these boats a mock combat was perpetually carried on ;—their respective commanders, two blooming youths, being habited to represent Eros and Anteros ; the former, the Celestial Love of the Platonists, and the latter, that more earthly spirit which usurps the name of Love among the Epicureans. Throughout the whole evening their conflict was maintained with various success ; the timid distance at which Eros kept aloof from his lively antagonist being his only safeguard against those darts of fire, with showers of which the other assailed him, but which, falling short of their mark upon the lake, only scorched the few flowers on which they fell, and were extinguished.

In another part of the gardens, on a wide glade, illuminated only by the moon, was performed an imitation of the torch-race of the Panathenæa, by young boys chosen for their fleetness, and arrayed with wings, like Cupids ; while, not far off, a group of seven nymphs, with each a star on her forehead, represented the movements of the planetary choir, and embodied the dream of Pythagoras into real motion and song.

At every turning some new enchantment broke unexpectedly on the eye or ear; and now, from the depth of a dark grove, from which a fountain at the same time issued, there came a strain of sweet music, which, mingled with the murmur of the water, seemed like the voice of the spirit that presided over its flow ;—while, at other times, the same strain appeared to come breathing from among flowers, or was heard suddenly from underground, as if the foot had just touched some spring that set its melody in motion.

It may seem strange that I should now dwell upon all these trifling details ; but they were, to me, full of the future ; and everything connected with that memorable night — even its long-repented follies— must for ever live fondly and sacredly in my memory. The festival concluded with a banquet, at which, as master of the Sect, I presided ; and being, myself, in every sense, the ascendant spirit of the whole scene, gave life to all around me, and saw my own happiness reflected in that of others.

## CHAPTER II.

THE festival was over;—the sounds of the song and dance had ceased, and I was now left in those luxurious gardens, alone. Though so ardent and active a votary of pleasure, I had, by nature, a disposition full of melancholy;—an imagination that, even in the midst of mirth and happiness, presented saddening thoughts, and threw the shadow of the future over the gayest illusions of the present. Melancholy was, indeed, twin-born in my soul with Passion; and not even in the fullest fervour of the latter, were they ever separated. From the first moment that I was conscious of thought and feeling, the same dark thread had run across the web; and images of death and annihilation came to mingle themselves with even the most smiling scenes through which love and enjoyment led me. My very passion for pleasure but deepened these gloomy thoughts. For, shut out, as I was by my creed, from a future life, and having no hope beyond the narrow horizon of this, every minute of earthly delight assumed, in my eyes, a mournful preciousness; and pleasure, like the flower of the cemetery, grew but more luxuriant from the neighbourhood of death.

This very night my triumph, my happiness, had seemed complete. I had been the presiding genius of that voluptuous scene. Both my ambition and my love of pleasure had drunk deep of the rich cup for which they thirsted. Looked up to, as I was, by the learned, and loved by the beautiful and the young, I had seen, in every eye that met mine, either the acknowledgment of bright triumphs already won, or the promise of others, still brighter, that awaited me. Yet, even in the midst of all this, the same dark thoughts had presented themselves;—the perishableness of myself and all around me had every instant recurred to my mind. Those hands I had pressed— those eyes, in which I had seen sparkling a spirit of light and life that should never die—those voices, that had talked of eternal love—all, all, I felt, were but a mockery of the moment, and would leave nothing eternal but the silence of their dust!

> Oh, were it not for this sad voice
>     Stealing amid our mirth to say,
> That all, in which we most rejoice,
>     Ere night may be the earth-worm's prey ;—
> *But* for this bitter—only this—
> Full as the world is brimm'd with bliss,
> And capable as feels my soul
> Of draining to its depth the whole,
> I should turn earth to heaven, and be,
> If bliss made gods, a deity !

Such was the description I gave of my own feelings, in one of those wild, passionate songs, to which this mixture of gaiety and melancholy, in a spirit so buoyant, naturally gave birth.

And seldom had my heart surrendered itself to this sort of vague sadness more unresistingly than at the present moment, when, as I paced thoughtfully among the fading lights and flowers of the banquet, the echo of my own step was all that now sounded, where so many gay forms had lately been revelling. The moon was still up, the morning had not yet glimmered, and the calm glories of night still rested on all around. Unconscious whither my pathway led, I wandered along, till I, at length, found myself before that fair statue of Venus, with which the chisel of Alcamenes had embellished our Garden;—that image of deified woman, the only idol to which I had ever yet bent the knee. Leaning against the pedestal of the statue, I raised my eyes to heaven, and, fixing them sadly and intently on the ever-burning stars, as if I sought to read the mournful secret in their light, asked, wherefore was it that Man alone must fade and perish, while they, so much less wonderful, less godlike than he, thus still live on in radiance un-changeable and for ever! "Oh, that there were some spell, some talisman," I exclaimed, "to make the spirit that burns within us deathless as those stars, and open to it a career like theirs, burning and inextinguishable throughout all time!"

While thus indulging in wild and melancholy fancies, I felt that lassitude which earthly pleasure, however sweet, leaves behind, come insensibly over me, and at length sunk at the base of the statue to sleep.

But even in sleep, the same fancies still haunted me; and a dream, so distinct and vivid as to leave behind it the impression of reality, thus presented itself to my mind. I found myself suddenly transported to a wide and desolate plain, where nothing appeared to breathe, or move, or live. The very sky that hung above it looked pale and extinct, giving the idea, not of darkness, but of light that had died ; and had that whole region been the remains of some older world, left broken up and sunless, it could not have presented an aspect more dead and desolate. The only thing that bespoke life, throughout this melancholy waste, was a small spark of light, that at first glimmered in the distance, but, at length, slowly approached the bleak spot where I stood. As it drew nearer, I could see that its small, but steady, gleam came from a taper in the hand of an ancient and venerable man, who now stood, like a pale messenger from the grave, before me. After a few moments of awful silence, during which he looked at me with a sadness that thrilled my very soul, he said, "Thou, who seekest eternal life, go unto the shores of the dark Nile—go unto the shores of the dark Nile, and thou wilt find the eternal life thou seekest!"

No sooner had he uttered these words than the deathlike hue of his cheek at once brightened into a smile of more than human promise; while the small torch he held in his hand sent forth a glow of radiance, by which suddenly the whole surface of the desert was illuminated;—the light spreading even as far as the distant horizon's edge, along whose line were now seen gardens, palaces, and spires, all as bright as the rich architecture of the clouds at sunset. Sweet music, too, came floating in every direction, through the air, and, from all sides, such varieties of enchantment broke upon me, that, with the excess alike of harmony and of radiance, I awoke.

That infidels should be superstitious is an anomaly neither unusual nor strange. A belief in superhuman agency seems natural and necessary to the mind ; and, if not suffered to flow in the obvious channels, it will find a vent in some other. Hence, many who have doubted the existence of a God, have yet implicitly placed themselves under the patronage of Fate or the stars. Much the same inconsistency I was conscious of in my own feelings. Though rejecting all belief in a Divine Providence, I had yet a faith in dreams that all my philosophy could not conquer. Nor was experience wanting to confirm me in my delusion ; for, by some of those accidental coincidences which make the fortune of soothsayers and prophets, dreams, more than once, had been to me

Oracles, truer far than oak,
Or dove, or tripod, ever spoke.

It was not wonderful, therefore, that the vision of that night—touching, as it did, a chord so ready to vibrate —should have affected me with more than ordinary power, and even sunk deeper into my memory with every effort I made to forget it. In vain was it that I mocked at my own weakness ;—such self-derision is seldom sincere. In vain did I pursue my accustomed pleasures. Their zest was, as usual, for ever new; but still, in the midst of all my enjoyment, came the cold and saddening consciousness of mortality, and, along with it, the recollection of this visionary promise, to which my fancy, in defiance of reason, still continued to cling.

At times, indulging in reveries, that were little else than a continuation of my dream, I even contemplated the possible existence of some mighty secret, by which our youth, if not perpetuated, might be at least prolonged, and that dreadful vicinity of death, within whose circle love pines and pleasure sickens, might be for a while averted. "Who can tell," I would ask, "but that in Egypt, that region of wonders, where Mystery hath yet unfolded but half her treasures,— where still remain, undeciphered, upon the pillars of Seth, so many written secrets of the antediluvian world—who knows but that some powerful charm, some amulet, may there lie hid, whose discovery, as this phantom hath promised, but awaits my coming,— some compound of the same pure atoms, that shine in the living stars, and whose infusion into the frame

of man might render him also unfading and immortal!"

Thus did I sometimes speculate, in those fond
rambling moods, when the life of excitement in which
I was engaged, acting upon a warm heart and vivid
fancy, produced an intoxication of spirit, during which
I was not wholly master of myself. I felt this bewilderment, too, not a little increased by the constant
struggle between my own natural feelings, and the
cold, mortal creed of my sect—in endeavouring to
escape from whose deadening bondage I but broke
loose into the realms of fantasy and romance.

Even in my calmest and soberest moments, however, that strange vision for ever haunted me ; and
every effort I made to chase it from my recollection
was unavailing. The deliberate conclusion, therefore,
to which I came at last, was, that to visit Egypt was
now my only resource ; that, without seeing that land
of wonders, I could not rest, nor, until convinced of
my folly by disappointment, be reasonable. Without
delay, accordingly, I announced to my friends of the
Garden, the intention I had formed to pay a visit to
the land of Pyramids. To none of them, however,
did I dare to confess the vague, visionary impulse
that actuated me ;—knowledge being the object that
I alleged, while Pleasure was that for which they gave
me credit. The interests of the School, it was feared,
might suffer by my absence ; and there were some
tenderer ties, which had still more to fear from separ-

ation. But for the former inconvenience a temporary remedy was provided ; while the latter a skilful distribution of vows and sighs alleviated. Being furnished with recommendatory letters to all parts of Egypt, I set sail in the summer of the year 257, A.D., for Alexandria.

## CHAPTER III.

To one, who so well knew how to extract pleasure from every moment on land, a sea-voyage, however smooth and favourable, appeared the least agreeable mode of losing time that could be devised. Often, indeed, did my imagination, in passing some isle of those seas, people it with fair forms and loving hearts, to which most willingly would I have paused to offer homage. But the wind blew direct towards the land of Mystery; and, still more, I heard a voice within me, whispering for ever, "On!"

As we approached the coast of Egypt, our course became less prosperous; and we had a specimen of the benevolence of the divinities of the Nile, in the shape of a storm, or rather whirlwind, which had nearly sunk our vessel, and which the Egyptians on board declared to be the work of their deity Typhon. After a day and night of danger, during which we were driven out of our course to the eastward, some benigner influence prevailed above; and, at length, as the morning freshly broke, we saw the beautiful city of Alexandria rising from the sea, with its proud Palace of Kings, its portico of four hundred columns, and the fair Pillar of Pillars, towering in the midst to heaven.

After passing in review this splendid vision, we shot rapidly round the Rock of Pharos, and, in a few minutes, found ourselves in the harbour of Eunostus. The sun had risen, but the light on the Great Tower of the Rock was still burning; and there was a languor in the first waking movements of that voluptuous city—whose houses and temples lay shining in silence around the harbour—that sufficiently attested the festivities of the preceding night.

We were soon landed on the quay; and, as I walked, through a line of palaces and shrines, up the street which leads from the sea to the Gate of Canopus, fresh as I was from the contemplation of my own lovely Athens, I yet felt a glow of admiration at the scene around me, which its novelty, even more than its magnificence, inspired. Nor were the luxuries and delights, which such a city promised, among the least of the considerations upon which my fancy dwelt. On the contrary, everything around me seemed prophetic of love and pleasure. The very forms of the architecture, to my Epicurean imagination, appeared to call up images of living grace; and even the dim seclusion of the temples and groves spoke only of tender mysteries to my mind. As the whole bright scene grew animated around me, I felt

c

that though Egypt might not enable me to lengthen life, she could teach the next best art, that of multiplying its enjoyments.

The population of Alexandria, at this period, consisted of the most motley miscellany of nations, religions, and sects, that had ever been brought together in one city. Beside the school of the Grecian Platonist was seen the oratory of the cabalistic Jew ; while the church of the Christian stood, undisturbed, over the crypts of the Egyptian Hierophant. Here, the adorer of Fire, from the East, laughed at the less elegant superstition of the worshipper of cats, from the West. Here Christianity, too, had learned to emulate the pious vagaries of Paganism ; and while, on one side, her Ophite professor was seen bending his knee gravely before a serpent, on the other was heard a Nicosian contending, with no less gravity, that there was no chance whatever of salvation out of the pale of the Greek alphabet. Still worse, the uncharitableness of Christian schism was already, with equal vigour, distinguishing itself ; and I heard everywhere, on my arrival, of the fierce rancour and hate with which the Greek and Latin churchmen were then persecuting each other, because, forsooth, the one fasted on the seventh day of the week, and the others fasted upon the fourth and sixth !

To none, however, of these different creeds and sects, except in as far as they furnished food for ridicule, had I time to pay much attention. I was now in the most luxurious city of the universe, and gave way, without reserve, to the various seductions that surrounded me. My reputation, both as a philosopher and a man of pleasure, had preceded my coming; and Alexandria, the second Athens of the world, welcomed me as her own. I found my celebrity, indeed, act as a talisman, that opened all hearts and doors at my approach. The usual novitiate of acquaintance was dispensed with in my favour, and not only intimacies, but loves and friendships, ripened as rapidly in my path as vegetation springs up where the Nile has flowed. The dark beauty of the Egyptian women possessed a novelty in my eyes that enhanced its other charms : and the hue left by the sun on their rounded cheeks seemed but an earnest of the genial ardour he had kindled in their hearts—

> Th' imbrowning of the fruit, that tells
> How rich within the soul of sweetness dwells.

Some weeks now passed in such constant and ever changing pleasures, that even the melancholy voice deep within my heart, though it still spoke, was but seldom listened to, and soon died away in the sound of the siren songs that surrounded me. At length, as the novelty of these gay scenes wore off, the same vague and gloomy bodings began to mingle with all my joys; and an incident that occurred at this time, during one of my gayest revels, conduced still more to deepen their gloom.

The celebration of the annual festival of Serapis

happened to take place during my stay, and I was, more than once, induced to join the gay multitudes that flocked to the shrine at Canopus on the occasion. Day and night, as long as this festival lasted, the great canal, which led from Alexandria to Canopus, was covered with boats full of pilgrims of both sexes, all hastening to avail themselves of this pious licence, which lent the zest of a religious sanction to pleasure, and gave a holiday to the passions and follies of earth, in honour of heaven.

I was returning, one lovely night, to Alexandria. The north wind, that welcome visitor, had cooled and freshened the air, while the banks, on either side of the stream, sent forth, from groves of orange and henna, the most delicious odours. As I had left all the crowd behind me at Canopus, there was not a boat to be seen on the canal but my own ; and I was just yielding to the thoughts which solitude at such an hour inspires, when my reveries were suddenly broken by the sound of some female voices, coming, mingled with laughter and screams, from the garden of a pavilion, that stood, brilliantly illuminated, upon the bank of the canal.

On rowing nearer, I perceived that both the mirth and the alarm had been caused by the efforts of some playful girls to reach a hedge of jasmine which grew near the water, and in bending towards which they had nearly fallen into the stream. Hastening to proffer my assistance, I soon recognised the voice of one of my fair Alexandrian friends, and, springing on the bank, was surrounded by the whole group, who insisted on my joining their party in the pavilion, and, having flung the tendrils of jasmine, which they had just plucked, around me, led me, no unwilling captive, to the banquet-room.

I found here an assemblage of the very flower of Alexandrian society. The unexpectedness of the meeting added new zest to it on both sides; and seldom had I ever felt more enlivened, myself, or contributed more successfully to circulate life among others.

Among the company were some Greek women, who, according to the fashion of their country, wore veils; but, as usual, rather to set off than conceal their beauty, some bright gleams of which were continually escaping from under the cloud. There was, however, one female, who particularly attracted my attention, on whose head was a chaplet of dark-coloured flowers, and who sat veiled and silent during the whole of the banquet. She took no share, I observed, in what was passing around : the viands and the wine went by her untouched, nor did a word that was spoken seem addressed to her ear. This abstraction from a scene so sparkling with gaiety, though apparently unnoticed by any one but myself, struck me as mysterious and strange. I inquired of my fair neighbour the cause of it, but she looked grave and was silent.

In the mean time, the lyre and the cup went round; and a young maid from Athens, as if inspired by the presence of her countryman, took her lute, and sung to it some of the songs of Greece, with a warmth of feeling that bore me back to the banks of the Ilissus, and, even in the bosom of present pleasure, drew a sigh from my heart for that which had passed away. It was daybreak ere our delighted party rose, and most unwillingly re-embarked to return to the city.

We were scarce afloat, when it was discovered that the lute of the young Athenian had been left behind; and, with a heart still full of its sweet sounds, I most readily sprang on shore to seek it. I hastened at once to the banquet-room, which was now dim and solitary, except that there, to my astonishment, was still seated that silent figure, which had awakened my curiosity so strongly during the night. A vague feeling of awe came over me, as I now slowly approached it. There was no motion, no sound of breathing, in that form; — not a leaf of the dark chaplet upon its brow stirred. By the light of a dying lamp which stood before the figure, I raised, with a hesitating hand, the veil, and saw—what my fancy had already anticipated—that the shape underneath was lifeless, was a skeleton! Startled and shocked, I hurried back with the lute to the boat, and was almost as silent as that shape itself during the remainder of the voyage.

This custom among the Egyptians of placing a mummy, or skeleton, at the banquet-table, had been for some time disused, except at particular ceremonies; and, even on such occasions, it had been the practice of the luxurious Alexandrians to disguise this memorial of mortality in the manner just described. But to me, who was wholly unprepared for such a spectacle, it gave a shock from which my imagination did not speedily recover. This silent and ghastly witness of mirth seemed to imbody, as it were, the shadow in my own heart. The features of the grave were thus stamped upon the idea that had long haunted me, and this picture of what I was *to be*, now associated itself constantly with the sunniest aspect of what I *was*.

The memory of the dream now recurred to me more livelily than ever. The bright, assuring smile of that venerable Spirit, and his words, "Go to the shores of the dark Nile, and thou wilt find the eternal life thou seekest," were for ever before my mind. But as yet, alas, I had done nothing towards realizing the proud promise. Alexandria was not Egypt;—the very soil on which it now stood was not in existence when already Thebes and Memphis had numbered ages of glory.

"No!" I exclaimed; "beneath the Pyramids of Memphis, or in the mystic Halls of the Labyrinth, can I alone hope to find those holy arcana of science, of which the antediluvian world has made Egypt its heir, and among which—blest thought !—the key to eternal life may lie."

Having formed my determination, I took leave of my many Alexandrian friends, and departed for Memphis.

## CHAPTER IV.

EGYPT was, perhaps, the country beyond all others, from that mixture of the melancholy and the voluptuous which marked the character of her people, her religion, and her scenery, to affect deeply a fancy and temperament like mine, and keep both for ever tremblingly alive. Wherever I turned, I beheld the desert and the garden, mingling together their desolation and bloom. I saw the love-bower and the tomb standing side by side, as if, in that land, Pleasure and Death kept hourly watch upon each other. In the very luxury of the climate there was the same saddening influence. The monotonous splendour of the days, the solemn radiance of the nights—all tended to cherish that ardent melancholy, the offspring of passion and of thought, which had been so long the familiar inmate of my soul.

When I sailed from Alexandria, the inundation of the Nile was at its full. The whole valley of Egypt lay covered by its flood : and, as, looking around me,

I saw in the light of the setting sun, shrines, palaces, and monuments, encircled by the waters, I could almost fancy that I beheld the sinking island of Atalantis, on the last evening its temples were visible above the wave. Such varieties, too, of animation as presented themselves on every side !—

> While, far as sight could reach, beneath as clear
> And blue a heaven as ever bless'd this sphere,
> Gardens, and pillar'd streets, and porphyry domes,
> And high-built temples, fit to be the homes
> Of mighty gods,—and pyramids, whose hour
> Outlasts all time, above the waters tower !
>
> Then, too, the scenes of pomp and joy, that make
> One theatre of this vast peopled lake,
> Where all that Love, Religion, Commerce gives
> Of life and motion, ever moves and lives.
> Here, up the steps of temples, from the wave
> Ascending, in procession slow and grave,
> Priests, in white garments, go, with sacred wands
> And silver cymbals gleaming in their hands :
> While, there, rich barks—fresh from those sunny tracts
> Far off, beyond the sounding cataracts—
> Glide with their precious lading to the sea :
> Plumes of bright birds, rhinoceros' ivory,
> Gems from the Isle of Meröe, and those grains
> Of gold, wash'd down by Abyssinian rains.
>
> Here, where the waters wind into a bay
> Shadowy and cool, some pilgrims on their way
> To Saïs or Bubastus, among beds
> Of lotus-flowers, that close above their heads,
> Push their light barks, and hid, as in a bower,
> Sing, talk, or sleep away the sultry hour ;
> While haply, not far off, beneath a bank
> Of blossoming acacias, many a prank

Is play'd in the cool current by a train
Of laughing nymphs, lovely as she whose chain
Around two conquerors of the world was cast,
But, for a third too feeble, broke at last !

Enchanted with the whole scene, I lingered de-
lightedly on my voyage, visiting all those luxurious
and venerable places, whose names have been consecrated by the wonder of ages. At Saïs I was present
during her Festival of Lamps, and read, by the blaze
of innumerable lights, those sublime words on the
temple of Neïtha :—" I am all that has been, that is,
and that will be, and no man hath ever lifted my
veil." I wandered among the prostrate obelisks of
Heliopolis, and saw, not without a sigh, the sun
smiling over her ruins, as if in mockery of the mass of
perishable grandeur, that had once called itself, in its
pride, " The City of the Sun." But to the Isle of the
Golden Venus was, I own, my favourite pilgrimage ;
and there, as I rambled through its shades, where
bowers are the only temples, I felt how far more
worthy to form the shrine of a Deity are the ever-
living stems of the garden and the grove, than the
most stately columns that the inanimate quarry can
supply.

Everywhere new pleasures, new interests, awaited
me ; and though Melancholy stood, as usual, for ever
near, her shadow fell but half-way over my vagrant
path, leaving the rest but more welcomely brilliant
from the contrast. To relate my various adventures,

during this short voyage, would only detain me from events, far, far more worthy of record. Amidst all this endless variety of attractions, the great object of my journey had been forgotten ;—the mysteries of this land of the sun still remained, to me, as much mysteries as ever, and as yet I had been initiated in nothing but its pleasures.

It was not till that memorable evening when I first stood before the Pyramids of Memphis, and beheld them towering aloft, like the watch-towers of Time, from whose summit, when about to expire, he will take his last look,—it was not till this moment that the great secret announced in my dream, again rose in all its inscrutable darkness, upon my thoughts. There was a solemnity in the sunshine resting upon those monuments—a stillness, as of reverence, in the air that breathed around them, which stole, like the music of past times, into my heart. I thought what myriads of the wise, the beautiful, and the brave, had sunk into dust since earth first saw those wonders ; and, in the sadness of my soul, I exclaimed,—" Must man alone, then, perish ? must minds and hearts be annihilated, while pyramids endure ? Oh, Death, Death! even upon these everlasting tablets—the only approach to immortality that kings themselves could purchase—thou hast written our doom, awfully and intelligibly, saying,—' There is for man no eternal mansion but the grave !' "

My heart sunk at the thought ; and, for the moment,

I yielded to that desolate feeling which overspreads
the soul that hath no light from the future. But
again the buoyancy of my nature prevailed, and
again, the willing dupe of vain dreams, I deluded myself into the belief of all that my heart most wished,
with that happy facility which enables imagination to
stand in the place of happiness. "Yes!" I cried; "immortality *must* be within man's reach; and, as wisdom
alone is worthy of such a blessing, to the wise alone
must the secret have been revealed. It is said, that
deep under yonder pyramid has lain for ages concealed the Table of Emerald, on which the Thrice-
Great Hermes, in times before the flood, engraved the
secret of Alchemy which gives gold at will. Why,
then, may not the mightier, the more god-like secret
that gives *life* at will, be recorded there also? It was
by the power of gold, of endless gold, that the kings,
who now repose in those massy structures, scooped
earth to its very centre, and raised quarries into the
air, to provide for themselves tombs that might outstand the world. Who can tell but that the gift of
immortality was also theirs? who knows but that they
themselves, triumphant over decay, are still living;—
those mighty mansions, which we call tombs, being
rich and everlasting palaces, within whose depths, concealed from this withering world, they still wander,
with the few Elect who have been sharers of their
gift, through a sunless, but ever-illuminated elysium
of their own? Else, wherefore those structures?

wherefore that subterranean realm, by which the
whole valley of Egypt is undermined? Why, else,
those labyrinths, which none of earth hath ever
beheld — which none of heaven, except that God
who stands with finger on his hushed lip,* hath ever
trodden ? "

While thus I indulged in fond dreams, the sun,
already half-sunk beneath the horizon, was taking,
calmly and gloriously, his last look of the Pyramids,
as he had done, evening after evening, for ages, till
they had become familiar to him as the earth itself.
On the side turned to his ray they now presented a
front of dazzling whiteness, while, on the other, their
great shadows, lengthening away to the eastward,
looked like the first steps of Night, hastening to
envelop the hills of Araby in her shade.

No sooner had the last gleam of the sun disappeared, than, on every house-top in Memphis, gay,
gilded banners were seen waving aloft, to proclaim
his setting, while, at the same moment, a full burst
of harmony was heard to peal from all the temples
along the shores.

Startled from my musing by these sounds, I at
once recollected, that, on that very evening, the great
festival of the Moon was to be celebrated. On a little

* "Enfin Harpocrates représentoit aussi le soleil. Il est vrai que
c'étoit le Dieu du silence ; il mettoit le doigt sur la bouche parce qu'on
adoroit le soleil avec un respectueux silence, et c'est de là qu'est venu
le Sigé des Basilidiens, qui tiroient leur origine de l'Egypte." —
BEAUSOBRE.

island, half-way over between the gardens of Memphis and the eastern shore, stood the temple of that goddess,

> whose beams
> Bring the sweet time of night-flowers and dreams.
> *Not* the cold Dian of the North, who chains
> In vestal ice the current of young veins ;
> But she, who haunts the gay, Bubastian grove,
> And owns she sees, from her bright heav'n above,
> Nothing on earth, to match that heav'n, but love !

Thus did I exclaim, in the words of one of their own Egyptian poets, as, anticipating the various delights of the festival, I cast away from my mind all gloomy thoughts, and, hastening to my little bark, in which I now lived the life of a Nile-bird, on the waters, steered my course to the island-temple of the Moon.

## CHAPTER V.

THE rising of the Moon, slow and majestic, as if conscious of the honours that awaited her upon earth, was welcomed with a loud acclaim from every eminence, where multitudes stood watching for her first light. And seldom had that light risen upon a more beautiful scene. The city of Memphis,—still grand, though no longer the unrivalled Memphis, that had borne away from Thebes the crown of supremacy, and worn it undisputed through ages,—now, softened by the mild moonlight that harmonized with her decline, shone forth among her lakes, her pyramids, and her shrines, like a dream of human glory that must ere long pass away. Even already ruin was visible around her. The sands of the Libyan desert were gaining upon her like a sea; and, among solitary columns and sphinxes, already half sunk from sight, Time seemed to stand waiting till all that now flourished around him should fall beneath his desolating hand, like the rest.

On the waters all was life and gaiety. As far as eye could reach, the lights of innumerable boats were seen studding, like rubies, the surface of the stream. Vessels of every kind,—from the light coracle, built for shooting down the cataracts, to the large yacht that glides slowly to the sound of flutes,—all were afloat for this sacred festival, filled with crowds of the young and the gay, not only from Memphis and Babylon, but from cities still farther removed from the festal scene.

As I approached the island, I could see, glittering through the trees on the bank, the lamps of the pilgrims hastening to the ceremony. Landing in the direction which those lights pointed out, I soon joined the crowd; and, passing through a long alley of sphinxes, whose spangling marble shone out from the dark sycamores around them, reached in a short time the grand vestibule of the temple, where I found the ceremonies of the evening already commenced.

In this vast hall, which was surrounded by a double range of columns, and lay open overhead to the stars of heaven, I saw a group of young maidens, moving in a sort of measured step, between walk and dance, round a small shrine, upon which stood one of those sacred birds, that, on account of the variegated colour of their wings, are dedicated to the worship of the moon. The vestibule was dimly lighted,—there being but one lamp of naphtha hung on each of the great pillars that encircled it. But, having taken my station beside one of those pillars, I had a clear view of the young dancers, as in succession they passed me.

D

The drapery of all was white as snow; and each wore loosely, beneath the bosom, a dark-blue zone, or bandelet, studded, like the skies at midnight, with small silver stars. Through their dark locks was wreathed the white lily of the Nile,—that sacred flower being accounted no less welcome to the moon than the golden blossoms of the bean-flower are known to be to the sun. As they passed under the lamp, a gleam of light flashed from their bosoms, which, I could perceive, was the reflection of a small mirror, that, in the manner of the women of the East, each of the dancers wore beneath her left shoulder.

There was no music to regulate their steps ; but, as they gracefully went round the bird on the shrine, some, by the beat of the castanet, some, by the shrill ring of a sistrum, which they held uplifted in the attitude of their own divine Isis, continued harmoniously to time the cadence of their feet ; while others, at every step, shook a small chain of silver, whose sound, mingling with those of the castanets and sistrums, produced a wild but not unpleasing harmony.

They seemed all lovely ; but there was one—whose face the light had not yet reached, so downcast she held it,—who attracted, and, at length, riveted, all my looks and thoughts. I know not why, but there was a something in those half-seen features,—a charm in the very shadow that hung over their imagined beauty,—which took my fancy more than all the out-shining loveliness of her companions. So enchained was I by this coy mystery, that her alone, of all the group, could I either see or think of—her alone I watched, as, with the same downcast brow, she glided gently and aërially round the altar, as if her presence, like that of a spirit, was something to be felt, not seen.

Suddenly, while I gazed, the loud crash of a thousand cymbals was heard;—the massy gates of the Temple flew open, as if by magic, and a flood of radiance from the illuminated aisle filled the whole vestibule; while, at the same instant, as if the light and the sounds were born together, a peal of rich harmony came mingling with the radiance.

It was then,—by that light, which shone full upon the young maiden's features, as, starting at the sudden blaze, she raised her eyes to the portal, and as quickly let fall their lids again,—it was then I beheld, what even my own ardent imagination, in its most vivid dreams of beauty, had never pictured. Not Psyche herself, when pausing on the threshold of heaven, while its first glories fell on her dazzled lids, could have looked more purely beautiful, or blushed with a more innocent shame. Often as I had felt the power of looks, none had ever entered into my soul so deeply. It was a new feeling—a new sense—coming as suddenly upon me as that radiance into the vestibule, and, at once, filling my whole being;—and had that bright vision but lingered another moment before my eyes, I should, in my transport, have wholly forgotten who I was and where, and thrown myself, in prostrate adoration, at her feet.

But scarcely had that gush of harmony been heard, when the sacred bird, which had, till now, been standing motionless as an image, spread wide his wings, and flew into the Temple: while his graceful young worshippers, with a fleetness like his own, followed,—and she, who had left a dream in my heart never to be forgotten, vanished along with the rest. As she went rapidly past the pillar against which I leaned, the ivy that encircled it caught in her drapery, and disengaged some ornament which fell to the ground. It was the small mirror which I had seen shining on her bosom. Hastily and tremulously I picked it up, and hurried to restore it;—but she was already lost to my eyes in the crowd.

In vain did I try to follow;—the aisles were already filled, and numbers of eager pilgrims pressed towards the portal. But the servants of the Temple denied all further entrance, and still, as I presented myself, their white wands barred the way. Perplexed and irritated amidst that crowd of faces, regarding all as enemies that impeded my progress, I stood on tip-toe, gazing into the busy aisles, and with a heart beating as I caught, from time to time, a glimpse of some spangled zone, or lotus wreath, which led me to fancy that I had discovered the fair object of my search. But it was all in vain;—in every direction, files of sacred nymphs were moving, but nowhere could I discover the form which alone I sought.

In this state of breathless agitation did I stand for some time,—bewildered with the confusion of faces and lights, as well as with the clouds of incense that rolled around me,—till, fevered and impatient, I could endure it no longer. Forcing my way out of the vestibule into the cool air, I hurried back through the alley of sphinxes to the shore, and flung myself into my boat.

There lies, to the north of Memphis, a solitary lake (which, at this season of the year, mingles with the rest of the waters), upon whose shore stands the Necropolis, or City of the Dead—a place of melancholy grandeur, covered over with shrines and pyramids, where many a kingly head, proud even in death, has lain awaiting through long ages the resurrection of its glories. Through a range of sepulchral grots underneath, the humbler denizens of the tomb are deposited,—looking out on each successive generation that visits them, with the same face and features they wore centuries ago. Every plant and tree that is consecrated to death, from the asphodel-flower to the mystic plantain, lends its sweetness or shadow to this place of tombs; and the only noise that disturbs its eternal calm is the low humming sound of the priests at prayer, when a new inhabitant is added to the silent city.

It was towards this place of death that, in a mood of mind, as usual, half gloomy, half bright, I now, almost unconsciously, directed my bark. The form of the young Priestess was continually before me. That one bright look of hers, the very remembrance of which was worth all the actual smiles of others, never for a moment left my mind. Absorbed in such thoughts, I continued to row on, scarce knowing whither I went, till, at length, startled to find myself within the shadow of the City of the Dead, I looked up, and beheld, rising in succession before me, pyramid beyond pyramid, each towering more loftily than the other, while all were out-topped in grandeur by one, upon whose summit the midnight moon appeared to rest as on a pedestal.

Drawing nearer to the shore, which was sufficiently elevated to raise this silent city of tombs above the level of the inundation, I rested my oar, and allowed the boat to rock idly upon the water, while, left equally without direction, my thoughts fluctuated as idly. How various and vague were the dreams that then floated through my mind—that bright vision of the temple still mingling itself with all! Sometimes she stood before me, like an aërial spirit, as pure as if that element of music and light, into which she had then vanished, was her only dwelling. Sometimes, animated with passion, and kindling into a creature of earth, she seemed to lean towards me with looks of tenderness, which it were worth worlds, but for one instant, to inspire; and again—as the dark fancies, that ever haunted me, recurred—I saw her cold, parched, and blackening, amid the gloom of those eternal sepulchres before me!

Turning away, with a shudder, from the cemetery at this thought, I heard the sound of an oar plying swiftly through the water, and, in a few moments, saw, shooting past me towards the shore, a small boat in which sat two female figures, muffled up and veiled. Having landed them not far from the spot where, under the shadow of a tomb on the bank, I lay concealed, the boat again departed, with the same fleetness, over the flood.

Never had the prospect of an adventure come more welcome to me than at this moment, when my busy fancy was employed in weaving such chains for my heart, as threatened a bondage, of all others, the most difficult to break. To become enamoured thus of a creature of my own imagination, was the worst, because the most lasting, of follies. It is only reality that can afford any chance of dissolving such spells, and the idol I was now creating to myself must for ever remain ideal. Any pursuit, therefore, that seemed likely to divert me from such thoughts—to bring back my imagination to earth and reality, from the vague region in which it had been wandering, was a relie too seasonable not to be welcomed with eagerness.

I had watched the course which the two figures took, and, having hastily fastened my boat to the bank, stepped gently on shore, and, at a little distance, followed them. The windings through which they led were intricate ; but, by the bright light of the moon, I was enabled to keep their forms in view, as, with rapid step, they glided among the monuments. At length, in the shade of a small pyramid, whose peak barely surmounted the plane-trees that grew nigh, they vanished from my sight. I hastened to the spot, but there was not a sign of life around ; and, had my creed extended to another world, I might have fancied that these mysterious forms were spirits, sent from thence to mock me,—so instantaneously had they disappeared. I searched through the neighbouring grove, but all there was still as death. At length, in examining one of the sides of the pyramid, which, for a few feet from the ground, was furnished with steps, I found, midway between peak and base, a part of the surface, which, although presenting to the eye an appearance of smoothness, gave to the touch, I thought, indications of a concealed opening.

After a variety of efforts and experiments, I, at last, more by accident than skill, pressed the spring that commanded this hidden aperture. In an instant the portal slid aside, and disclosed a narrow stairway within, the two or three first steps of which were discernible by the moonlight, while the rest were all lost in utter darkness. Though it was difficult to conceive that the persons whom I had been pursuing would have ventured to pass through this gloomy opening, yet to account for their disappearance otherwise was still more difficult. At all events, my curiosity was now too eager in the chase to relinquish it ;—the spirit of adventure, once raised, could not be so easily

laid.   Accordingly, having sent up a gay prayer to
that bliss-loving Queen whose eye alone was upon
me, I passed through the portal, and descended into
the pyramid.

## CHAPTER VI.

At the bottom of the stairway I found myself in a low, narrow passage through which, without stooping almost to the earth, it was impossible to proceed. Though leading through a multiplicity of dark windings, this way seemed but little to advance my progress,—its course, I perceived, being chiefly circular, and gathering, at every turn, but a deeper intensity of darkness.

"Can any thing human," thought I, "sojourn here?"—and had scarcely asked myself the question, when the path opened into a long gallery, at the farthest end of which a gleam of light was visible. This welcome glimmer appeared to issue from some cell or alcove, in which the right-hand wall of the gallery terminated, and, breathless with expectation, I stole gently towards it.

Arrived at the end of the gallery, a scene presented itself to my eyes, for which my fondest expectations of adventure could not have prepared me. The place from which the light proceeded was a small chapel, of whose interior, from the dark recess in which I stood, I could take, unseen myself, a full and distinct view. Over the walls of this oratory were painted some of those various symbols, by which the mystic wisdom of the Egyptians loves to shadow out the History of the Soul,—the winged globe with a serpent—the rays descending from above, like a glory—and the Theban beetle, as he comes forth after the waters have passed away, and the first sunbeam falls on his regenerated wings.

In the middle of the chapel, on a low altar of granite, lay a lifeless female form, enshrined within a case of crystal,—as it is the custom to preserve the dead in Ethiopia,—and looking as freshly beautiful as if the soul had but a few hours departed. Among the emblems of death, on the front of the altar, were a slender lotus-branch broken in two, and a bird just winging its flight from the spray.

To these memorials of the dead, however, I paid but little attention ; for there was a living object there upon which my eyes were now intently fixed.

The lamp, by which the whole of the chapel was illuminated, was placed at the head of the pale image in the shrine ; and, between its light and me, stood a female form, bending over the monument, as if to gaze upon the silent features within. The position in which this figure was placed, intercepting a strong light, afforded me, at first, but an imperfect and shadowy view of it. Yet even at this mere outline I

felt my heart beat high,—and memory had no less
share, as it proved, in this feeling than imagination.
For, on the head changing its position, so as to let a
gleam fall upon the features, I saw, with a transport
which had almost led me to betray my lurking-place,
that it was she—the young worshipper of Isis—the
same, the very same, whom I had seen, brightening
the holy place where she stood, and looking like an
inhabitant of some purer world.

The movement by which she had now afforded me
an opportunity of recognising her, was made in raising
from the shrine a small cross * of silver, which lay
directly over the bosom of the lifeless figure. Bringing it close to her lips, she kissed it with a religious
fervour ; then, turning her eyes mournfully upwards,
held them fixed with a degree of inspired earnestness,
as if, at that moment, in direct communion with
Heaven, they saw neither roof nor any other earthly
barrier between them and the skies.

What a power is there in innocence! whose very
helplessness is its safeguard—in whose presence even
Passion himself stands abashed, and turns worshipper
at the very altar which he came to despoil! She,
who, but a short hour before, had presented herself to
my imagination as something I could have risked immortality to win,—she, whom gladly, from the floor
of her own lighted temple, in the very face of its
proud ministers, I would have borne away in triumph,

* A cross was, among the Egyptians, the emblem of a future life.

and defied all punishments, both human and sacred, to make her mine,—that creature was now before me, thrown, as if by fate itself, into my power—standing there, beautiful and alone, with nothing but her innocence for her guard! Yet, no—so touching was the purity of the whole scene, so calm and august that protection which the dead extended over the living, that every earthly feeling was forgotten as I gazed, and love itself became exalted into reverence.

Entranced, indeed, as I felt in witnessing such a scene, thus to enjoy it by stealth seemed a wrong, a sacrilege—and, rather than let her eyes meet the flash of mine, or disturb, by a whisper, that sacred silence, in which Youth and Death held communion through undying Love, I would have suffered my heart to break, without a murmur, where I stood. As gently as if life itself depended upon my every movement, I stole away from that tranquil and holy scene—leaving it still holy and tranquil as I had found it—and, gliding back through the same passages and windings by which I had entered, regained the narrow stairway, and again ascended into light.

The sun had just risen, and, from the summit of the Arabian hills, was pouring down his beams into that vast valley of waters,—as if proud of last night's homage to his own divine Isis, now fading away in the superior splendour of her Lord. My first impulse was to fly at once from this dangerous spot, and seek, in new loves and pleasures, oblivion of the wondrous scene I had just witnessed. "Once out of the circle of this enchantment," I exclaimed, "I know my own susceptibility to new impressions too well, to doubt that I shall soon break the spell that is now around me."

But vain were all my efforts and resolves. Even while swearing to fly, I found my steps still lingering fondly round the pyramid—my eyes still turned towards the portal which severed this enchantress from the world of the living. Hour after hour did I wander through that City of Silence, till, already, it was mid-day, and, under the eye of the meridian sun, the mighty pyramid of pyramids stood, like a great spirit, shadowless.

Again did those wild and passionate feelings, which, for a moment, her presence had subdued into reverence, return to take possession of my imagination and my senses. I even reproached myself for the awe that had held me spell-bound before her. "What would my companions of the Garden say, did they know that their chief—he whose path Love had strewed with trophies—was now pining for a simple Egyptian girl, in whose presence he had not dared to give utterance to a single sigh, and who had vanquished the victor, without even knowing her triumph!"

A blush came over my cheek at the humiliating thought, and I determined, at all risks, to await her coming. That she should be an inmate of those gloomy caverns seemed inconceivable ; nor did there appear to be any issue from their depths but by the pyramid. Again, therefore, like a sentinel of the dead, did I pace up and down among those tombs, contrasting mournfully the burning fever within my own veins with the cold quiet of those who were slumbering around.

At length the intense glow of the sun over my head, and, still more, that ever-restless agitation in my heart, became too much for even strength like mine to endure. Exhausted, I threw myself down at the base of the pyramid—choosing my place directly under the portal, where, even should slumber surprise me, my heart, if not my ear, might still keep watch, and her footstep, light as it was, could not fail to awake me.

After many an ineffectual struggle against drowiness, I at length sunk into sleep—but not into forgetfulness. The same image still haunted me, in every variety of shape, with which imagination, assisted by memory, could invest it. Now, like the goddess Neïtha, upon her throne at Saïs, she seemed to sit, with the veil just raised from that brow, which till then no mortal had ever beheld,—and now, like the beautiful enchantress Rhodope, I saw her rise from out the pyramid in which she had dwelt for ages,—

> " Fair Rhodope, as story tells,
> The bright unearthly nymph, who dwells
> 'Mid sunless gold and jewels hid,
> The Lady of the Pyramid ! "

So long had my sleep continued, amidst that unbroken silence, that I found the moon again resplendent above the horizon when I awoke. All around looked still and lifeless as before, nor did a print upon the herbage betray that any foot, since my own, had passed over it. Refreshed by my long rest, and with a fancy still more excited by the mystic wonders of which I had been dreaming, I now resolved to revisit the chapel in the pyramid, and put an end, if possible, to this strange mystery that haunted me.

Having learned, from the experience of the preceding night, the inconvenience of encountering those labyrinths without a light, I now hastened to provide myself with a lamp from my boat. Tracking my way back with some difficulty to the shore, I there found not only my lamp, but also some dates and dried fruits, with a store of which I was always provided for my roving life upon the waters, and which now, after so many hours of abstinence, were a most welcome and necessary relief.

Thus prepared, I again ascended the pyramid, and was proceeding to search out the secret spring, when a loud, dismal noise was heard at a distance, to which all the melancholy echoes of the cemetery gave answer. The sound came, I knew, from the Great Temple on the shore of the lake, and was the sort of shriek which its gates—the Gates of Oblivion, as they are called—used to send forth from their hinges, when opening at night, to receive the newly landed dead.

I had heard that sound before, and always with sadness ; but, at this moment, it thrilled through me like a voice of ill omen, and I almost doubted whether I should not abandon my enterprise. The hesitation, however, was but momentary ;—even while it passed through my mind, I had touched the spring of the portal. In a few seconds more, I was again in the passage beneath the pyramid ; and, being enabled by the light of my lamp to follow the windings of the way more rapidly, soon found myself at the door of the small chapel in the gallery.

I entered, still awed, though there was now, alas, nothing living within. The young Priestess had vanished, like a spirit into the darkness ; and all the rest remained as I had left it on the preceding night. The lamp still stood burning upon the crystal shrine ; the cross was lying where the hands of the young mourner had placed it, and the cold image, within the shrine, wore still the same tranquil look, as if resigned to the solitude of death—of all lone things the lone-liest. Remembering the lips that I had seen kiss that cross, and kindling with the recollection, I raised it passionately to my own ;—but the dead eyes, at the same moment, I thought, met mine, and, awed and saddened in the midst of my ardour, I replaced the cross upon the shrine.

I had now lost every clue to the object of my pur-suit, and was about to retrace slowly my steps to earth, with all that gloomy satisfaction which certainty,

E

even when unwelcome, brings,—when, as I held forth
my lamp, on leaving the chapel, I could perceive that
the gallery, instead of terminating here, took a sudden
and snake-like bend to the left, which had before
eluded my observation, and which gave promise of a
pathway still further into those recesses. Re-animated
by this discovery, which opened a new source of hope
to my heart, I cast, for a moment, a hesitating look
at my lamp, as if to inquire whether it would be faithful through the gloom I was about to encounter, and
then, without further consideration, rushed eagerly
forward.

## CHAPTER VII.

THE path led, for a while, through the same sort of narrow windings as those which I had before encountered in descending the stairway; and at length opened, in a similar manner, into a straight and steep gallery, along each side of which stood, closely ranged and upright, a file of lifeless bodies, whose glassy eyes appeared to glare upon me preternaturally as I passed.

Arrived at the end of this gallery, I found my hopes, for the second time, vanish; as the path, it was plain, extended no further. The only object I could discern, by the glimmering of my lamp, which now, every minute, burned fainter and fainter, was the mouth of a huge well that lay gaping before me—a reservoir of darkness, black and unfathomable. It now crossed my memory that I had once heard of such wells, as being used occasionally for passages by the priests. Leaning down, therefore, over the edge, I examined anxiously all within, in order to discover whether there was any way of descending into the chasm. But the sides, I could see, were hard and smooth as glass, being varnished all over with that sort of dark pitch which the Dead Sea throws out upon its slimy shore.

After a more attentive scrutiny, however, I observed, at a depth of a few feet, a sort of iron step, projecting dimly from the side, and, below it, another, which, though hardly perceptible, was just sufficient to encourage an adventurous foot to the trial. Though all hope of tracing the young Priestess was now at an end,—it being impossible that female foot should have ventured on this descent,—yet, as I had so far engaged in the adventure, and there was, at least, a mystery to be unravelled, I determined, at all hazards, to explore the chasm. Placing my lamp, therefore, (which was hollowed at the bottom, so as to fit like a helmet) firmly upon my head, and having thus both hands at liberty for exertion, I set my foot cautiously on the iron step, and descended into the well.

I found the same footing, at regular intervals, to a considerable depth; and had already counted near a hundred of these steps, when the ladder altogether ceased, and I could descend no further. In vain did I stretch down my foot in search of support—the hard, slippery sides were all that it encountered. At length, stooping my head, so as to let the light fall below, I observed an opening or window directly above the step on which I stood, and, taking for granted that the way must lie in that direction, clambered with no small difficulty through the aperture.

I now found myself on a rude and narrow stairway, the steps of which were cut out of the living rock, and wound spirally downward in the same direction as the well. Almost dizzy with the descent, which seemed as if it would never end, I, at last, reached the bottom, where a pair of massy iron gates were closed directly across my path, as if to forbid any further progress. Massy, however, and gigantic as they were, I found, to my surprise, that the hand of an infant might have opened them with ease—so readily did their stupendous folds give way to my touch,

> "Light as a lime-bush, that receives
> Some wandering bird among its leaves."

No sooner, however, had I passed through, than the din, with which the gates clashed together again, was such as might have awakened death itself. It seemed as if every echo throughout that vast subterranean world, from the Catacombs of Alexandria to Thebes's Valley of Kings, had caught up and repeated the thundering sound.

Startled as I was by the crash, not even this supernatural clangour could divert my attention from the sudden light that now broke around me—soft, warm, and welcome as are the stars of his own South to the eyes of the mariner who has long been wandering through the cold seas of the North. Looking for the source of this splendour, I saw, through an archway opposite, a long illuminated alley, stretching away as far as the eye could reach, and fenced, on one side, with thickets of odoriferous shrubs, while along the other extended a line of lofty arcades, from which the light, that filled the whole area, issued. As soon, too, as the din of the deep echoes had subsided, there stole gradually on my ear a strain of choral music, which appeared to come mellowed and sweetened in its passage through many a spacious hall within those shining arcades; while, among the voices I could distinguish some female tones, which, towering high and clear above all the rest, formed the spire, as it were, into which the harmony tapered, as it rose.

So excited was my fancy by this sudden enchantment, that—though never had I caught a sound from the fair Egyptian's lips—I yet persuaded myself that the voice I now heard was hers, sounding highest and most heavenly of all that choir, and calling to me, like a distant spirit from its sphere. Animated by this thought, I flew forward to the archway, but found, to my mortification, that it was guarded by a trellis-work, whose bars, though invisible at a distance, resisted all my efforts to force them.

While occupied in these ineffectual struggles, I perceived, to the left of the archway, a dark, cavernous opening, which seemed to lead in a direction parallel to the lighted arcades. Notwithstanding, however, my impatience, the aspect of this passage, as I looked shudderingly into it, chilled my very blood. It was not so much darkness, as a sort of livid and ghastly twilight, from which a damp, like that of death-vaults, exhaled, and through which, if my eyes did not deceive me, pale, phantom-like shapes were, at that very moment, hovering.

Looking anxiously round, to discover some less formidable outlet, I saw, over the vast folding-gates through which I had just passed, a blue, tremulous flame, which, after playing for a few seconds over the dark ground of the pediment, settled gradually into characters of light, and formed the following words:—

> You, who would try
>   Yon terrible track,
> To live, or to die,
>   But ne'er to look back, —
>
> You, who aspire
>   To be purified there,
> By the terrors of Fire,
>   Of Water, and Air,—
>
> If danger, and pain,
>   And death you despise,
> On—for again
>   Into light you shall rise ;
>
> Rise into light
>   With that Secret Divine,
> Now shrouded from sight
>   By the Veils of the Shrine !
>
> But if——

Here the letters faded away into a dead blank, more awfully intelligible than the most eloquent words.

A new hope now flashed across me. The dream of the Garden, which had been for some time almost forgotten, returned freshly to my mind. " Am I then," I exclaimed, " in the path to the promised mystery ? and shall the great secret of Eternal Life *indeed* be mine ? "

" Yes ! " seemed to answer out of the air, that spirit-voice, which still was heard far-off, crowning the choir with its single sweetness. I hailed the omen with transport. Love and Immortality, both beckoning me onward—who would give even a thought to fear, with two such bright hopes in prospect ? Having invoked and blessed that unknown enchantress, whose steps had led me to this abode of mystery and knowledge, I instantly plunged into the chasm.

Instead of that vague, spectral twilight which had at first met my eye, I now found, as I entered, a thick darkness, which, though far less horrible, was, at this moment, still more disconcerting, as my lamp, which had been, for some time, almost useless, was now fast expiring. Resolved, however, to make the most of its last gleam, I hastened, with rapid step, through this gloomy region, which appeared to be wider and more open to the air than any I had yet passed. Nor was it long before the sudden appearance of a bright blaze in the distance announced to me that my first great Trial was at hand. As I drew nearer, the flames before me burst high and wide on all sides ;—and the spectacle that then presented itself was such as might have daunted even hearts far more accustomed to dangers than mine.

There lay before me, extending completely across my path, a thicket, or grove, of the most combustible trees of Egypt—tamarind, pine, and Arabian balm; while around their stems and branches were coiled serpents of fire, which, twisting themselves rapidly from bough to bough, spread the contagion of their own wild-fire as they went, and involved tree after tree in one general blaze. It was, indeed, rapid as the burning of those reed-beds of Ethiopia, whose light is seen at a distance, brightening, at night, the foamy cataracts of the Nile.

Through the middle of this blazing grove, I now perceived my only pathway lay. There was not a moment to be lost—for the conflagration gained rapidly on either side, and already the narrowing path between was strewed with vivid fire. Casting away my now useless lamp, and holding my robe as some slight protection over my head, I ventured, with trembling limbs, into the blaze.

Instantly, as if my presence had given new life to the flames, a fresh outbreak of combustion arose on all sides. The trees clustered into a bower of fire above my head, while the serpents that hung hissing from the red branches shot showers of sparkles down upon me as I passed. Never were decision and activity of more avail;—one minute later, and I must have perished. The narrow opening, of which I had so promptly availed myself, closed instantly behind me ; and, as I looked back, to contemplate the ordeal which I had passed, I saw that the whole grove was already one mass of fire.

Rejoiced to have escaped this first trial, I instantly plucked from one of the pine-trees a bough that was but just kindled, and, with this for my only guide, hastened breathlessly forward. I had gone but a few paces, when the path turned suddenly off,—leading downwards, as I could perceive by the glimmer of my brand, into a more confined space, through which a chilling air, as if from some neighbouring waters, blew over my brow. Nor had I proceeded in this course very far, when the sound of torrents—mingled, as I thought, from time to time, with shrill wailings, like the cries of persons in danger or distress—fell mournfully upon my ear. At every step the noise of the dashing waters increased, and I now perceived that I had entered an immense rocky cavern, through the middle of which, headlong as a winter-torrent, the flood, to whose roar I had been listening, poured its dark waters ; while upon its surface floated grim spectre-like shapes, which, as they went by, sent forth those dismal shrieks I had heard—as if in fear of some awful precipice towards whose brink they were hurrying.

I saw plainly that across that torrent lay my only course. It was, indeed, fearful ; but in courage now lay my only hope. What awaited me on the opposite shore, I knew not; for all there was immersed in impenetrable gloom, nor could the feeble light which I carried send its glimmer half so far. Dismissing, however, all thoughts but that of pressing onward, I sprung from the rock on which I stood into the flood, —trusting that, with my right hand, I should be able to buffet the current, while, with the other, as long as a gleam of my brand remained, I might hold it aloft to guide me safely to the shore.

Long, formidable, and almost hopeless was the struggle I had now to maintain; and more than once, overpowered by the rush of the waters, I had given myself up as destined to follow those pale, deathlike apparitions, that still went past me, hurrying with mournful cries, to find their doom in some invisible gulf beyond.

At length, just as my strength was nearly exhausted, and the last remains of the pine-branch were falling from my hand, I saw, outstretching towards me into the water, a light double balustrade, with a flight of steps between, ascending almost perpendicularly from the wave, till they seemed lost in a dense mass of clouds above. This glimpse—for it was nothing more, as my light expired in giving it—lent new spring to my courage. Having now both hands at liberty, so desperate were my efforts, that, after a few minutes' struggle, I felt my brow strike against the stairway, and, in another instant, my feet were on the steps.

Rejoiced at my rescue from that perilous flood, though I knew not whither this stairway led, I promptly ascended the steps. But this feeling of confidence was of short duration. I had not mounted far, when, to my horror, I perceived, that each successive step, as my foot left it, broke away from beneath me,—leaving me in mid-air, with no other alternative than that of still continuing to mount by the same momentary footing, and with the appalling doubt whether it would even endure my tread.

And thus did I, for a few seconds, continue to ascend, with nothing beneath me but that awful river, in which—so tranquil had it now become—I could hear the plash of the falling fragments, as every step in succession gave way from under my feet. It was a most trying moment,—but even still worse remained. I now found the balustrade, by which I had held during my ascent, and which had hitherto seemed firm, grow tremulous in my hand,—while the step, to which I was about to trust myself, tottered under my foot. Just then, a momentary flash, as if of lightning, broke around me, and I perceived, hanging out of the clouds, and barely within my reach, a huge brazen ring. Instinctively I stretched forth my arm to seize it, and, at the same instant, both balustrade and steps gave way beneath me, and I was left swinging by my hands in the dark void. As if, too, this massy ring, which I grasped, was by some magic power linked with all the winds in heaven, no sooner had I seized it than, like the touching of a spring, it seemed to give loose to every variety of gusts and tempests that ever strewed the sea-shore with wrecks or dead ; and, as I swung about, the sport of this elemental strife, every new burst of its fury threatened to shiver me, like a storm-sail, to atoms !

Nor was even this the worst ;—for, still holding, I know not how, by the ring, I felt myself caught up, as if by a thousand whirlwinds, and then, round and round, like a stone-shot in a sling, continued to be whirled in the midst of all this deafening chaos, till my brain grew dizzy, my recollection became confused, and I almost fancied myself on that wheel of the infernal world, whose rotations Eternity alone can number !

Human strength could no longer sustain such a trial. I was on the point, at last, of loosing my hold, when suddenly the violence of the storm moderated ; —my whirl through the air gradually ceased, and I felt the ring slowly descend with me, till—happy as a shipwrecked mariner at the first touch of land—I found my feet once more upon firm ground.

At the same moment, a light of the most delicious softness filled the whole air. Music, such as is heard in dreams, came floating at a distance ; and as my eyes gradually recovered their powers of vision, a scene of glory was revealed to them, almost too bright for imagination, and yet living and real. As far as the sight could reach, enchanting gardens were seen, opening away through long tracts of light and verdure, and sparkling everywhere with fountains, that circulated, like streams of life, among the flowers. Not a charm was here wanting, that the fancy of poet or prophet, in their warmest pictures of Elysium, has ever yet dreamed or promised. Vistas, opening into scenes of indistinct grandeur,—streams, shining out at intervals, in their shadowy course,—and labyrinths of flowers, leading, by mysterious windings, to green, spacious glades full of splendour and repose. Over all this, too, there fell a light, from some unseen source, resembling nothing that illumines our upper world—a sort of golden moonlight, mingling the warm radiance of day with the calm and melancholy lustre of night.

Nor were there wanting inhabitants for this sunless Paradise. Through all the bright gardens were wandering, with the serene air and step of happy spirits, groups both of young and old, of venerable and of lovely forms, bearing, most of them, the Nile's white flowers on their heads, and branches of the eternal palm in their hands; while, over the verdant turf, fair children and maidens went dancing to aërial music, whose source was, like that of the light, invisible, but which filled the whole air with its mystic sweetness.

Exhausted as I was by the painful trials I had undergone, no sooner did I perceive those fair groups in the distance, than my weariness, both of frame

and spirit, was forgotten. A thought crossed me
that she, whom I sought, might possibly be among
them ; and notwithstanding the awe, with which
that unearthly scene inspired me, I was about to fly,
on the instant, to ascertain my hope. But in the
act of making the effort, I felt my robe gently pulled,
and, turning, beheld an aged man before me, whom,
by the sacred hue of his garb, I knew to be a
Hierophant. Placing a branch of the consecrated
palm in my hand, he said, in a solemn voice,
"Aspirant of the Mysteries, welcome!"—Then, regarding me for a few seconds with grave attention,
added, in a tone of courteousness and interest, "The
victory over the body hath been gained!—Follow
me, young Greek, to thy resting-place."

I obeyed in silence,—and the Priest, turning away
from this scene of splendour, into a secluded path,
where the light faded away as we advanced, conducted me to a small pavilion, by the side of a
whispering stream, where the very spirit of slumber
seemed to preside, and, pointing silently to a bed of
dried poppy-leaves, left me to repose.

## CHAPTER VIII.

THOUGH the sight of that splendid scene whose glories opened upon me, like a momentary glimpse into another world, had, for an instant, re-animated my strength and spirit, yet so completely was my whole frame subdued by fatigue, that, even had the form of the young Priestess herself then stood before me, my limbs would have sunk in the effort to reach her. No sooner had I fallen on my leafy couch, than sleep, like a sudden death, came over me ; and I lay, for hours, in that deep and motionless rest, which not even a shadow of life disturbs.

On awaking I saw, beside me, the same venerable personage, who had welcomed me to this subterranean world on the preceding night. At the foot of my couch stood a statue, of Grecian workmanship, representing a boy with wings, seated gracefully on a lotus-flower, and having the forefinger of his right hand pressed to his lips. This action, together with the glory round his brows, denoted, as I already knew, the God of Silence and Light.

Impatient to know what further trials awaited me, I was about to speak, when the Priest exclaimed, anxiously, "Hush!"—and, pointing to the statue at the foot of the couch, said,—"Let the spell of that Spirit be upon thy lips, young stranger, till the wisdom of thy instructors shall think fit to remove it. Not unaptly doth the same deity preside over Silence and Light; since it is only out of the depth of contemplative silence that the great light of the soul, Truth, can arise!"

Little used to the language of dictation or instruction, I was now preparing to rise, when the Priest again restrained me; and, at the same moment, two boys, beautiful as the young Genii of the stars, entered the pavilion. They were habited in long garments of the purest white, and bore each a small golden chalice in his hand. Advancing towards me, they stopped on opposite sides of the couch, and one of them, presenting me his chalice of gold, said, in a tone between singing and speaking :—

> " Drink of this cup—Osiris sips
>   The same in his halls below ;
> And the same he gives, to cool the lips
>   Of the Dead who downward go.

> " Drink of this cup—the water within
>   Is fresh from Lethe's stream ;
> 'Twill make the past, with all its sin,
>   And all its pain and sorrows, seem
> Like a long-forgotten dream !

F

" The pleasure, whose charms
　　Are steep'd in woe ;
　The knowledge, that harms
　　The soul to know ;

" The hope, that, bright
　　As the lake of the waste,
　Allures the sight,
　　But mocks the taste ;

" The love that binds
　　Its innocent wreath,
　Where the serpent winds,
　　In venom, beneath ;—

" All that, of evil or false, by thee
　　Hath ever been known or seen,
　Shall melt away in this cup, and be
　　Forgot, as it never had been ! "

Unwilling to throw a slight on this strange ceremony, I leaned forward, with all due gravity, and
tasted the cup ; which I had no sooner done than
the young cup-bearer, on the other side, invited my
attention ; and, in his turn, presenting the chalice
which he held, sung, with a voice still sweeter than
that of his companion, the following strain :—

" Drink of this cup—when Isis led
　　Her boy, of old, to the beaming sky,
　She mingled a draught divine, and said—
　　' Drink of this cup, thou'lt never die ! '

" Thus do I say and sing to thee,
　　Heir of that boundless heav'n on high,
　Though frail, and fall'n, and lost thou be,
　　Drink of this cup, thou'lt never die ! "

Much as I had endeavoured to keep my philosophy

on its guard against the illusions with which, I knew, this region abounded, the young cup-bearer had here touched a spring of imagination, over which my philosophy, as has been seen, had but little control. No sooner had the words, "thou shalt never die," struck on my ear, than the dream of the Garden came fully to my mind, and, starting half-way from the couch, I stretched forth my hands to the cup. Instantly, however, recollecting myself, and fearing I had betrayed to others a weakness fit only for my own secret indulgence, with a smile of affected in-difference I sunk back again on my couch, while the young minstrel, but little interrupted by my movement, still continued his strain, of which I heard but the concluding words :—

> " And Memory, too, with her dreams shall come,
> Dreams of a former, happier day,
> When Heaven was still the Spirit's home,
> And her wings had not yet fallen away ;

> " Glimpses of glory, ne'er forgot,
> That tell, like gleams on a sunset sea,
> What once hath been, what now is not,
> But, oh, what again shall brightly be !"

Though the assurances of immortality contained in these verses would at any other moment—vain and visionary as I thought them—have sent my fancy wandering into reveries of the future, the effort of self-control I had just made enabled me to hear them with indifference.

Having gone through the form of tasting this second cup, I again looked anxiously to the Hierophant, to ascertain whether I might be permitted to rise. His assent having been given, the young pages brought to my couch a robe and tunic, which, like their own, were of linen of the purest white ; and, having assisted to clothe me in this sacred garb, they then placed upon my head a chaplet of myrtle, in which the symbol of Initiation, a golden grasshopper, was seen shining out from among the dark leaves.

Though sleep had done much to refresh my frame, something more was still wanting to restore its strength ; and it was not without a smile at my own reveries I reflected how much more welcome than even the young page's cup of immortality was the unpretending, but real, repast now set before me, consisting of fresh fruits from the Isle of Gardens in the Nile, the delicate flesh of the desert antelope, and wine from the Vineyard of the Queens at Anthylla, which one of the pages fanned with a palm-leaf, to keep it cool.

Having done justice to these dainties, it was with pleasure I heard the proposal of the Priest, that we should walk forth together and meditate among the scenes without. I had not forgotten the splendid Elysium that last night welcomed me,—those rich gardens, that soft unearthly music and light, and, above all, those fair forms I had seen wandering about,—as if, in the very midst of happiness, still seeking it. The hope, which had then occurred to me, that, among those bright groups, might possibly be found the young maiden I sought, now returned with increased strength. I had little doubt that my guide was leading me to the same Elysian scene, and that the form, so fit to inhabit it, would again appear before my eyes.

But far different, I found, was the region to which he now conducted me;—nor could the whole world have produced a scene more gloomy, or more strange. It had the appearance of a small solitary valley, enclosed, on every side, by rocks, which seemed to rise, almost perpendicularly, till they reached the very sky; for it was, indeed, the blue sky that I saw shining between their summits, and whose light, dimmed and nearly lost in its descent thus far, formed the melancholy daylight of this nether world.* Down the side of these rocky walls descended a cataract, whose source was upon earth, and on whose waters, as they rolled glassily over the edge above, a gleam of radiance rested, showing how brilliant and pure was the sunshine they had left behind. From thence, gradually growing darker and frequently broken, in its long descent, by alternate chasms and projections, the stream fell, at last, in a pale and thin mist—the

* "On s'était même avisé, depuis la première construction de ces demeures, de percer en plusieurs endroits jusqu'au haut les terres qui les couvroient ; non pas à la vérité, pour tirer un jour qui n'auroit jamais été suffisant, mais pour recevoir un air salutaire, &c."—SETHOS.

phantom of what it had been on earth—into a small still lake that lay at the base of the rock to receive it.

Nothing was ever so bleak and saddening as the appearance of this lake. The usual ornaments of the waters of Egypt were not wanting to it: the tall lotus here uplifted her silvery flowers, and the crimson flamingo floated over the tide. But they looked not the same as in the world above;—the flower had exchanged its whiteness for a livid hue, and the wings of the bird hung heavy and colourless. Everything wore the same half-living aspect; and the only sounds that disturbed the mournful stillness were the wailing cry of a heron among the sedges, and that din of the falling waters, in their midway struggle, above.

There was, indeed, an unearthly sadness in the whole scene, of which no heart, however light, could resist the influence. Perceiving how I was affected by it, " Such scenes," remarked the Priest, "suit best that solemn complexion of mind which becomes him who approaches the Great Mystery of futurity. Behold,"—and, in saying thus, he pointed to the opening over our heads, through which, though the sun had but just passed his meridian, I could perceive a star or two twinkling in the heavens,—" as from this gloomy depth we can see those fixed stars, which are invisible now to the dwellers upon the bright earth, even so, to the sad and self-humbled spirit, doth many a mystery of Heaven reveal itself, of which they, who walk in the light of the proud world, know not ! "

He now led me towards a rustic seat or alcove, beside which stood an image of that dark Deity, that God without a smile, who presides over the silent kingdom of the Dead.* The same livid and lifeless hue was upon his features that seemed to hang over everything in this dim valley ; and, with his right hand, he pointed directly downwards, to denote that his melancholy kingdom lay there. A plantain—that favourite tree of the genii of Death—stood behind the statue, and spread its branches over the alcove, in which the Priest now seated himself, and made sign that I should take my place by his side.

After a long pause, as if of thought and preparation, —"Nobly," said he, "young Greek, hast thou sustained the first trials of Initiation. What still remains, though of vital import to the soul, brings with it neither pain nor peril to the body. Having now proved and chastened thy mortal frame, by the three ordeals of Fire, of Water, and of Air, the next task to which we are called is the purification of thy spirit,— the cleansing of that inward and immortal part, so as to render it fit for the reception of the last luminous revealment, when the Veils of the Sanctuary shall be thrown aside, and the Great Secret of Secrets unfolded to thy view ! Towards this object, the primary and most important step is, instruction. What the three purifying elements thou hast passed through, have done for thy body, instruction will effect for——"

* Osiris.

"But that lovely maiden!" I exclaimed, bursting from my silence, having fallen, during his speech, into a deep reverie, in which I had forgotten him, myself, the Great Secret, everything—but her.

Startled by this profane interruption, he cast a look of alarm towards the statue, as if fearful lest the God should have heard my words. Then, turning to me, in a tone of mild solemnity, "It is but too plain," said he, "that thoughts of the vain upper world, and of its shadowy delights, still engross thee far too much to allow the lessons of Truth to sink profitably into thy heart. A few hours of meditation amid this solemn scenery—of that wholesome meditation, which purifies, by saddening—may haply dispose thee to receive, with due feelings of reverence, the holy and imperishable knowledge that is in store for thee. With this hope I now leave thee to thy own thoughts, and to that God, before whose calm and mournful eye all the vanities of the world, from which thou comest, wither!"

Thus saying, he turned slowly away, and passing behind the statue, towards which he had pointed during the last sentence, suddenly, and as if by enchantment, disappeared from my sight.

## CHAPTER IX.

BEING now left to my own solitary thoughts, I had full leisure to reflect, with some degree of coolness, upon the inconveniences, if not dangers, of the situation into which my love of adventure had hurried me. However prompt my imagination was to kindle, in its own ideal sphere, I have ever found that, when brought into contact with reality, it as suddenly cooled ;—like those meteors, that appear to be stars, while in the air, but, the moment they touch earth, are extinguished. And such was the feeling of disenchantment that now succeeded to the wild dreams in which I had been indulging. As long as fancy had the field of the future to herself, even immortality did not seem too distant a race for her. But when human instruments interposed, the illusion all vanished. From mortal lips the promise of immortality seemed a mockery, nor had imagination herself any wings that could carry beyond the grave.

Nor was this disappointment the only feeling that occupied me ;—the imprudence of the step on which

I had ventured now appeared in its full extent before my eyes. I had here thrown myself into the power of the most artful priesthood in the world, without a chance of being able to escape from their toils, or to resist any machinations with which they might beset me. It appeared evident, from the state of preparation in which I had found all that wonderful apparatus, by which the terrors and splendours of Initiation are produced, that my descent into the pyramid was not unexpected. Numerous, indeed, and active as were the spies of the Sacred College of Memphis, it could little be doubted that all my movements, since my arrival, had been watchfully tracked ; and the many hours I had employed in wandering and exploring around the pyramid, betrayed a curiosity and a spirit of adventure which might well suggest to these wily priests the hope of inveigling an Epicurean into their superstitious toils.

I was well aware of their hatred to the sect of which I was Chief ;—that they considered the Epicureans as, next to the Christians, the most formidable enemies of their craft and power. " How thoughtless, then," I felt, " to have placed myself in a situation where I am equally helpless against their fraud and violence, and must either pretend to be the dupe of their impostures, or else submit to become the victim of their vengeance !" Of these alternatives, bitter as they were, the latter appeared by far the more welcome. It was with a blush that I even looked back upon the mockeries I had already yielded to ; and the prospect of being put through still further ceremonials, and of being tutored and preached to by hypocrites I so much despised, appeared to me, in my present temper, a trial of patience, to which the flames and whirlwinds I had already encountered were but pastime.

Often and impatiently did I look up, between those rocky walls, to the bright sky that appeared to rest upon their summits, as, pacing round and round, through every part of the valley, I endeavoured to find some outlet from its gloomy precincts. But vain were all my endeavours ;—that rocky barrier, which seemed to end but in heaven, interposed itself everywhere. Neither did the image of the young maiden, though constantly in my mind, now bring with it the least consolation or hope. Of what avail was it that she, perhaps, was an inhabitant of this region, if I could neither behold her smile, nor catch the sound of her voice,—if, while among preaching priests I wasted away my hours, her presence was, alas, diffusing its enchantment elsewhere.

At length exhausted, I lay down by the brink of the lake, and gave myself up to all the melancholy of my fancy. The pale semblance of daylight, which had hitherto glimmered around, grew, every moment, more dim and dismal. Even the rich gleam, at the summit of the cascade, had faded ; and the sunshine, like the water, exhausted in its descent, had now dwindled into a ghostly glimmer, far worse than darkness. The birds upon the lake, as if about to die with the dying light, sunk down their heads; and as I looked to the statue, the deepening shadows gave such an expression to its mournful features as chilled my very soul.

The thought of death, ever ready to present itself to my imagination, now came, with a disheartening weight, such as I had never before felt. I almost fancied myself already in the dark vestibule of the grave,—separated, for ever, from the world above, and with nothing but the blank of an eternal sleep before me. It had often, I knew, happened that the visitants of this mysterious realm were, after their descent from earth, never seen or heard of;—being condemned, for some failure in their initiatory trials, to pine away their lives in those dark dungeons, with which, as well as with altars, this region abounded. Such, I shuddered to think, might probably be my own destiny; and so appalling was the thought that even the spirit by which I had been hitherto sustained died within me, and I was already giving myself up to helplessness and despair.

At length, after some hours of this gloomy musing, I heard a rustling in the sacred grove behind the statue; and, soon after, the sound of the Priest's voice—more welcome than I had ever thought such voice could be—brought the assurance that I was not yet, at least, wholly abandoned. Finding his way to me through the gloom, he now led me to the spot on which we had parted so many hours before ; and, addressing me in a voice that retained no trace of displeasure, bespoke my attention, while he should reveal to me some of those divine truths, by whose infusion, he said, into the soul of man, its purification can alone be effected.

The valley had now become so dark that we were no longer able to discern each other's face. There was a melancholy in the voice of my instructor that well accorded with the gloom around us : and, saddened and subdued, I now listened with resignation, if not with interest, to those sublime, but, alas, I thought, vain tenets, which, with all the warmth of a true believer, this Hierophant expounded to me.

He spoke of the pre-existence of the soul,—of its abode, from all eternity, in a place of splendour and bliss, of which all that we have most beautiful in our conceptions here is but a dim transcript, a clouded remembrance. In the blue depths of ether, he said, lay that "Country of the Soul,"—its boundary alone visible in that line of milky light, which separates it, as by a barrier of stars, from the dark earth. " Oh, realm of purity ! Home of the yet unfallen Spirit !— where, in the days of her first innocence, she wandered ; ere yet her beauty was soiled by the touch of earth, or her resplendent wings had begun to wither away. Methinks I see," he cried, " at this moment, those fields of radiance,—I look back, through the mists of life, into that luminous world, where the souls that have never lost their high, heavenly rank, still soar, without a stain, above the shadowless stars, and there dwell together in infinite perfection and bliss!"

As he spoke these words, a burst of pure, brilliant light, like a sudden opening of heaven, broke through the valley; and, as soon as my eyes were able to endure the splendour, such a vision of glory and love-liness opened upon them, as took even my sceptical spirit by surprise, and made it yield, at once, to the potency of the spell.

Suspended, as I thought, in air, and occupying the whole of the opposite region of the valley, there appeared an immense orb of light, within which, through a haze of radiance, I could see distinctly fair groups of young female spirits, who, in silent, but harmonious movement, like that of the stars, wound slowly through a variety of fanciful evolutions; seeming, as they linked and unlinked each other's arms, to form a living labyrinth of beauty and grace. Though their feet appeared to glide along a field of light, they had also wings of the most brilliant hue, which, like rainbows over waterfalls, when played with by the breeze, reflected, every moment, a new variety of glory.

As I stood, gazing with wonder, the orb, with all its ethereal inmates, began gradually to recede into the dark void, lessening, as it went, and becoming more bright, as it lessened;—till, at length, distant, to all appearance, as a retiring comet, this little world of

Spirits, in one small point of intense radiance, shone its last and vanished. "Go," exclaimed the rapt Priest, "ye happy souls, of whose dwelling a glimpse is thus given to our eyes; go, wander, in your orb, through the boundless Heaven, nor ever let a thought of this perishable world come to mingle its dross with your divine nature, or allure you down earthward to that mortal fall by which spirits, no less bright and admirable, have been ruined!"

A pause ensued, during which, still under the influence of wonder, I sent my fancy wandering after the inhabitants of that orb,—almost wishing myself credulous enough to believe in a heaven, of which creatures so much like those I worshipped upon earth were inmates.

At length, the Priest, with a mournful sigh at the sad contrast he was about to draw between the happy spirits we had just seen and the fallen ones of earth, resumed again his melancholy History of the Soul. Tracing it gradually from the first moment of earthward desire, to its final eclipse in the shadows of this world, he dwelt upon every stage of its darkening descent, with a pathos that sent sadness into the very depths of the heart. The first downward look of the Spirit towards earth—the tremble of her wings on the edge of Heaven—the giddy slide, at length, down that fatal descent, and the Lethean cup, midway in the sky, of which when she has once tasted, Heaven is forgot,—through all these gradations he traced mournfully her fall, to the last stage of darkness, when, wholly immersed in this world, her celestial nature is changed, she no longer can rise above earth, nor can remember her former home, but by glimpses so vague, that, at length, mistaking for hope what is only recollection, she believes them to be a light from the Future, not the Past.

"To retrieve this ruin of the once blessed Soul,— to clear away from around her the clouds of earth, and, restoring her lost wings,* facilitate their return to Heaven,—such," said the reverend man, "is the great task of our religion, and such the triumph of those divine Mysteries, in whose inmost depths the life and essence of our holy religion lie treasured. However sunk and changed and clouded may be the Spirit, yet as long as a single trace of her original light remains, there is still hope that——"

Here his voice was interrupted by a strain of mournful music, of which the low, distant breathings had been, for some minutes, heard, but which now gained upon the ear too thrillingly to let it listen to any more earthly sound. A faint light, too, at that instant broke through the valley, and I could perceive, not far from the spot where we sat, a female figure, veiled, and crouching to earth, as if subdued by sorrow, or under the influence of shame.

The feeble light, by which I saw her, came from a

---

* In the language of Plato, Hierocles, &c., to "restore to the soul its wings," is the main object both of religion and philosophy.

pale, moonlike meteor, which had gradually formed itself in the air as the music approached, and now shed over the rocks and the lake a glimmer as cold as that by which the Dead, in their own kingdom, gaze upon each other. The music, too, which appeared to rise directly out of the lake, and to come full of the breath of its dark waters, spoke a despondency in every note which no language could express ;—and, as I listened to its tones, and looked upon that fallen Spirit (for such, the holy man whispered, was the form before us), so entirely did the illusion of the scene take possession of me, that, with breathless anxiety, I now awaited the result.

Nor had I gazed long before that form rose slowly from its drooping position ;—the air around it grew bright, and the pale meteor overhead assumed a more cheerful and living light. The veil, which had before shrouded the face of the figure, became every minute more transparent, and the features, one by one, gradually disclosed themselves. Having tremblingly watched the progress of the apparition, I now started from my seat, and half exclaimed, "It is she!" In another minute, this veil had, like a thin mist, melted away, and the young Priestess of the Moon stood, for the third time, revealed before my eyes!

To rush instantly towards her was my first impulse —but the arm of the Priest held me firmly back. The fresh light, which had begun to flow in from all sides, collected itself in a glory round the spot where

G

she stood. Instead of melancholy music, strains of the most exalted rapture were heard ; and the young maiden, buoyant as the inhabitants of the fairy orb, amid a blaze of light like that which fell upon her in the Temple, ascended into the air.

"Stay, beautiful vision, stay !" I exclaimed, as, breaking from the hold of the Priest, I flung myself prostrate on the ground,—the only mode by which I could express the admiration, even to worship, with which I was filled. But the vanishing spirit heard me not :—receding into the darkness, like that orb, whose track she seemed to follow, her form lessened away till she was seen no more. Gazing, till the last luminous speck had disappeared, I suffered myself unconsciously to be led away by my reverend guide, who, placing me once more on my bed of poppy-leaves, left me to such repose as it was now possible, after such a scene, to enjoy.

## CHAPTER X.

THE apparition with which I had been blessed in that Valley of Visions—for so the place where I had witnessed these wonders was called—brought back to my heart all the hopes and fancies in which during my descent from earth I had indulged. I had now seen once more that matchless creature, who had been my guiding star into this mysterious world; and that she must be, in some way, connected with the further revelations that awaited me, I saw no reason to doubt. There was a sublimity, too, in the doctrines of my reverend teacher, and even a hope in the promises of immortality held out by him, which, in spite of reason, won insensibly both upon my fancy and my pride.

The Future, however, was now but of secondary consideration;—the Present, and that deity of the Present, woman, were the objects that engrossed my whole soul. For the sake, indeed, of such beings alone did I consider immortality desirable, nor, without them, would eternal life have appeared to me worth a prayer. To every further trial of my patience and faith, I now made up my mind to submit without a murmur. Some kind chance, I fondly persuaded myself, might yet bring me nearer to the object of my adoration, and enable me to address, as mortal woman, one who had hitherto been to me but as a vision, a shade.

The period of my probation, however, was nearly at an end. Both frame and spirit had now been tried ; and, as the crowning test of the purification of the latter was that power of seeing into the world of spirits, with which I had proved myself, in the Valley of Visions, to be endowed, there remained now, to perfect my Initiation, but this one night more, when, in the Temple of Isis, and in the presence of her unveiled image, the last grand revelation of the Secret of Secrets was to be laid open to me.

I passed the morning of this day in company with the same venerable personage, who had, from the first, presided over the ceremonies of my instruction ; and who, to inspire me with due reverence for the power and magnificence of his religion, now conducted me through the long range of illuminated galleries and shrines, that extend under the site upon which Memphis and the Pyramids stand, and form a counterpart underground to that mighty city of temples upon earth.

He then descended with me, still lower, into those winding crypts, where lay the Seven Tables of stone

*The Ring*

found by Hermes in the valley of Hebron. "On these tables," said he, "is written all the knowledge of the antediluvian race,—the decrees of the stars from the beginning of time, the annals of a still earlier world, and all the marvellous secrets, both of heaven and earth, which would have been

> '*but* for this key,
> Lost in the Universal Sea.'"

Returning to the region from which we had descended, we next visited, in succession, a series of small shrines representing the various objects of adoration through Egypt, and thus furnishing to the Priest an occasion for explaining the mysterious nature of animal worship, and the refined doctrines of theology that lay veiled under its forms. Every shrine was consecrated to a particular faith, and contained a living image of the deity which it adored. Beside the goat of Mendes, with his refulgent star upon his breast, I saw the crocodile, as presented to the eyes of its idolaters at Arsinoë, with costly gems in its loathsome ears, and rich bracelets of gold encircling its feet. Here, floating through a tank in the centre of a temple, the sacred carp of Lepidotum showed its silvery scales ; while, there, the Isiac serpents trailed languidly over the altar, with that sort of movement which is thought most favourable to the aspirations of their votaries. In one of the small chapels we found a beautiful child, feeding and watching over those golden beetles, which are adored for their brightness, as emblems of the sun ; while, in another, stood a sacred ibis upon its pedestal, so like, in plumage and attitude, to the bird of the young Priestess, that most gladly would I have knelt down and worshipped it for her sake.

After visiting all these various shrines, and hearing the reflections which they suggested, I was next led by my guide to the Great Hall of the Zodiac, on whose ceiling, in bright and undying colours, was delineated the map of the firmament, as it appeared at the first dawn of time. Here, in pointing out the track of the sun among the spheres, he spoke of the analogy that exists between moral and physical darkness—of the sympathy with which all spiritual creatures regard the sun, so as to sadden and decline when he sinks into his wintry hemisphere, and to rejoice when he resumes his own empire of light. Hence, the festivals and hymns, with which most of the nations of the earth are wont to welcome the resurrection of his orb in spring, as an emblem and pledge of the re-ascent of the soul to heaven. Hence, the songs of sorrow, the mournful ceremonies,—like those Mysteries of the Night, upon the Lake of Saïs, —in which they brood over his autumnal descent into the shades, as a type of the Spirit's fall into this world of death.

In discourses such as these the hours passed away ; and though there was nothing in the light of this sunless region to mark to the eye the decline of day,

my own feelings told me that the night drew near ;—
nor, in spite of my incredulity, could I refrain from a
slight flutter of hope, as that promised moment of
revelation approached, when the Mystery of Mysteries
was to be made all my own. This consummation,
however, was less near than I expected. My patience
had still further trials to encounter. It was necessary,
I now found, that, during the greater part of the night,
I should keep watch in the Sanctuary of the Temple,
alone and in utter darkness,—thus preparing myself,
by meditation, for the awful moment, when the
irradiation from behind the sacred Veils was to burst
upon me.

At the appointed hour, we left the Hall of the
Zodiac, and proceeded through a long line of marble
galleries, where the lamps were more thinly scattered
as we advanced, till, at length, we found ourselves in
total darkness. Here the Priest, taking me by the
hand, and leading me down a flight of steps, into a
place where the same deep gloom prevailed, said, with
a voice trembling, as if from excess of awe,—" Thou
art now within the Sanctuary of our goddess, Isis, and
the veils, that conceal her sacred image, are before
thee ! "

After exhorting me earnestly to that train of
thought which best accorded with the spirit of the
place where I stood, and, above all, to that full and
unhesitating faith, with which alone, he said, the
manifestation of such mysteries should be approached,

the holy man took leave of me, and re-ascended the steps;—while, so spell-bound did I feel by that deep darkness, that the last sound of his footsteps died upon my ear, before I ventured to stir a limb from the position in which he had left me.

The prospect of the long watch I had now to look forward to was dreadful. Even danger itself, if in an active form, would have been far preferable to this sort of safe, but dull, probation, by which patience was the only virtue put to the proof. Having ascertained how far the space around me was free from obstacles, I endeavoured to beguile the time by pacing up and down within those limits, till I became tired of the monotonous echoes of my own tread. Finding my way, then, to what I felt to be a massive pillar, and, leaning wearily against it, I surrendered myself to a train of thoughts and feelings, far different from those with which the good Hierophant had hoped to inspire me.

" Why," I again asked, " if these priests possess the secret of life, why are they themselves the victims of death ? why sink into the grave with the cup of immortality in their hands ? But no, safe boasters, the eternity they so lavishly promise is reserved for *another*, a future world—that ready resource of all priestly promises—that depository of the airy pledges of all creeds. Another world!—alas, where does it lie ? or, what spirit hath ever come to say that Life is there ? "

The conclusion at which, half sadly, half passionately, I arrived, was that, life being but a dream of the
moment never to come again, every bliss so vaguely
promised for hereafter ought to be secured by the
wise man here. And, as no heaven I had ever heard
of from these visionary priests opened half such certainty of happiness as that smile which I beheld last
night,—" Let me," I exclaimed, impatiently, striking
the massy pillar till it rung, " let me but make that
beautiful Priestess my own, and I here willingly exchange for her every chance of immortality that the
combined wisdom of Egypt's Twelve Temples can
offer me ! "

No sooner had I uttered these words, than a tremendous peal, like that of thunder, rolled over the Sanctuary, and seemed to shake its very walls. On every
side, too, a succession of blue, vivid flashes pierced,
like lances of light, through the gloom, revealing to
me, at intervals, the mighty dome in which I stood,—
its ceiling of azure, studded with stars,—its colossal
columns, towering aloft, and those dark, awful veils,
whose massy drapery hung from the roof to the floor,
covering the rich glories of the Shrine beneath their
folds.

So weary had I grown of my tedious watch that
this stormy and fitful illumination, during which the
Sanctuary seemed to rock to its base, was by no
means an unwelcome interruption of the monotonous
trial my patience had to suffer. After a short interval,

however, the flashes ceased ;—the sounds died away, like exhausted thunder, through the abyss, and darkness and silence, like that of the grave, succeeded.

Resting my back once more against the pillar, and fixing my eyes upon that side of the Sanctuary from which the promised irradiation was to burst, I now resolved to await the awful moment in patience. Resigned and almost immovable, I had remained thus, for nearly another hour, when suddenly, along the edges of the mighty Veils, I perceived a thin rim of light, as if from some brilliant object under them; —resembling that border which encircles a cloud at sunset, when the rich radiance from behind is escaping at its edges.

This indication of concealed glories grew every instant more strong ; till, at last, vividly marked as it was upon the darkness, the narrow fringe of lustre almost pained the eye, giving promise of a fulness of splendour too bright to be endured. My expectations were now wound to the highest pitch, and all the scepticism, into which I had been cooling down my mind, was forgotten. The wonders that had been presented to me since my descent from earth,—that glimpse into Elysium on the first night of my coming, —those visitants from the Land of Spirits in the mysterious valley,—all led me to expect, in this last and brightest revelation, such visions of glory and knowledge as might transcend even fancy itself, nor leave a doubt that they belonged less to earth than heaven.

While, with an imagination thus excited, I stood
waiting the result, an increased gush of light still
more awakened my attention; and I saw, with an
intenseness of interest which made my heart beat
aloud, one of the corners of the mighty Veil slowly
raised. I now felt that the Great Secret, whatever it
might be, was at hand. A vague hope even crossed
my mind—so wholly had imagination now resumed
her empire—that the splendid promise of my dream
was on the very point of being realized!

With surprise, however, and, for the moment, with
some disappointment, I perceived, that the massy
corner of the Veil was but lifted sufficiently from the
ground to allow a female figure to emerge from under
it,—and then fell over its mystic splendours as utterly
dark as before. By the strong light, too, that issued
when the drapery was raised, and illuminated the
profile of the emerging figure, I either saw, or fancied
that I saw, the same bright features, that had already
so often mocked me with their momentary charm, and
seemed destined to haunt my fancy as unavailingly as
even the fond, vain dream of Immortality itself.

Dazzled as I had been by that short gush of
splendour, and distrusting even my senses, when
under the influence of an imagination so much
excited, I had but just begun to question myself as to
the reality of my impression, when I heard the sounds
of light footsteps approaching me through the gloom.
In a second or two more, the figure stopped before

me, and, placing the end of a riband gently in my
hand, said, in a tremulous whisper, "Follow, and be
silent."

So sudden and strange was the adventure, that, for
a moment, I hesitated,—fearing that my eyes might
possibly have been deceived as to the object they had
seen. Casting a look towards the Veil, which seemed
bursting with its luminous secret, I was almost doubting to which of the two chances I should commit
myself, when I felt the riband in my hand pulled
softly at the other extremity. This movement, like a
touch of magic, at once decided me. Without any
further deliberation, I yielded to the silent summons,
and, following my guide, who was already at some
distance before me, found myself led up the same
flight of marble steps by which the Priest had conducted me into the Sanctuary. Arrived at their summit, I felt the pace of my conductress quicken, and
giving one more look to the Veiled Shrine, whose
glories we left burning uselessly behind us, hastened
onward into the gloom, full of confidence in the
belief, that she, who now held the other end of that
clue, was one whom I was ready to follow devotedly
through the world.

## CHAPTER XI.

WITH such rapidity was I hurried along by my unseen guide, full of wonder at the speed with which
she ventured through these labyrinths, that I had but
little time left for reflection upon the strangeness of the
adventure in which I had embarked. My knowledge
of the character of the Memphian priests, as well as
some fearful rumours that had reached me, concerning
the fate that often attended unbelievers in their hands,
awakened a momentary suspicion of treachery in my
mind. But, when I recalled the face of my guide, as
I had seen it in the small chapel, with that divine
look, the very memory of which brought purity into
the heart, I found my suspicions all vanish, and felt
shame at having harboured them but an instant.

In the meanwhile, our rapid course continued without any interruption, through windings even more
capriciously intricate than any I yet had passed, and
whose thick gloom seemed never to have been broken
by a single glimmer of light. My unseen conductress
was still at some distance before me, and the slight

clue, to which I clung as if it were Destiny's own thread, was still kept, by her flying speed, at full stretch between us. At length, suddenly stopping she said, in a breathless whisper, " Seat thyself here ; " and, at the same moment, led me by the hand to a sort of low car, in which, obeying her command, I lost not a moment in placing myself, while the maiden, no less promptly, took her seat by my side.

A sudden click, like the touching of a spring, was then heard, and the car,—which, I had felt in entering it, leaned half-way over a steep descent,—on being loosed from its station, shot down, almost perpendicularly, into the darkness, with a rapidity which, at first, nearly deprived me of breath. The wheels slid smoothly and noiselessly in grooves, and the impetus which the car acquired in descending was sufficient, I perceived, to carry it up an eminence that succeeded, —from the summit of which it again rushed down another declivity, even still more long and precipitous than the former. In this manner we proceeded, by alternate falls and rises, till, at length, from the last and steepest elevation, the car descended upon a level of deep sand, where, after running for a few yards, it by degrees lost its motion and stopped.

Here, the maiden alighting again placed the riband in my hands,—and again I followed her, though with more slowness and difficulty than before, as our way now led up a flight of damp and time-worn steps, whose ascent seemed to the weary and insecure foot interminable. Perceiving with what languor my guide advanced, I was on the point of making an effort to assist her progress, when the creak of an opening door above, and a faint gleam of light which, at the same moment, shone upon her figure, apprized me that we were at last arrived within reach of sunshine.

Joyfully I followed through this opening, and, by the dim light, could discern that we were now in the sanctuary of a vast, ruined temple,—having entered by a secret passage under the pedestal upon which an image of the idol of the place once stood. The first movement of the young maiden, after closing again the portal under the pedestal was, without even a single look towards me, to cast herself down upon her knees, with her hands clasped and uplifted, as if in thanksgiving or prayer. But she was unable, evidently, to sustain herself in this position ;—her strength could hold out no longer. Overcome by agitation and fatigue, she sunk senseless upon the pavement.

Bewildered as I was myself by the strange events of the night, I stood for some minutes looking upon her in a state of helplessness and alarm. But, re-minded, by my own feverish sensations, of the reviving effects of the air, I raised her gently in my arms, and crossing the corridor that surrounded the sanctuary, found my way to the outer vestibule of the temple. Here, shading her eyes from the sun, I placed her, reclining, upon the steps, where the cool north-wind, then blowing freshly between the pillars, might play, with free draught, over her brow.

It was, indeed—as I now saw, with certainty—the same beautiful and mysterious girl, who had been the cause of my descent into that subterranean world, and who now, under such strange and unaccountable circumstances, was my guide back again to the realms of day. I looked around to discover where we were, and beheld such a scene of grandeur, as, could my eyes have been then attracted to any object but the pale form reclining at my side, might well have induced them to dwell on its splendid beauties.

I was now standing, I found, on the small island in the centre of Lake Mœris; and that sanctuary, where we had just emerged from darkness, formed part of the ruins of an ancient temple, which was (as I have since learned), in the grander days of Memphis, a place of pilgrimage for worshippers from all parts of Egypt. The fair Lake, itself, out of whose waters once rose pavilions, palaces, and even lofty pyramids, was still, though divested of many of these wonders, a scene of interest and splendour such as the whole world could not equal. While the shores still sparkled with mansions and temples, that bore testimony to the luxury of a living race, the voice of the Past, speaking out of unnumbered ruins, whose summits, here and there, rose blackly above the wave, told of times long fled and generations long swept away,

before whose gigantic remains all the glory of the
present stood humbled. Over the southern bank of
the Lake hung the dark relics of the Labyrinth ;—its
twelve Royal Palaces, representing the mansions of
the Zodiac—its thundering portals and constellated
halls, having left nothing now behind but a few frown-
ing ruins, which, contrasted with the soft groves of
acacia and olive around them, seemed to rebuke the
luxuriant smiles of nature, and threw a melancholy
grandeur over the whole scene.

The effects of the air, in re-animating the young
Priestess, were less speedy than I had expected ;—her
eyes were still closed, and she remained pale and
insensible. Alarmed, I now rested her head (which
had been for some time supported by my arm) against
the base of one of the columns, with my cloak for its
pillow, while I hastened to procure some water from
the Lake. The temple stood high, and the descent to
the shore was precipitous. But, my Epicurean habits
having but little impaired my activity, I soon descended, with the lightness of a desert deer, to the
bottom. Here, plucking from a lofty bean-tree, whose
flowers stood, shining like gold, above the water, one
of those large hollowed leaves that serve as cups for
the Hebes of the Nile, I filled it from the Lake, and
hurried back with the cool draught towards the
temple. It was not, however, without some difficulty
that I succeeded at last in bearing my rustic chalice
steadily up the steep ; more than once did an unlucky

H

slip waste all its contents, and as often did I return impatiently to refill it.

During this time, the young maiden was fast recovering her animation and consciousness ; and, at the moment when I appeared above the edge of the steep, was just rising from the steps, with her hand pressed to her forehead, as if confusedly recalling the recollection of what had occurred. No sooner did she observe me, than a short cry of alarm broke from her lips. Looking anxiously round, as though she sought for protection, and half audibly uttering the words, "Where is he?" she made an effort, as I approached, to retreat into the temple.

Already, however, I was by her side, and taking gently her hand in mine, as she turned away from me, asked, " Whom dost thou seek, fair Priestess ? " —thus, for the first time, breaking the silence she had enjoined, and in a tone that might have reassured the most timid spirit. But my words had no effect in calming her apprehension. Trembling, and with her eyes still averted towards the Temple, she continued in a voice of suppressed alarm,—" Where *can* he be ? —that venerable Athenian, that philosopher, who——"

" Here, here," I exclaimed, anxiously, interrupting her,—" behold him still by thy side,—the same, the very same, who saw thee steal from under the Veils of the Sanctuary, whom thou hast guided by a clue through those labyrinths below, and who now only waits his command from those lips, to devote himself through life and death to thy service." As I spoke these words, she turned slowly round, and looking timidly in my face, while her own burned with blushes, said, in a tone of doubt and wonder, " Thou ! " and then hid her eyes in her hands.

I knew not how to interpret a reception so unexpected. That some mistake or disappointment had occurred was evident ; but so inexplicable did the whole adventure appear to me, that it was in vain to think of unravelling any part of it. Weak and agitated, she now tottered to the steps of the Temple, and there seating herself, with her forehead against the cold marble, seemed for some moments absorbed in the most anxious thought ; while silent and watchful I awaited her decision, though, at the same time, with a feeling which proved to be prophetic,—that my destiny must, from thenceforth, be linked inseparably with hers.

The inward struggle by which she was agitated, though violent, was not of long continuance. Starting suddenly from her seat, with a look of terror towards the Temple, as if the fear of immediate pursuit had alone decided her, she pointed eagerly towards the East, and exclaimed, " To the Nile, without delay ! " —clasping her hands, after she had thus spoken, with the most suppliant fervour, as if to soften the abruptness of the mandate she had given, and appealing to me at the same time with a look that would have taught Stoics themselves tenderness.

I lost not a moment in obeying the welcome command. With a thousand wild hopes naturally crowding upon my fancy, at the thoughts of a voyage under such auspices, I descended rapidly to the shore, and hailing one of those boats that ply upon the Lake for hire, arranged speedily for a passage down the canal to the Nile. Having learned, too, from the boatmen, a more easy path up the rock, I hastened back to the Temple for my fair charge ; and without a word or look that could alarm, even by its kindness, or disturb the innocent confidence which she now evidently reposed in me, led her down by the winding path to the boat.

Everything around looked sunny and smiling as we embarked. The morning was now in its first freshness, and the path of the breeze might clearly be traced over the Lake, as it went wakening up the waters from their sleep of the night. The gay, golden-winged birds that haunt these shores, were, in every direction, skimming along the Lake; while, with a graver consciousness of beauty, the swan and the pelican were seen dressing their white plumage in the mirror of its wave. To add to the liveliness of the scene, there came, at intervals, on the breeze, a sweet tinkling of musical instruments from boats at a distance, employed thus early in pursuing the fish of these waters, that allow themselves to be decoyed into the nets by music.

The vessel I had selected for our voyage was one

of those small pleasure-boats or yachts,—so much in use among the luxurious navigators of the Nile,—in the centre of which rises a pavilion of cedar or cypress wood, adorned richly on the outside with religious emblems, and gaily fitted up within for feasting and repose. To the door of this pavilion I now led my companion, and, after a few words of kindness,—tempered cautiously with as much reserve as the deep tenderness of my feeling towards her would admit of,—left her in solitude to court that restoring rest which the agitation of her spirits so much required.

For myself, though repose was hardly less necessary to me, the state of ferment in which my thoughts had been so long kept appeared to render it hopeless. Throwing myself on the deck of the vessel, under an awning which the sailors had raised for me, I continued, for some hours, in a sort of vague day-dream ; —sometimes passing in review the scenes of that subterranean drama, and sometimes, with my eyes fixed in drowsy vacancy, receiving passively the impressions of the bright scenery through which we passed.

The banks of the canal were then luxuriantly wooded. Under the tufts of the light and towering palm were seen the orange and the citron, interlacing their boughs ; while, here and there, huge tamarisks thickened the shade, and, at the very edge of the bank, the willow of Babylon stood bending its graceful branches into the water. Occasionally, out of the depth of these groves, there shone a small temple or pleasure-house ;—while, now and then, an opening in their line of foliage allowed the eye to wander over extensive fields, all covered with beds of those pale, sweet roses, for which this district of Egypt is so celebrated.

The activity of the morning hour was visible in every direction. Flights of doves and lapwings were fluttering among the leaves, and the white heron, which had been roosting all night in some date-tree, now stood sunning its wings upon the green bank, or floated, like living silver, over the flood. The flowers, too, both of land and water, looked all just freshly awakened ;—and, most of all, the superb lotus, which, having risen along with the sun from the wave, was now holding up her chalice for a full draught of his light.

Such were the scenes that now successively presented themselves, mingling with the vague reveries that floated through my mind, as our boat, with its high, capacious sail, swept along the flood. Though the occurrences of the last few days appeared to me one continued series of wonders, yet by far the most striking marvel of all was, that she whose first look had sent wild-fire into my heart,—whom I had thought of ever since with a restlessness of passion that would have dared anything on earth to obtain its object,— was now resting sacredly within that small pavilion, while guarding her, even from myself, I lay calmly at its threshold,

Meanwhile, the sun had reached his meridian height. The busy hum of the morning had died gradually away, and all around was sleeping in the hot stillness of noon. The Nile-goose, having folded up her splendid wings, was lying motionless on the shadow of the sycamores in the water. Even the nimble lizards upon the bank appeared to move more languidly as the light fell upon their gold and azure hues. Overcome as I was with watching, and weary with thought, it was not long before I yielded to the becalming influence of the hour. Looking fixedly at the pavilion,—as if once more to assure myself that I was not already in a dream, but that the young Egyptian was really there,—I felt my eyes close as I gazed, and in a few minutes sunk into a profound sleep.

## CHAPTER XII.

IT was by the canal through which we now sailed, that, in the more prosperous days of Memphis, the commerce of Upper Egypt and Nubia was transported to her magnificent Lake, and from thence, having paid tribute to the queen of cities, was poured out again, through the Nile, into the ocean. The course of this canal to the river was not direct, but ascending in a south-easterly direction towards the Saïd; and in calms, or with adverse winds, the passage was tedious. But as the breeze was now blowing freshly from the north, there was every prospect of our reaching the river before nightfall. Rapidly, too, as our galley swept along the flood, its motion was so smooth as to be hardly felt; and the quiet gurgle of the waters, and the drowsy song of the boatman at the prow, were the only sounds that disturbed the deep silence which prevailed.

The sun, indeed, had nearly sunk behind the Libyan hills, before the sleep, into which these sounds had contributed to lull me, was broken; and the first

*The Nile*

object on which my eyes rested, in waking, was that fair young Priestess,—seated within a porch which shaded the door of the pavilion, and bending intently over a small volume that lay unrolled on her lap.

Her face was but half turned towards me ; and as she, once or twice, raised her eyes to the warm sky, whose light fell, softened through the trellis, over her cheek, I found all those feelings of reverence, which she had inspired me with in the chapel, return. There was even a purer and holier charm around her countenance, thus seen by the natural light of day, than in those dim and unhallowed regions below. She was now looking, too, direct to the glorious sky, and her pure eyes and that heaven, so worthy of each other, met.

After contemplating her for a few moments with little less than adoration, I rose gently from my resting-place, and approached the pavilion. But the mere movement had startled her from her devotion, and, blushing and confused, she covered the volume with the folds of her robe.

In the art of winning upon female confidence I had, of course, long been schooled ; and, now that to the lessons of gallantry the inspiration of love was added, my ambition to please and to interest could hardly, it may be supposed, fail of success. I soon found, however, how much less fluent is the heart than the fancy, and how different from each other may be the operations of making love and feeling it. In the few words of greeting now exchanged between us, it was evident that the gay, the enterprising Epicurean was little less embarrassed than the secluded Priestess ;—and, after one or two ineffectual efforts to bring our voices acquainted with each other, the eyes of both turned bashfully away, and we relapsed into silence.

From this situation—the result of timidity on one side, and of a feeling altogether new on the other—we were at length relieved, after an interval of estrangement, by the boatmen announcing that the Nile was in sight. The countenance of the young Egyptian brightened at this intelligence ; and the smile with which I congratulated her upon the speed of our voyage was responded to by another from her, so full of gratitude that already an instinctive sympathy seemed established between us.

We were now on the point of entering that sacred river, for a draught of whose sweet flood the royal daughters of the Ptolemies, when far away on foreign thrones, have been known to sigh in the midst of their splendour. As our boat, with slackened sail, was gliding into the current, an inquiry from the boatmen, whether they should anchor for the night in the Nile, first reminded me of the ignorance in which I still remained, with respect to either the motive or destination of our voyage. Embarrassed by their question, I directed my eyes towards the Priestess, whom I saw waiting for my answer with a look of anxiety, which this silent reference to her wishes at once dispelled. Unfolding eagerly the volume with which I had seen her so much occupied, she took from between its folds a small leaf of papyrus, on which there appeared to be some faint lines of drawing, and, after looking upon it thoughtfully for a few moments, placed it, with an agitated hand, in mine.

In the meantime, the boatmen had taken in their sail, and the yacht drove slowly down the river with the current, while, by a light which had been kindled at sunset on the deck, I stood examining the leaf that the Priestess had given me,—her dark eyes fixed anxiously on my countenance all the while. The lines traced upon the papyrus were so faint as to be almost invisible, and I was for some time wholly unable to form a conjecture as to their import. At length, however, I succeeded in discovering that they were the outlines, or map—traced slightly and un-steadily with a Memphian reed—of a part of that mountainous ridge by which Upper Egypt is bounded to the east, together with the names, or rather em-blems, of the chief towns in its immediate neigh-bourhood.

It was thither, I now saw clearly, that the young Priestess wished to pursue her course. Without further delay, therefore, I ordered the boatmen to set our yacht before the wind, and ascend the current. My command was promptly obeyed : the white sail again rose into the region of the breeze, and the satisfaction that beamed in every feature of the fair Egyptian

showed that the quickness with which I had attended
to her wishes was not unfelt by her.  The moon had
now risen ; and, though the current was against us,
the Etesian wind of the season blew strongly up the
river, and we were soon floating before it, through the
rich plains and groves of the Saïd.

The love with which this simple girl had inspired
me, was, perhaps, from the mystic scenes and situa-
tions in which I had seen her, not unmingled with
a tinge of superstitious awe, under the influence of
which I felt the natural buoyancy of my spirit re-
pressed.  The few words that had passed between
us on the subject of our route had somewhat loosened
this spell ; and what I wanted of vivacity and confidence was more than compensated by the tone of
deep sensibility which love had awakened in their
place.

We had not proceeded far before the glittering of
lights at a distance, and the shooting up of fireworks,
at intervals, into the air, apprized us that we were
then approaching one of those night-fairs, or marts,
which it is the custom, at this season, to hold upon the
Nile.  To me the scene was familiar ; but to my young
companion it was evidently a new world ; and the
mixture of alarm and delight with which she gazed,
from under her veil, upon the busy scene into which we
now sailed, gave an air of innocence to her beauty,
which still more heightened its every charm.

It was one of the widest parts of the river ; and

the whole surface, from one bank to the other, was covered with boats. Along the banks of a green island, in the middle of the stream, lay anchored the galleys of the principal traders,—large floating bazas, bearing each the name of its owner, emblazoned in letters of flame, upon the stern. Over their decks were spread out, in gay confusion, the products of the loom and needle of Egypt,—rich carpets of Memphis, and those variegated veils for which the female embroiders of the Nile are so celebrated, and to which the name of Cleopatra lends a traditional charm. In each of the other galleys was exhibited some branch of Egyptian workmanship—vases of the fragrant porcelain of On,—cups of that frail crystal whose hues change like those of the pigeon's plumage,—enamelled amulets graven with the head of Anubis, and necklaces and bracelets of the black beans of Abyssinia.

While Commerce was thus displaying all her luxuries in one quarter, in every other Pleasure swarmed, in her thousand shapes, over the waters. Nor was the festivity confined to the river alone ; as along the banks of the island and on the shores there were seen illuminated mansions glittering through the trees, whence sounds of music and merriment came. In some of the boats were bands of minstrels, who, from time to time, answered each other, like echoes, across the wave ; and the notes of the lyre, the flageolet, and the sweet lotus-wood flute, were heard, in the pauses of revelry, dying along the waters.

Meanwhile, from other boats stationed in the least lighted places, the workers of fire sent forth their wonders into the air. Bursting out suddenly from time to time, as if in the very exuberance of joy, these sallies of flame appeared to reach the sky, and there, breaking into a shower of sparkles, shed such a splendour around as brightened even the white Arabian hills,—making them shine like the brow of Mount Atlas at night when the fire from his own bosom is playing around its snows.

The opportunity this mart afforded us of providing ourselves with some less remarkable habiliments than those in which we had escaped from that nether world, was too seasonable not to be gladly taken advantage of by both. For myself, the strange mystic garb which I wore was sufficiently concealed by my Grecian mantle, which I had fortunately thrown round me on the night of my watch. But the thin veil of my companion was a far less efficient disguise. She had, indeed, flung away the golden beetles from her hair ; but the sacred robe of her order was still too visible, and the stars of the bandelet shone brightly through her veil.

Most gladly, therefore, did she avail herself of this opportunity of a change ; and, as she took from out a casket—which, with the volume I had seen her reading, appeared to be her only treasure—a small jewel, to give in exchange for the simple garments she had chosen, there fell out, at the same time, the very cross of silver, which I had seen her kiss, as may be remembered, in the monumental chapel, and which was afterwards pressed to my own lips. This link between us (for such it now appeared to my imagination) called up again in my heart all the burning feelings of that moment;—and, had I not abruptly turned away, my agitation would, but too plainly, have betrayed itself.

The object for which we had delayed in this gay scene having been accomplished, the sail was again spread, and we proceeded on our course up the river. The sounds and the lights we left behind died gradually away, and we now floated along in moon-light and silence once more. Sweet dews, worthy of being called "the tears of Isis," fell refreshingly through the air, and every plant and flower sent its fragrance to meet them. The wind, just strong enough to bear us smoothly against the current, scarce stirred the shadow of the tamarisks on the water. As the inhabitants from all quarters were collected at the night-fair, the Nile was more than usually still and solitary. Such a silence, indeed, prevailed, that, as we glided near the shore, we could hear the rustling of the acacias as the chameleons ran up their stems. It was, altogether, such a night as only the climate of Egypt can boast, when the whole scene around lies lulled in that sort of bright tranquillity, which may be imagined to light the slumbers of those happy spirits, who are said to rest in the Valley of the Moon, on their way to heaven.

By such a light, and at such an hour, seated, side by side, on the deck of that bark, did we pursue our course up the lonely Nile—each a mystery to the other—our thoughts, our objects, our very names a secret ;—separated, too, till now, by destinies so different ; the one, a gay voluptuary of the Garden of Athens, the other, a secluded Priestess of the Temples of Memphis ;—and the only relation yet established between us being that dangerous one of love, passionate love, on one side, and the most feminine and confiding dependence on the other.

The passing adventure of the night-fair had not only dispelled still more our mutual reserve, but had supplied us with a subject on which we could converse without embarrassment. From this topic I took care to lead on, without interruption, to others,— fearful lest our former silence should return, and the music of her voice again be lost to me. It was, indeed, only by thus indirectly unburdening my heart that I was enabled to refrain from the full utterance of all I thought and felt ; and the restless rapidity with which I flew from subject to subject was but an effort to escape from the only one in which my heart was interested.

" How bright and happy," said I,—pointing up to Sothis, the fair Star of the Waters, which was just then shining brilliantly over our heads,—" How bright and happy this world ought to be, if—as your Egyptian sages assert—yon pure and beautiful luminary was its birth-star!" Then, still leaning back, and letting my eyes wander over the firmament, as if seeking to disengage them from the fascination which they dreaded—"To the study," I exclaimed, "for ages, of skies like this, may the pensive and mystic character of your nation be traced. That mixture of pride and melancholy which naturally arises, at the sight of those eternal lights shining out of darkness; —that sublime, but saddened, anticipation of a Future, which comes over the soul in the silence of such an hour, when, though Death seems to reign in the repose of earth, there are yet those beacons of Immortality burning in the sky—— "

Pausing, as I uttered the word "immortality," with a sigh to think how little my heart echoed to my lips, I looked in the face of my companion, and saw that it had lighted up, as I spoke, into a glow of holy animation, such as Faith alone gives—such as Hope herself wears when she is dreaming of heaven. Touched by the contrast, and gazing upon her with mournful tenderness, I found my arms half opened, to clasp her to my heart, while the words died away inaudibly upon my lips,—"Thou, too, beautiful maiden! must thou, too, die for ever?"

My self-command, I felt, had nearly deserted me. Rising abruptly from my seat, I walked to the middle of the deck, and stood, for some moments, unconsciously gazing upon one of those fires, which— according to the custom of all who travel by night

I

on the Nile—our boatmen had kindled, to scare away
the crocodiles from the vessel.    But it was in vain
that I endeavoured to compose my spirit.   Every
effort I made but more deeply convinced me, that,
till the mystery which hung round that maiden should
be solved—till the secret, with which my own bosom
laboured, should be disclosed—it was fruitless to
attempt even a semblance of tranquillity.

My resolution was therefore taken ;—to lay open
at least my own heart, as far as such a revelation
might be risked, without startling the timid innocence
of my companion.   Thus resolved, I resumed my
seat, with more composure, by her side, and taking
from my bosom the small mirror which she had
dropped in the Temple, and which I had ever since
worn suspended round my neck, presented it with a
trembling hand to her view.    The boatmen had just
kindled one of their night-fires near us, and its light,
as she leaned forward towards the mirror, fell upon
her face.

The quick blush of surprise with which she recognised it to be hers, and her look of bashful, yet eager,
inquiry, in raising her eyes to mine, were appeals
which I was not, of course, tardy in answering. Beginning with the first moment when I saw her in the
Temple, and passing hastily, but with words that
burned as they went, over the impression which she
had then left upon my heart and fancy, I proceeded
to describe the particulars of my descent into the

pyramid—my surprise and adoration at the door of the chapel—my encounter with the Trials of Initiation, so mysteriously prepared for me, and all the various visionary wonders I had witnessed in that region, till the moment when I had seen her stealing from under the Veils to approach me.

Though, in detailing these events, I had said but little of the feelings they had awakened in me,—though my lips had sent back many a sentence un-uttered, there was still enough that could neither be subdued nor disguised, and which, like that light from under the veils of her own Isis, glowed through every word that I spoke. When I told of the scene in the chapel,—of the silent interview which I had witnessed between the dead and the living,—the maiden leaned down her head and wept, as from a heart full of tears. It seemed a pleasure to her, however, to listen ; and, when she looked at me again, there was an earnest and affectionate cordiality in her eyes, as if the knowledge of my having been present at that mourn-ful scene had opened a new source of sympathy and intelligence between us. So neighbouring are the fountains of Love and Sorrow, and so imperceptibly do they often mingle their streams.

Little, indeed, as I was guided by art or design, in my manner and conduct towards this innocent girl, not all the most experienced gallantry of the Garden could have dictated a policy half so seductive as that which my new master, Love, now taught me. The same ardour which, if shown at once, and without reserve, might probably have startled a heart so little prepared for it, being now checked and softened by the timidity of real love, won its way without alarm, and, when most diffident of success, was then most surely on its way to triumph. Like one whose slumbers are gradually broken by music, the maiden's heart was awakened without being disturbed. She followed the course of the charm, unconscious whither it led, nor was even aware of the flame she had lighted in another's bosom till startled by the reflection of it glimmering in her own.

Impatient as I was to appeal to her generosity and sympathy for a similar proof of confidence to that which I had just given, the night was now too far advanced for me to impose upon her such a task. After exchanging a few words, in which, though little met the ear, there was a tone and manner, on both sides, that spoke far more than language, we took a lingering leave of each other for the night, with every prospect, I fondly hoped, of being still together in our dreams.

## CHAPTER XIII.

IT was so near the dawn of day when we parted that
we found the sun sinking westward when we rejoined
each other. The smile, so frankly cordial, with which
she now met me, might have been taken for the greeting of a long mellowed friendship, did not the blush
and the cast-down eyelid that followed give symptoms
of a feeling newer and less calm. For myself, lightened
as I was, in some degree, by the confession which I
had made, I was yet too conscious of the new aspect
thus given to our intercourse, not to feel some alarm
at the prospect of returning to the theme. We were
both, therefore, alike willing to suffer our attention to
be diverted, by the variety of strange objects that
presented themselves on the way, from a subject that
both equally trembled to approach.

The river was now all full of motion and life.
Every instant we met with boats descending the
current, so wholly independent of aid from sail or oar
that the mariners sat idly upon the deck as they shot
along, either singing or playing upon their double-

reeded pipes. The greater number of these boats came laden with those large emeralds, from the mine in the desert, whose colours, it is said, are brightest at the full of the moon ; while some of them brought cargoes of frankincense from the acacia-groves near the Red Sea. On the decks of others, that had been, as we learned, to the Golden Mountains beyond Syene, were heaped blocks and fragments of that sweet-smelling wood which is yearly washed down by the Green Nile of Nubia at the season of the floods.

Our companions up the stream were far less numerous. Occasionally a boat, returning lightened from the fair of last night, shot rapidly past us, with those high sails that catch every breeze from over the hills ;—while, now and then, we overtook one of those barges full of bees, that are sent at this season to colonise the gardens of the south, and take advantage of the first flowers after the inundation has passed away.

For a short time, this constant variety of objects enabled us to divert so far our conversation as to keep it from lighting upon the one, sole subject, round which it constantly hovered. But the effort, as might be expected, was not long successful. As evening advanced the whole scene became more solitary. We less frequently ventured to look upon each other, and our intervals of silence grew more long.

It was near sunset, when, in passing a small temple

on the shore, whose porticoes were now full of the evening light, we saw issuing from a thicket of acanthus near it, a train of young maidens gracefully linked together in the dance by stems of the lotus held at arms' length between them. Their tresses were also wreathed with this gay emblem of the season, and in such profusion were its white flowers twisted round their waists and arms that they might have been taken, as they lightly bounded along the bank, for Nymphs of the Nile, then freshly risen from their bright gardens under the wave.

After looking for a few minutes at this sacred dance, the maiden turned away her eyes, with a look of pain, as if the remembrances it recalled were of no welcome nature. This momentary retrospect, this glimpse into the past, appeared to offer a sort of clue to the secret for which I panted ;—and accordingly I proceeded, as gradually and delicately as my impatience would allow, to avail myself of the opening. Her own frankness, however, relieved me from the embarrassment of much questioning. She seemed even to feel that the confidence I sought was due to me ; and, beyond the natural hesitation of maidenly modesty, not a shade of reserve or evasion appeared.

To attempt to repeat, in her own touching words, the simple story which she now related to me, would be like endeavouring to note down some strain of unpremeditated music, with all those fugitive graces, those felicities of the moment, which no art can restore, as they first met the ear. From a feeling, too, of humility, she had omitted in her short narrative several particulars relating to herself, which I afterwards learned ;—while others, not less important, she but slightly passed over, from a fear of offending the prejudices of her heathen hearer.

I shall, therefore, give her story, not as she, herself, sketched it, but as it was afterwards filled up by a pious and venerable hand,—far, far more worthy than mine of being associated with the memory of such purity.

## STORY OF ALETHE.

" THE mother of this maiden was the beautiful Theora
of Alexandria, who, though a native of that city, was
descended from Grecian parents. When very young,
Theora was one of the seven maidens selected to note
down the discourses of the eloquent Origen, who, at
that period, presided over the School of Alexandria,
and was in all the fulness of his fame both among
Pagans and Christians. Endowed richly with the
learning of both creeds, he brought the natural light
of philosophy to illustrate the mysteries of faith, and
was then only proud of his knowledge of the wisdom
of this world when he found it minister usefully to
the triumph of divine truth.

" Though he had courted in vain the crown of
martyrdom, it was, throughout his whole life, held
suspended over his head, and he had more than
once shown himself ready to die for that faith which
he lived but to uphold and adorn. On one of these
occasions, his tormentors, having habited him like an
Egyptian priest, placed him upon the steps of the

Temple of Serapis, and commanded that he should, in the manner of the Pagan ministers, present palm-branches to the multitude who went up into the shrine. But the courageous Christian disappointed their views. Holding forth the branches with an un-shrinking hand, he cried aloud, 'Come hither and take the branch, not of an Idol Temple, but of Christ.'

" So indefatigable was this learned Father in his studies, that, while composing his Commentary on the Scriptures, he was attended by seven scribes or notaries, who relieved each other in recording the dictates of his eloquent tongue ; while the same number of young females, selected for the beauty of their penmanship, were employed in arranging and transcribing the precious leaves.

"Among the scribes so selected, was the fair young Theora, whose parents, though attached to the Pagan worship, were not unwilling to profit by the accom-plishments of their daughter, thus devoted to a task which they looked on as purely mechanical. To the maid herself, however, her employment brought far other feelings and consequences. She read anxiously as she wrote, and the divine truths, so eloquently illustrated, found their way, by degrees, from the page to her heart. Deeply, too, as the written words affected her, the discourses from the lips of the great teacher himself, which she had frequent opportunities of hearing, sunk still more deeply into her mind.

There was, at once, a sublimity and gentleness in his views of religion, which, to the tender hearts and lively imaginations of women, never failed to appeal with convincing power. Accordingly, the list of his female pupils was numerous; and the names of Barbara, Juliana, Heraïs, and others, bear honourable testimony to his influence over that sex.

"To Theora the feeling with which his discourses inspired her was like a new soul,—a consciousness of spiritual existence never before felt. By the eloquence of the comment she was awakened into admiration of the text; and when, by the kindness of a catechumen of the school, who had been struck by her innocent zeal, she, for the first time, became possessor of a copy of the Scriptures, she could not sleep for thinking of her sacred treasure. With a mixture of pleasure and fear she hid it from all eyes, and was like one who had received a divine guest under her roof, and felt fearful of betraying its divinity to the world.

"A heart so awake would have been with ease secured to the faith had her opportunities of hearing the sacred word continued. But circumstances arose to deprive her of this advantage. The mild Origen, long harassed and thwarted in his labours by the tyranny of Demetrius, Bishop of Alexandria, was obliged to relinquish his school and fly from Egypt. The occupation of the fair scribe was, therefore, at an end: her intercourse with the followers of the new faith ceased ; and the growing enthusiasm of her heart gave way to more worldly impressions.

"Among other feelings love conduced not a little to wean her thoughts from the true religion. While still very young, she became the wife of a Greek adventurer, who had come to Egypt as a purchaser of that rich tapestry in which the needles of Persia are rivalled by the looms of the Nile. Having taken his young bride to Memphis, which was still the great mart of this merchandise, he there, in the midst of his speculations, died,—leaving his widow on the point of becoming a mother, while, as yet, but in her nineteenth year.

" For single and unprotected females, it has been, at all times, a favourite resource to seek for employment in the service of some of those great temples by which so large a portion of the wealth and power of Egypt is absorbed. In most of these institutions there exists an order of Priestesses, which, though not hereditary, like that of the Priests, is provided for by ample endowments, and confers that dignity and station, with which, in a government so theocratic, Religion is sure to invest even her humblest hand-maids. From the general policy of the Sacred College of Memphis, we may take for granted, that an accomplished female, like Theora, found but little difficulty in being elected one of the Priestesses of Isis ; and it was in the service of the subterranean shrines that her ministry chiefly lay.

" Here, a month or two after her admission, she gave birth to Alethe, who first opened her eyes among the unholy pomps and specious miracles of this mysterious region. Though Theora, as we have seen, had been diverted by other feelings from her first enthusiasm for the Christian faith, she had never wholly forgot the impression then made upon her. The sacred volume, which the pious catechumen had given her, was still treasured with care ; and, though she seldom opened its pages, there was always an idea of sanctity associated with it in her memory, and often would she sit to look upon it with reverential pleasure, recalling the happiness she had felt when it was first made her own.

" The leisure of her new retreat, and the lone melancholy of widowhood, led her still more frequently to indulge in such thoughts, and to recur to those consoling truths which she had heard in the school of Alexandria. She now began to peruse eagerly the sacred volume, drinking deep of the fountain of which she before but tasted, and feeling —what thousands of mourners since her have felt— that Christianity is the true and only religion of the sorrowful.

" This study of her secret hours became still more dear to her, from the very peril with which, at that period, it was attended, as well as from the necessity she felt herself under of concealing from all those around her the precious light that had been thus kindled in her own heart. Too timid to encounter the fierce persecution, which awaited all who were suspected of a leaning to Christianity, she continued to officiate in the pomps and ceremonies of the Temple ;—though, often, with such remorse of soul that she would pause, in the midst of the rites, and pray inwardly to God that He would forgive her this profanation of His Spirit.

" In the meantime her daughter, the young Alethe, grew up still lovelier than herself, and added, every hour, to her happiness and her fears. When arrived at a sufficient age, she was taught, like the other children of the priestesses, to take a share in the service and ceremonies of the shrines. The duty of some of these young servitors was to look after the flowers for the altar ;—of others, to take care that the sacred vases were filled every day with fresh water from the Nile. The task of some was to preserve, in perfect polish, those silver images of the Moon which the priests carried in processions ; while others were, as we have seen, employed in feeding the consecrated animals, and in keeping their plumes and scales bright for the admiring eyes of their worshippers.

"The office allotted to Alethe—the most honourable of these minor ministries—was to wait upon the sacred birds of the Moon, to feed them daily with those eggs from the Nile which they loved, and provide for their use that purest water, which alone these delicate birds will touch. This employment was the delight

of her childish hours ; and that ibis, which Alciphron
(the Epicurean) saw her dance round in the Temple,
was, of all the sacred flock, her especial favourite, and
had been daily fondled and fed by her from infancy.

" Music, as being one of the chief spells of this enchanted region, was an accomplishment required of
all its ministrants; and the harp, the lyre, and the
sacred flute, sounded nowhere so sweetly as through
these subterranean gardens. The chief object, indeed,
in the education of the youth of the Temple, was to
fit them, by every grace of art and nature, to give
effect to the illusion of those shows and phantasms, in
which the entire charm and secret of Initiation lay.

" Among the means employed to support the old
system of superstition, against the infidelity and, still
more, the new Faith that menaced it, was an increased
prodigality of splendour and marvels in those Mysteries for which Egypt has so long been celebrated.
Of these ceremonies so many imitations had, under
various names, multiplied throughout Europe, that the
parent superstition ran a risk of being eclipsed by its
progeny ; and, in order still to rank as the first Priesthood in the world, it became necessary for those of
Egypt to continue still the best impostors.

" Accordingly, every contrivance that art could
devise, or labour execute,—every resource that the
wonderful knowledge of the Priests, in pyrotechny,
mechanics, and dioptrics, could command, — was
brought into action to heighten the effect of their

Mysteries, and give an air of enchantment to everything connected with them.

"The final scene of beatification, — the Elysium, into which the Initiate was received, — formed, of course, the leading attraction of these ceremonies ; and to render it captivating alike to the senses of the man of pleasure, and the imagination of the spiritualist, was the object to which the whole skill and attention of the Sacred College were devoted. By the influence of the Priests of Memphis over those of the other Temples they had succeeded in extending their subterranean frontier, both to the north and south, so as to include, within their ever-lighted Paradise, some of the gardens excavated for the use of the other Twelve Shrines.

"The beauty of the young Alethe, the touching sweetness of her voice, and the sensibility that breathed throughout her every look and movement, rendered her a powerful auxiliary in such appeals to the imagination. She had been, accordingly, in her very childhood, selected from among her fair companions, as the most worthy representative of spiritual loveliness, in those pictures of Elysium—those scenes of another world—by which not only the fancy, but the reason, of the excited Aspirants was dazzled.

"To the innocent child herself these shows were pastime. But to Theora, who knew too well the imposition to which they were subservient, this profanation of all that she loved was a perpetual source of

horror and remorse. Often would she—when Alethe
stood smiling before her, arrayed, perhaps, as a spirit
of the Elysian world,—turn away, with a shudder,
from the happy child, almost fancying that she already
saw the shadows of sin descending over that innocent
brow, as she gazed upon it.

" As the intellect of the young maid became more
active and inquiring, the apprehensions and difficulties
of the mother increased. Afraid to communicate her
own precious secret, lest she should involve her child
in the dangers that encompassed it, she yet felt it to
be no less a cruelty than a crime to leave her wholly
immersed in the darkness of Paganism. In this
dilemma, the only resource that remained to her was
to select, and disengage from the dross that surrounded them, those pure particles of truth which lie
at the bottom of all religions ;—those feelings, rather
than doctrines, of which God has never left His creatures destitute, and which, in all ages, have furnished,
to those who sought after it, some clue to His glory.

" The unity and perfect goodness of the Creator ;
the fall of the human soul into corruption ; its struggles with the darkness of this world, and its final
redemption and re-ascent to the source of all spirit ;—
these natural solutions of the problem of our existence,
these elementary grounds of all religion and virtue,
which Theora had heard illustrated by her Christian
teacher, lay also, she knew, veiled under the theology
of Egypt ; and to impress them, in their abstract

K

purity, upon the mind of her susceptible pupil, was, in default of more heavenly lights, her sole ambition and care.

"It was generally their habit, after devoting their mornings to the service of the Temple, to pass their evenings and nights in one of those small mansions above ground, allotted, within the precincts of the Sacred College, to some of the most favoured Priest-esses. Here, out of the reach of those gross supersti-tions, which pursued them, at every step, below, she endeavoured to inform, as far as she could venture, the mind of her beloved girl; and found it lean as naturally and instinctively to truth as plants long shut up in darkness will, when light is let in upon them, incline themselves to its rays.

"Frequently, as they sat together on the terrace at night, admiring that glorious assembly of stars, whose beauty first misled mankind into idolatry, she would explain to the young listener by what gradations it was that the worship, thus transferred from the Creator to the creature, sunk still lower and lower in the scale of being till man at length presumed to deify man, and, by the most monstrous of inversions, heaven became at last the mirror of earth, reflecting back all its most earthly features.

"Even in the Temple itself the anxious mother would endeavour to interpose her purer lessons among the idolatrous ceremonies in which they were engaged. When the favourite ibis of Alethe took its station on

the shrine, and the young maiden was seen approaching, with all the gravity of worship, the very bird
which she had played with but an hour before,—when
the acacia-bough, which she herself had plucked,
seemed to acquire a sudden sacredness in her eyes,
as soon as the priest had breathed upon it,—on all
such occasions Theora, though with fear and trembling,
would venture to suggest to the youthful worshipper
the distinction that should be drawn between the
sensible object of adoration, and that spiritual, unseen
Deity of which it was but the remembrancer or type.

" With sorrow, however, she soon discovered that,
in thus but partially letting in light upon a mind far
too ardent to rest satisfied with such glimmerings, she
but bewildered the heart which she meant to guide,
and cut down the feeble hope around which its faith
twined, without substituting any other support in its
place. As the beauty, too, of Alethe began to attract
all eyes, new fears crowded upon the mother's heart ;
—fears, in which she was but too much justified by
the characters of some of those around her.

" In this sacred abode, as may easily be conceived,
morality did not always go hand and hand with
religion. The hypocritical and ambitious Orcus, who
was, at this period, High Priest of Memphis, was a
man, in every respect, qualified to preside over a
system of such splendid fraud. He had reached that
effective time of life, when enough of the warmth and
vigour of youth remains to give animation to the

counsels of age. But, in his instance, youth had left only the baser passions behind, while age had brought with it a more refined maturity of mischief. The advantages of a faith appealing almost wholly to the senses, were well understood by him ; nor had he failed either to discover that, in order to render religion subservient to his own interests, he must shape it adroitly to the interests and passions of others.

" The state of remorse and misery in which the mind of Theora was constantly kept by the scenes, however artfully veiled, which she daily witnessed around her, became at length intolerable. No perils that the cause of truth could bring with it would be half so dreadful as this endurance of sinfulness and deceit. Her child was, as yet, pure and innocent ; but, without that sentinel of the soul, Religion, how long might she continue so ?

" This thought at once decided her : all other fears vanished before it. She resolved instantly to lay open to Alethe the whole secret of her soul ; to make this child, who was her only hope on earth, the sharer of all her hopes in heaven, and then fly with her, as soon as possible, from this unhallowed spot, to the far desert—to the mountains—to any place, however desolate, where God and the consciousness of innocence might be with them.

" The promptitude with which her young pupil caught from her the divine truths was even beyond what she expected. It was like the lighting of one torch at another, so prepared was Alethe's mind for the illumination. Amply was the anxious mother now repaid for all her misery, by this perfect communion of love and faith, and by the delight with which she saw her beloved child—like the young antelope, when first led by her dam to the well—drink thirstily by her side, at the source of all life and truth.

" But such happiness was not long to last. The anxieties that Theora had suffered began to prey upon her health. She felt her strength daily decline ; and the thoughts of leaving, alone and unguarded in the world, that treasure which she had just devoted to Heaven, gave her a feeling of despair which but hastened the ebb of life. Had she put in practice her resolution of flying from this place, her child might have been now beyond the reach of all she dreaded, and in the solitude of the desert would have found at least safety from wrong. But the very happiness she had felt in her new task diverted her from this project ;—and it was now too late, for she was already dying.

" She continued to conceal, however, her state from the tender and sanguine girl, who, though seeing the traces of disease upon her mother's cheek, little knew that they were the hastening footsteps of death, nor thought even of the possibility of losing what was so dear to her. Too soon, however, the moment of

separation arrived ; and while the anguish and dismay of Alethe were in proportion to the security in
which she had indulged, Theora, too, felt, with bitter
regret, that she had sacrificed to her fond consideration
much precious time, and that there now remained but
a few brief and painful moments for the communication of all those wishes and instructions on which the
future destiny of the young orphan depended.

" She had, indeed, time for little more than to place
the sacred volume solemnly in her hands, to implore
that she would, at all risks, fly from this unholy place,
and, pointing in the direction of the mountains of
the Saïd, to name, with her last breath, the venerable
man, to whom, under Heaven, she looked for the
protection and salvation of her child.

" The first violence of feeling to which Alethe gave
way was succeeded by a fixed and tearless grief, which
rendered her insensible, for some time, to the dangers
of her situation. Her only comfort was in visiting
that monumental chapel where the beautiful remains
of Theora lay. There, night after night, in contemplation of those placid features, and in prayers for the
peace of the departed spirit, did she pass her lonely,
and—however sad they were—happiest hours. Though
the mystic emblems that decorated that chapel were
but ill-suited to the slumber of a Christian saint, there
was one among them, the Cross, which, by a remarkable coincidence, is an emblem common alike to the
Gentile and the Christian,—being, to the former, a

shadowy type of that immortality, of which, to the latter, it is a substantial and assuring pledge.

"Nightly, upon this cross, which she had often seen her lost mother kiss, did she breathe forth a solemn and heartfelt vow, never to abandon the faith which that departed spirit had bequeathed to her. To such enthusiasm, indeed, did her heart at such moments rise, that, but for the last injunctions from those pallid lips, she would, at once, have avowed her perilous secret, and pronounced the words, 'I am a Christian!' among those benighted shrines!

"But the will of her to whom she owed more than life was to be obeyed. To escape from this haunt of superstition must now, she felt, be her first object; and, in devising the means of effecting it, her mind, day and night, was employed. It was with a loathing not to be concealed, that she now found herself compelled to resume her idolatrous services at the shrine. To some of the offices of Theora she succeeded, as is the custom, by inheritance; and in the performance of these tasks—sanctified as they were in her eyes by the pure spirit she had seen engaged in them—there was a sort of melancholy pleasure in which her sorrow found relief. But the part she was again forced to take, in the scenic shows of the Mysteries, brought with it a sense of wrong and degradation which she could no longer endure.

"Already had she formed, in her own mind, a plan of escape, in which her acquaintance with all the windings of this mystic realm gave her confidence, when the reception of Alciphron, as an Initiate, took place.

"From the first moment of the landing of that philosopher at Alexandria, he had become an object of suspicion and watchfulness to the inquisitorial Orcus, whom philosophy, in any shape, naturally alarmed, but to whom the sect over which the young Athenian presided was particularly obnoxious. The accomplishments of Alciphron, his popularity where-ever he went, and the bold freedom with which he indulged his wit at the expense of religion, were all faithfully reported to the High Priest by his spies, and awaked in his mind no kindly feelings towards the stranger. In dealing with an infidel, such a per-sonage as Orcus could know no other alternative but that of either converting or destroying him ; and though his spite, as a man, would have been more gratified by the latter proceeding, his pride, as a priest, led him to prefer the triumph of the former.

"The first descent of the Epicurean into the pyramid became speedily known, and the alarm was immediately given to the Priests below. As soon as they had discovered that the young philosopher of Athens was the intruder, and that he not only still continued to linger round the pyramid, but was observed to look often and wistfully towards the portal, it was concluded that his curiosity would impel him to try a second descent ; and Orcus, blessing the good chance which had thus brought the wild bird to his net, resolved not to suffer an opportunity so precious to be wasted.

"Instantly, the whole of that wonderful machinery, by which the phantasms and illusions of Initiation are produced, were put in active preparation throughout that subterranean realm; and the increased stir and vigilance awakened among its inmates, by this more than ordinary display of the resources of priestcraft, rendered the accomplishment of Alethe's purpose, at such a moment, peculiarly difficult. Wholly ignorant of the important share which it had been her own fortune to take in attracting the young philosopher down to this region, she but heard of him vaguely, as the Chief of a great Grecian sect, who had been led, by either curiosity or accident, to expose himself to the first trials of Initiation, and whom the priests, she could see, were endeavouring to insnare in their toils, by every art and lure with which their dark science had gifted them.

"To her mind, the image of a philosopher, such as Alciphron had been represented to her, came associated with ideas of age and reverence; and, more than once, the possibility of his being made instrumental to her deliverance flashed a hope across her heart in which she could not refrain from indulging. Often had she been told by Theora of the many Gentile sages, who had laid their wisdom down humbly at the foot of the Cross; and though this

Initiate, she feared, could hardly be among the number, yet the rumours which she had gathered from the servants of the Temple, of his undisguised contempt for the errors of heathenism, led her to hope she might find tolerance, if not sympathy, in her appeal to him.

"Nor was it solely with a view to her own chance of deliverance that she thus connected him in her thoughts with the plan which she meditated. The look of proud and self-gratulating malice, with which the High Priest had mentioned this 'infidel,' as he styled him, when instructing her in the scene she was to enact before the philosopher in the valley, but too plainly informed her of the destiny that hung over him. She knew how many were the hapless candidates for Initiation who had been doomed to a durance worse than that of the grave, for but a word, a whisper breathed against the sacred absurdities which they witnessed ; and it was evident to her that the venerable Greek (for such her fancy represented Alciphron) was no less interested in escaping from the perils of this region than herself.

"Her own resolution was, at all events, fixed. That visionary scene, in which she had appeared before Alciphron,—little knowing how ardent were the heart and imagination, over which her beauty, at that moment, exercised its influence,—was, she solemnly resolved, the very last unholy service that superstition or imposture should ever command of her.

"On the following night the Aspirant was to watch

in the Great Temple of Isis. Such an opportunity
of approaching and addressing him might never come
again. Should he, from compassion for her situation,
or a sense of the danger of his own, consent to lend
his aid to her flight, most gladly would she accept it,
—well assured that no danger or treachery she might
risk could be half so odious and fearful as those
which she left behind. Should he, on the contrary,
refuse, her determination was equally fixed—to trust
to that God whose eye watches over the innocent, and
go forth alone.

"To reach the island in Lake Mœris was her first
great object ; and there occurred fortunately, at this
time, a mode of effecting her purpose, by which both
the difficulty and dangers of the attempt would be
much diminished. The day of the annual visitation
of the High Priest to the Place of Weeping—as that
island in the centre of the Lake is called—was now
fast approaching ; and Alethe knew that the self-
moving car, by which the High Priest and one of the
Hierophants are conveyed to the chambers under the
Lake, stood then waiting in readiness. By availing
herself of this expedient, she would gain the double
advantage both of facilitating her own flight, and
retarding the speed of her pursuers.

"Having paid a last visit to the tomb of her beloved
mother, and wept there, long and passionately, till
her heart almost failed in the struggle,—having
paused, too, to give a kiss to her favourite ibis, which,

though too much a Christian to worship, she was still child enough to love,—she went early, with a trembling step, to the Sanctuary, and there hid herself in one of the recesses of the Shrine. Her intention was to steal out from thence to Alciphron while it was yet dark, and before the illumination of the great Statue behind the Veils had begun. But her fears delayed her till it was almost too late ;—already was the image lighted up, and still she remained trembling in her hiding-place.

"In a few minutes more the mighty Veils would have been withdrawn, and the glories of that scene of enchantment laid open,—when, at length, summoning all her courage, and taking advantage of a momentary absence of those employed in preparing this splendid mockery, she stole from under the Veil and found her way, through the gloom, to the Epicurean. There was then no time for explanation ;—she had but to trust to the simple words, 'Follow, and be silent ;' and the implicit readiness with which she found them obeyed filled her with no less surprise than the philosopher himself had felt in hearing them.

"In a second or two they were on their way through the subterranean windings, leaving the ministers of Isis to waste their splendours on vacancy, through a long series of miracles and visions which they now exhibited,—unconscious that he, whom they were taking such pains to dazzle, was already, under the guidance of the young Christian, far removed beyond he reach of their deceiving spells."

## CHAPTER XIV.

SUCH was the singular story, of which this innocent girl now gave me, in her own touching language, the outline.

The sun was just rising as she finished her narrative. Fearful of encountering the expression of those feelings with which, she could not but observe, I was affected by her recital, scarcely had she concluded the last sentence, when, rising abruptly from her seat, she hurried into the pavilion, leaving me with the words already crowding for utterance to my lips.

Oppressed by the various emotions thus sent back upon my heart, I lay down on the deck in a state of agitation that defied even the most distant approaches of sleep. While every word she had uttered, every feeling she expressed, but ministered new fuel to that flame which consumed me, and to describe which, passion is far too weak a word, there was also much of her recital that disheartened and alarmed me. To find a Christian thus under the garb of a Memphian Priestess, was a discovery that, had my heart been

less deeply interested, would but have more power-
fully stimulated my imagination and pride. But,
when I recollected the austerity of the faith she had
embraced,—the tender and sacred tie, associated with
it in her memory, and the devotion of woman's heart
to objects thus consecrated,—her very perfections but
widened the distance between us, and all that most
kindled my passion at the same time chilled my
hopes.

Were we to be left to each other, as on this silent
river, in such undisturbed communion of thoughts
and feelings, I knew too well, I thought, both her
sex's nature and my own, to feel a doubt that love
would ultimately triumph. But the severity of the
guardianship to which I must resign her,—that of
some monk of the desert, some stern Solitary,—the
influence such a monitor would gain over her mind,
—and the horror with which he might, ere long, teach
her to regard the reprobate infidel on whom she now
smiled,—in all this prospect I saw nothing but
despair. After a few short hours, my dream of happiness would be at an end, and such a dark chasm
must then open between our fates, as would dissever
them, wide as earth from heaven, asunder.

It was true, she was now wholly in my power. I
feared no witnesses but those of earth, and the
solitude of the desert was at hand. But though I
acknowledged not a heaven, I worshipped her who was,
to me, its type and substitute. If, at any moment,

a single thought of wrong or deceit, towards one so sacred arose in my mind, one look from her innocent eyes averted the sacrilege. Even passion itself felt a holy fear in her presence,—like the flame trembling in the breeze of the sanctuary,—and Love, pure Love, stood in place of Religion.

As long as I knew not her story, I could indulge, at least, in dreams of the future. But, now—what hope, what prospect remained? My single chance of happiness lay in the hope, however delusive, of being able to divert her thoughts from the fatal project which she meditated ; of weaning her, by persuasion and argument, from that austere faith, which I had before hated and now feared, and of attaching her, perhaps, alone and unlinked as she was in the world, to my own fortunes for ever !

In the agitation of these thoughts, I had started from my resting-place, and continued to pace up and down, under a burning sun, till, exhausted both by thought and feeling, I sunk down, amid that blaze of light, into a sleep, which to my fevered brain seemed a sleep of fire.

On awaking, I found the veil of Alethe laid carefully over my brow, while she, herself, sat near me, under the shadow of the sail, looking anxiously upon that leaf, which her mother had given her, and employed apparently in comparing its outlines with the course of the river, as well as with the forms of the rocky hills by which we were passing. She looked pale and troubled, and rose eagerly to meet me, as if she had long and impatiently waited for my waking.

Her heart, it was plain, had been disturbed from its security, and was beginning to take alarm at its own feelings. But, though vaguely conscious of the peril to which she was exposed, her reliance, as is usual in such cases, increased with her danger, and upon me, far more than on herself, did she seem to depend for saving her. To reach, as soon as possible, her asylum in the desert, was now the urgent object of her en-treaties and wishes; and the self-reproach which she expressed at having, for a single moment, suffered her thoughts to be diverted from this sacred purpose, not only revealed the truth, that she *had* forgotten it, but betrayed even a glimmering consciousness of the cause.

Her sleep, she said, had been broken by ill-omened dreams. Every moment the shade of her mother had stood before her, rebuking, with mournful looks, her delay, and pointing, as she had done in death, to the eastern hills. Bursting into tears at this accusing recollection, she hastily placed the leaf, which she had been examining, in my hands, and implored that I would ascertain, without a moment's delay, what portion of our voyage was still unperformed, and in what space of time we might hope to accomplish it.

I had, still less than herself, taken note of either place or distance; and, could we have been left to glide on in this dream of happiness, should never have thought of pausing to ask where it would end. But such confidence I felt was far too sacred to be deceived. Reluctant as I naturally was, to enter on an inquiry which might soon dissipate even my last hope, her wish was sufficient to supersede even the selfishness of love, and on the instant I proceeded to obey her will.

There stands on the eastern bank of the Nile, to the north of Antinöe, a high and steep rock, impending over the flood, which has borne, for ages, from a prodigy connected with it, the name of the Mountain of the Birds. Yearly, it is said, at a certain season and hour, large flocks of birds assemble in the ravine, of which this rocky mountain forms one of the sides, and are there observed to go through the mysterious ceremony of inserting each its beak into a particular cleft of the rock, till the cleft closes upon one of their number, when all the rest of the birds take wing, and leave the selected victim to die.

Through the ravine, rendered famous by this charm, —for such the multitude consider it,—there ran, in ancient times, a canal from the Nile, to some great and forgotten city, now buried in the desert. To a short distance from the river this canal still exists, but, after having passed through the defile, its scanty waters disappear, and are wholly lost under the sands.

It was in the neighbourhood of this place, as I could collect from the delineations on the leaf,—where

L

a flight of birds represented the name of the mountain,—that the abode of the Solitary, to whom Alethe was about to be consigned, was situated. Little as I knew of the geography of Egypt, it at once struck me, that we had long since left this mountain behind ; and, on inquiring of our boatmen, I found my conjecture confirmed. We had, indeed, passed it on the preceding night ; and, as the wind had been, ever since, blowing strongly from the north, and the sun was already sinking towards the horizon, we must be now, at least, a day's sail to the southward of the spot.

This discovery, I confess, filled my heart with a feeling of joy which I found it difficult to conceal. It seemed as if fortune was conspiring with love in my behalf, and by thus delaying the moment of our separation, afforded me a chance at least of happiness. Her look and manner, too, when informed of our mistake, rather encouraged than chilled this secret hope. In the first moment of astonishment, her eyes opened upon me with a suddenness of splendour, under which I felt my own wink as though lightning had crossed them. But she again, as suddenly, let their lids fall, and, after a quiver of her lip, which showed the conflict of feeling then going on within, crossed her arms upon her bosom, and looked down silently upon the deck ; her whole countenance sinking into an expression, sad, but resigned, as if she now felt that fate was on the side of wrong, and saw Love already stealing between her soul and heaven.

I was not slow, of course, in availing myself of
what I fancied to be the irresolution of her mind.
But, still, fearful of exciting alarm by any appeal to
feelings of regard or tenderness, I but addressed myself to her imagination, and to that love of novelty
and wonders which is ever ready to be awakened
within the youthful breast.  We were now approaching that region of miracles, Thebes.  " In a day or
two," said I, " we shall see, towering above the waters,
the colossal Avenue of Sphinxes, and the bright
Obelisks of the Sun.  We shall visit the plain of
Memnon, and behold those mighty statues that fling
their shadows at sunrise over the Libyan hills.  We
shall hear the image of the Son of the Morning
answering to the first touch of light.  From thence,
in a few hours, a breeze like this will transport us to
those sunny islands near the cataracts; there to
wander, among the sacred palm-groves of Philœ, or
sit, at noon-tide hours, in those cool alcoves which the
waterfall of Syene shadows under its arch.  Oh, who
is there that, with scenes of such loveliness within
reach, would turn coldly away to the bleak desert,
and leave this fair world, with all its enchantments,
shining unseen and unenjoyed ?  At least,"—I added,
taking tenderly her hand in mine,—" let a few more
days be stolen from the dreary fate to which thou
hast devoted thyself, and then—— "

She had heard but the last few words ;—the rest
had been lost upon her.  Startled by the tone of

tenderness into which, in despite of all my resolves, I had suffered my voice to soften, she looked for an instant with passionate earnestness into my face;— then, dropping upon her knees with her clasped hands upraised, exclaimed,—"Tempt me not, in the name of God I implore thee, tempt me not to swerve from my sacred duty. Oh! take me instantly to that desert mountain, and I will bless thee for ever."

This appeal, I felt, could not be resisted,—even though my heart were to break for it. Having silently intimated my assent to her prayer, by a slight pressure of her hand as I raised her from the deck, I proceeded immediately, as we were still in full career, for the south, to give orders that our sail should be instantly lowered, and not a moment lost in retracing our course.

In giving these directions, however, it, for the first time, occurred to me, that, as I had hired this yacht in the neighbourhood of Memphis, where it was probable the flight of the young Priestess would be most vigilantly tracked, we should run the risk of betraying to the boatmen the place of her retreat;—and there was now a most favourable opportunity for taking precautions against this danger. Desiring, therefore, that we should be landed at a small village on the shore, under pretence of paying a visit to some shrine in the neighbourhood, I there dismissed our barge, and was relieved from fear of further observation, by seeing it again set sail, and resume its course fleetly up the current.

From the boats of all descriptions that lay idle beside the bank I now selected one, in every respect suited to my purpose,—being, in its shape and accommodations, a miniature of our former vessel, but, at the same time, so light and small as to be manageable by myself alone, and requiring, with the advantage of the current, little more than a hand to steer it. This boat I succeeded, without much difficulty, in purchasing, and, after a short delay, we were again afloat down the current;—the sun just then sinking, in conscious glory, over his own golden shrines in the Libyan waste.

The evening was calmer and more lovely than any that had yet smiled upon our voyage; and, as we left the shore, a strain of sweet melody came soothingly over our ears. It was the voice of a young Nubian girl, whom we saw kneeling before an acacia, upon the bank, and singing, while her companions stood around, the wild song of invocation, which, in her country, they address to that enchanted tree :—

> " Oh ! Abyssinian tree,
>     We pray, we pray to thee ;
> By the glow of thy golden fruit,
>     And the violet hue of thy flower,
>         And the greeting mute
>         Of thy bough's salute
> To the stranger who seeks thy bower.*

---

* See an account of this sensitive tree, which bends down its branches to those who approach it, in M. Jomard's Description of Syene and the Cataracts.

## II.

"Oh ! Abyssinian tree,
How the traveller blesses thee,
When the night no moon allows,
And the sunset hour is near,
And thou bend'st thy boughs
To kiss his brows,
Saying, 'Come rest thee here.'
Oh ! Abyssinian tree,
Thus bow thy head to me !"

In the burden of this song the companions of the young Nubian joined ; and we heard the words, "Oh ! Abyssinian tree," dying away on the breeze, long after the whole group had been lost to our eyes.

Whether, in the new arrangement which I had made for our voyage, any motive, besides those which I professed, had a share, I can scarcely, even myself, —so bewildered were then my feelings,—determine. But no sooner had the current borne us away from all human dwellings, and we were alone on the waters, with not a soul near, then I felt how closely such solitude draws hearts together, and how much more we seemed to belong to each other, than when there were eyes around us.

The same feeling, but without the same sense of its danger, was manifest in every look and word of Alethe. The consciousness of the one great effort which she had made appeared to have satisfied her heart on the score of duty,—while the devotedness with which she saw I attended to her every wish, was felt with all that trusting gratitude which, in woman, is the day-spring of love. She was, therefore, happy, innocently happy ; and the confiding, and even affectionate, unreserve of her manner, while it rendered my trust more sacred, made it also far more difficult.

It was only, however, upon subjects unconnected with our situation or fate, that she yielded to such interchange of thought, or that her voice ventured to answer mine. The moment I alluded to the destiny that awaited us, all her cheerfulness fled, and she became saddened and silent. When I described to her the beauty of my own native land—its founts of inspiration and fields of glory—her eyes sparkled with sympathy, and sometimes even softened into fondness. But when I ventured to whisper, that, in that glorious country, a life full of love and liberty awaited her ; when I proceeded to contrast the adoration and bliss she might command, with the gloomy austerities of the life to which she was hastening,—it was like the coming of a sudden cloud over a summer sky. Her head sunk, as she listened ;—I awaited in vain for an answer ; and when, half playfully reproaching her for this silence, I stooped to take her hand, I could feel the warm tears fast falling over it.

But even this—feeble as was the hope it held out— was still a glimpse of happiness. Though it foreboded that I should lose her, it also whispered that I was loved. Like that lake, in the Land of Roses,* whose

* The province of Arsinoe, now Fioum.

waters are half sweet, half bitter, I felt my fate to be a compound of bliss and pain,—but its very pain well worth all ordinary bliss.

And thus did the hours of that night pass along; while every moment shortened our happy dream, and the current seemed to flow with a swifter pace than any that ever yet hurried to the sea. Not a feature of the whole scene but lives, at this moment, freshly in my memory;—the broken star-light on the water;—the rippling sound of the boat, as without oar or sail, it went, like a thing of enchantment, down the stream;—the scented fire, burning beside us upon the deck, and, then, that face, on which its light fell, revealing, at every moment, some new charm,—some blush or look, more beautiful than the last!

Often, while I sat gazing, forgetful of all else in this world, our boat, left wholly to itself, would drive from its course, and, bearing us away to the bank, get entangled in the water-flowers, or be caught in some eddy, ere I perceived where we were. Once, too, when the rustling of my oar among the flowers had startled away from the bank some wild antelopes, that had stolen, at that still hour, to drink of the Nile, what an emblem did I think it of the young heart then beside me,—tasting, for the first time, of hope and love, and so soon, alas, to be scared from their sweetness for ever!

## CHAPTER XV.

THE night was now far advanced ;—the bend of our course towards the left, and the closing in of the eastern hills upon the river, gave warning of our approach to the hermit's dwelling. Every minute now appeared like the last of existence ; and I felt a sinking of despair at my heart, which would have been intolerable, had not a resolution that suddenly, and as if by inspiration, occurred to me, presented a glimpse of hope which, in some degree, calmed my feelings.

Much as I had, all my life, despised hypocrisy,— the very sect I had embraced being chiefly recommended to me by the war they continued to wage upon the cant of all others,—it was, nevertheless, in hypocrisy that I now scrupled not to take refuge from that calamity which to me was far worse than either shame or death—my separation from Alethe. In my despair, I adopted the humiliating plan — deeply humiliating as I felt it to be, even amid the joy with which I welcomed it—of offering myself to this hermit, as a convert to his faith, and thus becoming the fellow-disciple of Alethe under his care!

From the moment I resolved upon this plan my spirit felt lightened. Though having fully before my eyes, the labyrinth of imposture into which it would lead me, I thought of nothing but the chance of our being still together. In this hope, all pride, all philosophy was forgotten, and everything seemed tolerable but the prospect of losing her.

Thus resolved, it was with somewhat less reluctant feelings that I now undertook, at the anxious desire of my companion, to ascertain the site of that well-known mountain, in the neighbourhood of which the dwelling of the anchoret lay. We had already passed one or two stupendous rocks, which stood, detached, like fortresses, over the river's brink, and which, in some degree, corresponded with the description on the leaf. So little was there of life now stirring along the shores, that I had begun almost to despair of any assistance from inquiry, when, on looking to the western bank, I saw a boatman among the sedges, towing his small boat, with some difficulty, up the current. Hailing him as we passed, I asked,—"Where stands the Mountain of the Birds?"—and he had hardly time to answer, as he pointed above us, "There," when we perceived that we were just then entering into the shadow which this mighty rock flings across the whole of the flood.

In a few moments we had reached the mouth of

the ravine, of which the Mountain of the Birds forms one of the sides, and through which the scanty canal from the Nile flows. At the sight of this awful chasm, within some of whose dreary recesses (if we had rightly interpreted the leaf) the dwelling of the Solitary was to be found, our voices sunk at once into a low whisper, while Alethe turned round to me with a look of awe and eagerness, as if doubtful whether I had not already disappeared from her side. A quick movement, however, of her hand towards the ravine, told too plainly that her purpose was still unchanged. Immediately checking, therefore, with my oars, the career of our boat, I succeeded, after no small exertion, in turning it out of the current of the river, and steering into this bleak and stagnant canal.

Our transition from life and bloom to the very depth of desolation was immediate. While the water on one side of the ravine lay buried in shadow, the white skeleton-like crags of the other stood aloft in the pale glare of moonlight. The sluggish stream through which we moved yielded sullenly to the oar, and the shriek of a few water-birds, which we had roused from their fastnesses, was succeeded by a silence, so dead and awful, that our lips seemed afraid to disturb it by a breath ; and half-whispered exclamations, " How dreary ! "—" How dismal ! "—were almost the only words exchanged between us.

We had proceeded for some time through this gloomy defile, when, at a short distance before us, among the rocks upon which the moonlight fell, we perceived, on a ledge but little elevated above the canal, a small hut or cave, which, from a tree or two planted around it, had some appearance of being the abode of a human being. " This, then," thought I, " is the home to which she is destined ! "—A chill of despair came again over my heart, and the oars, as I sat gazing, lay motionless in my hands.

I found Alethe, too, whose eyes had caught the same object, drawing closer to my side than she had yet ventured. Laying her hand agitatedly upon mine, " We must here," said she, " part for ever." I turned to her, as she spoke ; there was a tenderness, a despondency in her countenance, that at once saddened and inflamed my soul. " Part ! " I exclaimed passionately,—" No !—the same God shall receive us both. Thy faith, Alethe, shall, from this hour, be mine, and I will live and die in this desert with thee!"

Her surprise, her delight at these words, was like a momentary delirium. The wild, anxious smile, with which she looked into my face, as if to ascertain whether she had, indeed, heard my words aright, bespoke a happiness too much for reason to bear. At length the fulness of her heart found relief in tears ; and, murmuring forth an incoherent blessing on my name, she let her head fall languidly and powerlessly on my arm. The light from our boat-fire shone upon her face. I saw her eyes, which she had closed for a moment, again opening upon me with the

same tenderness, and—merciful Providence, how I
remember that moment!—was on the point of bending down my lips towards hers, when, suddenly, in the
air above us, as if it came direct from heaven, there
burst forth a strain of choral music, that with its
solemn sweetness filled the whole valley.

Breaking away from my caress at these supernatural sounds, the maiden threw herself trembling
upon her knees, and, not daring to look up, exclaimed
wildly, " My mother, oh my mother ! "

It was the Christian's morning hymn that we
heard ;—the same, as I learned afterwards, that, on
their high terrace at Memphis, she had been taught
by her mother to sing to the rising sun.

Scarcely less startled than my companion, I looked
up, and, at the very summit of the rock above us, saw
a light, appearing to come from a small opening or
window, through which the sounds also, that had
appeared to me so supernatural, issued. There could
be no doubt, that we had now found—if not the
dwelling of the anchoret—at least, the haunt of some
of the Christian brotherhood of these rocks, by whose
assistance we could not fail to find the place of his
retreat.

The agitation, into which Alethe had been thrown
by the first burst of that psalmody, soon yielded to
the softening recollections which it brought back ;
and a calm came over her brow, such as it had never
before worn, since we met. She seemed to feel that

she had now reached her destined haven, and to hail, as the voice of heaven itself, those solemn sounds by which she was welcomed to it.

In her tranquillity, however, I was very far from yet sympathizing. Impatient to learn all that awaited her as well as myself, I pushed our boat close to the base of the rock, so as to bring it directly under that lighted window on the summit, to find my way up to which was now my immediate object. Having hastily received my instructions from Alethe, and made her repeat again the name of the Christian whom we sought, I sprang upon the bank, and was not long in discovering a sort of path, or stairway, cut rudely out of the rock, and leading, as I found, by easy windings, up the steep.

After ascending for some time, I arrived at a level space or ledge, which the hand of labour had succeeded in converting into a garden, and which was planted, here and there, with fig-trees and palms. Around it, too, I could perceive, through the glimmering light, a number of small caves or grottos, into some of which, human beings might find an entrance; while others appeared of no larger dimensions than those tombs of the Sacred Birds which are seen ranged around Lake Mœris.

I was still, I found, but half-way up the ascent, nor could perceive any further means of continuing my course, as the mountain from hence rose, almost perpendicularly, like a wall. At length, however, on exploring around, I discovered behind the shade of a fig-tree a large ladder of wood, resting firmly against the rock, and affording an easy and safe ascent up the steep.

Having ascertained thus far, I again descended to the boat for Alethe, whom I found trembling already at her short solitude ; and having led her up the stairway to this quiet garden, left her lodged securely, amid its holy silence, while I pursued my way upward to the light on the rock.

At the top of the long ladder I found myself on another ledge or platform, somewhat smaller than the first, but planted in the same manner, with trees, and, as I could perceive by the mingled light of morning and the moon, embellished with flowers. I was now near the summit ;—there remained but another short ascent, and, as a ladder against the rock supplied, as before, the means of scaling it, I was in a few minutes at the opening from which the light issued.

I had ascended gently, as well from a feeling of awe at the whole scene, as from an unwillingness to disturb rudely the rites on which I intruded. My approach, therefore, being unheard, an opportunity was, for some moments, afforded me of observing the group within, before my appearance at the window was discovered.

In the middle of the apartment, which seemed once to have been a Pagan oratory, there was collected an assembly of about seven or eight persons, some male,

some female, kneeling in silence round a small altar ;
—while, among them, as if presiding over their ceremony, stood an aged man, who, at the moment of my
arrival, was presenting to one of the female worshippers an alabaster cup, which she applied, with
profound reverence, to her lips. The venerable
countenance of the minister, as he pronounced a
short prayer over her head, wore an expression of
profound feeling that showed how wholly he was
absorbed in that rite ; and when she had drank of the
cup,—which I saw had engraven on its side the image
of a head, with a glory round it,—the holy man bent
down and kissed her forehead.

After this parting salutation, the whole group rose
silently from their knees ; and it was then, for the
first time, that, by a cry of terror from one of the
women, the appearance of a stranger at the window
was discovered. The whole assembly seemed startled
and alarmed, except him, that superior person, who,
advancing from the altar, with an unmoved look,
raised the latch of the door adjoining to the window,
and admitted me.

There was, in this old man's features, a mixture of
elevation and sweetness, of simplicity and energy,
which commanded at once attachment and homage ;
and half hoping, half fearing, to find in him the
destined guardian of Alethe, I looked anxiously in
his face, as I entered, and pronounced the name "Melanius!"—"Melanius is my name, young stranger,"

he answered ; "and whether in friendship or in enmity thou comest, Melanius blesses thee." Thus saying, he made a sign with his right hand above my head, while, with involuntary respect, I bowed beneath the benediction.

"Let this volume," I replied, "answer for the peacefulness of my mission,"—at the same time, placing in his hands the copy of the Scriptures which had been his own gift to the mother of Alethe, and which her child now brought as the credential of her claims on his protection. At the sight of this sacred pledge, which he recognized instantly, the solemnity that had at first marked his reception of me softened into tenderness. Thoughts of other times appeared to pass through his mind ; and as, with a sigh of recollection, he took the book from my hands, some words on the outer leaf caught his eye. They were few,— but contained, most probably, the last wishes of the dying Theora ; for, as he read them over eagerly, I saw tears in his aged eyes. "The trust," he said, with a faltering voice, "is precious and sacred, and God will enable, I hope, His servant to guard it faithfully."

During this short dialogue, the other persons of the assembly had departed, being, as I afterwards learned, brethren from the neighbouring bank of the Nile, who came thus secretly before daybreak to join in worshipping their God. Fearful lest their descent down the rock might alarm Alethe, I hurried briefly

M

over the few words of explanation that remained, and, leaving the venerable Christian to follow at his leisure, hastened anxiously down to rejoin the young maiden.

## CHAPTER XVI.

MELANIUS was one of the first of those zealous Christians of Egypt, who, following the recent example of the hermit Paul, bade farewell to all the comforts of social existence, and betook themselves to a life of contemplation in the desert. Less selfish, however, in his piety, than most of these ascetics, Melanius forgot not the world, in leaving it. He knew that man was not born to live wholly for himself; that his relation to human kind was that of the link to the chain, and that even his solitude should be turned to the advantage of others. In flying, therefore, from the din and disturbance of life, he sought not to place himself beyond the reach of its sympathies, but selected a retreat where he could combine the advantage of solitude with those opportunities of being useful to his fellow-men which a neighbourhood to their populous haunts would afford.

That taste for the gloom of subterranean recesses, which the race of Misraim inherit from their Ethiopian ancestors, had, by hollowing out all Egypt into

caverns and crypts, supplied these Christian anchorets
with an ample choice of retreats.    Accordingly, some
found a shelter in the grottos of Elethya ;—others,
among the royal tombs of the Thebaïd.    In the
middle of the Seven Valleys, where the sun rarely
shines, a few have fixed their dim and melancholy
retreat ; while others have sought the neighbourhood
of the red Lakes of Nitria, and there, like those
Pagan solitaries of old, who fixed their dwelling
among the palm-trees near the Dead Sea, pass their
whole lives in musing amidst the sterility of nature,
and seem to find, in her desolation, peace.

It was on one of the mountains of the Saïd, to the
east of the river, that Melanius, as we have seen,
chose his place of seclusion,—having all the life and
fertility of the Nile on one side, and the lone, dismal
barrenness of the desert on the other.    Half-way
down this mountain, where it impends over the ravine,
he found a series of caves or grottos dug out of the
rock, which had, in other times, ministered to some
purpose of mystery, but whose use had long been
forgotten, and their recesses abandoned.

To this place, after the banishment of his great
master, Origen, Melanius, with a few faithful followers,
retired, and there, by the example of his innocent life,
as well as by his fervid eloquence, succeeded in winning crowds of converts to his faith.    Placed, as he
was, in the neighbourhood of the rich city, Antinoë,
though he mingled not with its multitude, his name

and his fame were ever among them, and, to all who sought after instruction or consolation, the cell of the hermit was always open.

Notwithstanding the rigid abstinence of his own habits, he was yet careful to provide for the comforts of others. Content with a rude pallet of straw himself, he had always for the stranger a less homely resting-place. From his grotto the wayfaring and the indigent never went unrefreshed ; and, with the aid of some of his brethren, he had formed gardens along the ledges of the mountain, which gave an air of life and cheerfulness to his rocky dwelling, and supplied him with the chief necessaries of such a climate—fruit and shade.

Though the acquaintance he had formed with the mother of Alethe, during the short period of her attendance at the school of Origen, was soon interrupted, and never afterwards renewed, the interest which he had then taken in her fate was far too lively to be forgotten. He had seen the zeal with which her young heart welcomed instruction ; and the thought that so promising a candidate for heaven should have relapsed into idolatry, came often, with disquieting apprehension, over his mind.

It was, therefore, with true pleasure, that, but a year or two before Theora's death, he had learned by a private communication from her, transmitted through a Christian embalmer of Memphis, that "not only had her own heart taken root in the faith. but that a new bud had flowered with the same divine hope, and that, ere long, he might see them both transplanted to the desert."

The coming, therefore, of Alethe was far less a surprise to him, than her coming thus alone was a shock and a sorrow; and the silence of their first meeting showed how painfully both remembered that the tie which had brought them together was no longer of this world,—that the hand, which should have been joined with theirs, was mouldering in the tomb. I now saw that not even religion was proof against the sadness of mortality. For, as the old man put the ringlets aside from her forehead, and contemplated in that clear countenance the reflection of what her mother had been, there was a mournfulness mingled with his piety, as he said, " Heaven rest her soul!" which showed how little even the certainty of a heaven for those we love can reconcile us to the pain of having lost them on earth.

The full light of day had now risen upon the desert, and our host, reminded, by the faint looks of Alethe, of the many anxious hours we had passed without sleep, proposed that we should seek, in the chambers of the rock, such rest as a hermit's dwelling could offer. Pointing to one of the largest of these openings, as he addressed me,—" Thou wilt find," he said, " in that grotto a bed of fresh doum leaves, and may the consciousness of having protected the orphan sweeten thy sleep ! "

I felt how dearly this praise had been earned, and already almost repented of having deserved it. There was a sadness in the countenance of Alethe, as I took leave of her, to which the forebodings of my own heart but too faithfully responded ; nor could I help fearing, as her hand parted lingeringly from mine, that I had, by this sacrifice, placed her beyond my reach for ever.

Having lighted for me a lamp, which, in these recesses, even at noon, is necessary, the holy man led me to the entrance of the grotto. And here, I blush to say, my career of hypocrisy began. With the sole view of obtaining another glance at Alethe, I turned humbly to solicit the benediction of the Christian, and, having conveyed to 'her, while bending reverently down, as much of the deep feeling of my soul as looks could express, I then, with a desponding spirit, hurried into the cavern.

A short passage led me to the chamber within,—the walls of which I found covered, like those of the grottos of Lycopolis, with paintings, which, though executed long ages ago, looked as fresh as if their colours were but laid on yesterday. They were, all of them, representations of rural and domestic scenes ; and, in the greater number, the melancholy imagination of the artist had called in, as usual, the presence of Death, to throw his shadow over the picture.

My attention was particularly drawn to one series of subjects, throughout the whole of which the same group—consisting of a youth, a maiden, and two aged persons, who appeared to be the father and mother of the girl,—were represented in all the details of their daily life. The looks and attitudes of the young people denoted that they were lovers ; and, sometimes, they were seen sitting under a canopy of flowers, with their eyes fixed on each other's faces, as though they could never look away ; sometimes, they appeared walking along the banks of the Nile,

> ————on one of those sweet nights
> When Isis, the pure star of lovers, lights
> Her bridal crescent o'er the holy stream,—
> When wandering youths and maidens watch her beam,
> And number o'er the nights she hath to run
> Ere she again embrace her bridegroom sun.

Through all these scenes of endearment the two elder persons stood by ; — their calm countenances touched with a share of that bliss in whose perfect light the young lovers were basking. Thus far, all was happiness ;—but the sad lesson of mortality was yet to come. In the last picture of the series, one of the figures was missing. It was that of the young maiden, who had disappeared from among them. On the brink of a dark lake stood the three who remained ; while a boat, just departing for the City of the Dead, told too plainly the end of their dream of happiness.

This memorial of a sorrow of other times—of a sorrow, ancient as death itself,—was not wanting to deepen the melancholy of my mind, or to add to the weight of the many bodings that pressed upon it.

After a night, as it seemed, of anxious and unsleeping thought, I rose from my bed and returned to the garden. I found the Christian alone,—seated, under the shade of one of his trees, at a small table, with a volume unrolled before him, while a beautiful antelope lay sleeping at his feet. Struck forcibly by the contrast which he presented to those haughty priests whom I had seen surrounded by the pomp and gorgeousness of temples, " Is this, then," thought I, " the faith before which the world now trembles—its temple the desert, its treasury a book, and its High Priest the solitary dweller of the rock ? "

He had prepared for me a simple, but hospitable repast, of which fruits from his own garden, the white bread of Olyra, and the juice of the honey-cane, were the most costly luxuries. His manner to me was even more cordial and fatherly than before ; but the absence of Alethe, and, still more, the ominous reserve with which he not only, himself, refrained from all mention of her name, but eluded the few inquiries by which I sought to lead to it, seemed to confirm all the apprehensions I had felt in parting from her.

She had acquainted him, it was evident, with the whole history of our flight. My reputation as a philosopher—my desire to become a Christian—all was already known to the zealous Anchoret, and the subject of my conversion was the very first on which he entered. Oh, pride of philosophy, how wert thou then humbled, and with what shame did I stand in

the presence of that venerable man, not daring to let
my eyes meet his, while, with ingenuous trust in the
sincerity of my intention, he welcomed me to a par-
ticipation of his holy hope, and imprinted the Kiss of
Charity on my infidel brow !

Embarrassed as I could not but feel by the humiliating consciousness of hypocrisy, I was even still more
perplexed by my almost total ignorance of the real
tenets of the faith to which I professed myself a convert.   Abashed and confused, and with a heart sick
at its own deceit, I listened to the animated and
eloquent gratulations of the Christian, as though they
were words in a dream, without any link or meaning ;
nor could disguise but by the mockery of a reverent
bow, at every pause, the total want of self-possession,
and even of speech, under which I laboured.

A few minutes more of such trial, and I must have
avowed my imposture.   But the holy man saw my
embarrassment ;—and, whether mistaking it for awe,
or knowing it to be ignorance, relieved me from my
perplexity by at once changing the theme.   Having
gently awakened his antelope from its sleep, "You
have doubtless," he said, "heard of my brother-
anchoret, Paul, who, from his cave in the marble
mountains, near the Red Sea, sends hourly the
blessed 'sacrifice of thanksgiving' to heaven.   Of *his*
walks, they tell me, a lion is the companion ; but, for
me," he added with a playful and significant smile.
"who try my powers of taming but on the gentler

animals, this feeble child of the desert is a far fitter playmate." Then, taking his staff, and putting the time-worn volume which he had been perusing into a large goat-skin pouch that hung by his side, " I will now," said he, " conduct thee over my rocky kingdom, —that thou mayest see in what drear and barren places that ' sweet fruit of the spirit,' Peace, may be gathered."

To speak of peace to a heart throbbing, as mine did, at that moment, was like talking of some distant harbour to the mariner sinking at sea. In vain did I look around for some sign of Alethe ;—in vain make an effort even to utter her name. Consciousness of my own deceit, as well as a fear of awakening in the mind of Melanius any suspicion that might tend to frustrate my only hope, threw a fetter over my spirit and checked my tongue. In humble silence, therefore, I followed, while the cheerful old man, with slow but firm step, ascended the rock, by the same ladders which I had mounted on the preceding night.

During the time when the Decian Persecution was raging, many Christians, as he told me, of the neighbourhood had taken refuge under his protection, in these grottos ; and the small chapel upon the summit, where I had found his flock at prayer, was, in those awful times of suffering, their usual place of retreat, where, by drawing up these ladders, they were enabled to secure themselves from pursuit.

From the top of the rock, the view, on either side,

embraced the two extremes of fertility and desolation ;
nor could the Epicurean and the Anchoret, who now
stood gazing from that height, be at any loss to indulge their respective tastes, between the living
luxuriance of the world on one side, and the dead,
pulseless repose of the desert on the other. When we
turned to the river, what a picture of animation presented itself ?  Near us, to the south, were the graceful colonnades of Antinoë, its proud, populous streets,
and triumphal monuments.  On the opposite shore,
rich plains, teeming with cultivation to the water's
edge, offered up, as from verdant altars, their fruits to
the sun ; while, beneath us, the Nile,

> ——the glorious stream,
> That late between its banks was seen to glide,—
> With shrines and marble cities, on each side,
> Glittering, like jewels strung along a chain,—
> Had now sent forth its waters, and o'er plain
> And valley, like a giant from his bed
> Rising with outstretch'd limbs, superbly spread.

From this scene, on one side of the mountain, we
had but to turn round our eyes to the other, and it
was as if Nature herself had become suddenly extinct ;
—a wide waste of sands, bleak and interminable,
wearying out the sun with its sameness of desolation ;
—black, burnt-up rocks, that stood as barriers, at
which life stopped ;—while the only signs of animation,
past or present, were the footprints, here and there, of
an antelope or ostrich, or the bones of dead camels,

as they lay whitening at a distance, marking out the track of the caravans over the waste.

After listening, while he contrasted, in a few eloquent words, the two regions of life and death on whose confines we stood, I again descended with my guide to the garden we had left. From thence, turning into a path along the mountain-side, he conducted me to another row of grottos, facing the desert, which had once, he said, been the abode of those brethren in Christ, who had fled with him to this solitude from the crowded world,—but which death had, within a few short months, rendered tenantless. A cross of red stone, and a few faded trees, were the only traces these solitaries had left behind.

A silence of some minutes succeeded, while we descended to the edge of the canal; and I saw opposite, among the rocks, that solitary cave which had so chilled me with its aspect on the preceding night. Beside the bank we found one of those rustic boats which the Egyptians construct of planks of wild thorn, bound rudely together with bands of papyrus. Placing ourselves in this boat, and rather impelling than rowing it across, we made our way through the foul and shallow flood, and landed directly under the site of the cave.

This dwelling, as I have already mentioned, was situated upon a ledge of the rock; and being provided with a sort of window or aperture to admit the light of heaven, was accounted, I found, more cheerful than the grottos on the other side of the ravine. But there was a dreariness in the whole region around, to which light only lent additional horror. The dead whiteness of the rocks, as they stood, like ghosts in the sunshine ;—that melancholy pool, half lost in the sands ;—all gave to my mind the idea of a wasting world. To dwell in such a place seemed to me like a living death ; and when the Christian, as we entered the cave, said, " Here is to be thy home," prepared as I had been for the worst, my resolution gave way ;—every feeling of disappointed passion and humbled pride, which had been gathering round my heart for the last few hours, found a vent at once, and I burst into tears.

Accustomed to human weakness, and perhaps guessing at some of the sources of mine, the good Hermit, without appearing to take any notice of this emotion, proceeded to expatiate, with a cheerful air, on, what he called, the comforts of my dwelling. Sheltered from the dry, burning wind of the south, my porch would inhale, he said, the fresh breeze of the Dog-star. Fruits from his own mountain-garden should furnish my repast. The well of the neighbour-ing rock would supply my beverage ; and " here," he continued,—lowering his voice into a more solemn tone, as he placed upon the table the volume which he had brought,—" here, my son, is that 'well of living waters,' in which alone thou wilt find lasting refreshment or peace!" Thus saying, he descended the rock to his boat, and after a few plashes of his oar had died upon my ear, the solitude and silence that reigned around me was complete.

## CHAPTER XVII.

WHAT a fate was mine!—but a few weeks since, presiding over that gay Festival of the Garden, with all
the luxuries of existence tributary in my train ; and
now,— self-humbled into a solitary outcast,— the
hypocritical pupil of a Christian anchoret,—without
even the excuse of religious fanaticism, or any other
madness, but that of love, wild love, to extenuate
my fall! Were there a hope that, by this humiliating waste of existence, I might purchase now and
then a momentary glimpse of Alethe, even the depths
of the desert, with such a chance, would be welcome.
But to live—and live thus—*without* her, was a misery
which I neither foresaw nor could endure.

Hating even to look upon the den to which I was
doomed, I hurried out into the air, and found my
way, along the rocks, to the desert. The sun was
going down, with that blood-red hue, which he so
frequently wears, in this climate, at his setting. I
saw the sands, stretching out, like a sea to the horizon,
as if their waste extended to the very verge of the
world,—and, in the bitterness of my feelings, rejoiced

to see so large a portion of creation rescued, even by this barren liberty, from the encroaching grasp of man. The thought seemed to relieve my wounded pride, and, as I wandered over the dim and boundless solitude, to be thus free, even amidst blight and desolation, appeared to me a blessing.

The only living thing I saw was a restless swallow, whose wings were of the hue of the gray sands over which he fluttered. "Why (thought I) may not the mind, like this bird, partake of the colour of the desert, and sympathize in its austerity, its freedom, and its calm?"—thus vainly endeavouring, between despondence and defiance, to encounter, with some degree of fortitude what yet my heart sickened to contemplate. But the effort was unavailing. Overcome by that vast solitude, whose repose was not the slumber of peace, but rather the sullen and burning silence of hate, I felt my spirit give way, and even love itself yielded to despair.

Seating myself on a fragment of a rock, and covering my eyes with my hands, I made an effort to shut out the overwhelming prospect. But all in vain—it was still before me, with every additional horror that fancy could suggest; and when, again looking forth, I saw the last red ray of the sun, shooting across the melancholy and lifeless waste, it appeared to me like the light of that comet which once desolated this world, and thus luridly shone out over the ruin that it had made!

N

Appalled by my own gloomy imaginations, I turned towards the ravine ; and, notwithstanding the disgust with which I had fled from my dwelling, was not ill pleased to find my way, over the rocks, to it again. On approaching the cave, to my astonishment, I saw a light within. At such a moment, any vestige of life was welcome, and I hailed the unexpected appearance with pleasure. On entering, however, I found the chamber all as lonely as I had left it. The light I had seen came from a lamp that burned brightly on the table ; beside it was unfolded the volume which Melanius had brought, and upon the open leaves—oh, joy and surprise—lay the well-known cross of Alethe!

What hand, but her own, could have prepared this reception for me ?—The very thought sent a hope into my heart, before which all despondency fled. Even the gloom of the desert was forgotten, and my rude cave at once brightened into a bower. She had here reminded me, by this sacred memorial, of the vow which I had pledged to her under the Hermit's rock ; and I now scrupled not to reiterate the same daring promise, though conscious that through hypocrisy alone could I fulfil it.

Eager to prepare myself for my task of imposture, I sat down to the volume, which I now found to be the Hebrew Scriptures ; and the first sentence on which my eyes fell was—" The Lord hath commanded the blessing, even Life for evermore ! " Startled by those words, in which it appeared to me as if the Spirit of

my dream had again pronounced his assuring predic-
tion, I raised my eyes from the page, and repeated
the sentence over and over, as if to try whether the
sounds had any charm or spell to re-awaken that
faded illusion in my soul. But, no—the rank frauds
of the Memphian priesthood had dispelled all my
trust in the promises of religion. My heart had again
relapsed into its gloom of scepticism, and, to the
word of "Life," the only answer it sent back was,
"Death!"

Impatient, however, to possess myself of the elements of a faith, upon which—whatever it might
promise for hereafter—I felt that all my happiness
here depended, I turned over the pages with an
earnestness and avidity such as never even the
most favourite of my studies had awakened in me.
Though, like all who seek but the surface of learning,
I flew desultorily over the leaves, lighting only on the
more prominent and shining points, I yet found myself, even in this undisciplined career, arrested, at
every page, by the awful, the supernatural sublimity,
the alternate melancholy and grandeur of the images
that crowded upon me.

I had, till now, known the Hebrew theology but
through the platonising refinement of Philo ;—as, in
like manner, for my knowledge of the Christian
doctrine I was indebted to by brother Epicureans,
Lucian and Celsus. Little, therefore, was my mind
prepared for the simple majesty, the high tone of

inspiration,—the poetry, in short, of heaven, that breathed throughout these oracles. Could admiration have kindled faith, I should, that night, have been a believer ; so elevated, so awed was my imagination by that wonderful book,—its warnings of woe, its announcements of glory, and its unrivalled strains of adoration and sorrow.

Hour after hour, with the same eager and desultory curiosity, did I turn over the leaves ;—and when, at length, I lay down to rest, my fancy was still haunted by the impressions it had received. I went again through the various scenes of which I had read; again called up, in sleep, the bright images that had passed before me, and, when awakened at dawn by the solemn hymn from the chapel, imagined that I was still listening to the sound of the winds, sighing mournfully through the harps of Israel on the willows.

Starting from my bed, I hurried out upon the rock, with a hope that, among the tones of that morning choir, I might be able to distinguish the sweet voice of Alethe. But the strain had ceased ;—I caught only the last notes of the hymn, as, echoing up that lonely valley, they died away into the silence of the desert.

With the first glimpse of light I was again eagerly at my study, and, notwithstanding the frequent distraction both of my thoughts and looks towards the distant, half-seen grottos of the Anchoret, continued my task with unabating perseverance through the day. Still alive, however, but to the eloquence, the poetry of what I read, of its claims to authority as a history I never paused to consider. My fancy alone being interested by it, to fancy I referred all that it contained; and, passing rapidly from annals to prophecy, from narration to song, regarded the whole but as a tissue of oriental allegories, in which the deep melancholy of Egyptian associations was interwoven with the rich and sensual imagery of the East.

Towards sunset I saw the venerable Hermit, on his way, across the canal, to my cave. Though he was accompanied only by his graceful antelope, which came snuffing the wild air of the desert, as if scenting its home, I felt his visit, even thus, to be a most welcome relief. It was the hour, he said, of his evening ramble up the mountain,—of his accustomed visit to those cisterns of the rock from which he nightly drew his most precious beverage. While he spoke, I observed in his hand one of those earthen cups in which it is the custom of the inhabitants of the wilderness to collect the fresh dew among the rocks. Having proposed that I should accompany him in his walk, he proceeded to lead me, in the direction of the desert, up the side of the mountain that rose above my dwelling, and which formed the southern wall or screen of the defile.

Near the summit we found a seat, where the old man paused to rest. It commanded a full view over

the desert, and was by the side of one of those
hollows in the rock, those natural reservoirs, in which
are treasured the dews of night for the refreshment
of the dwellers in the wilderness. Having learned
from me how far I had advanced in my study,—"In
yonder light," said he, pointing to a small cloud in
the east, which had been formed on the horizon by
the haze of the desert, and was now faintly reflecting
the splendours of sunset,—"in the midst of that light
stands Mount Sinai, of whose glory thou hast read ;
upon whose summit was the scene of one of those
awful revelations, in which the Almighty has renewed
from time to time his communication with Man, and
kept alive the remembrance of his own Providence in
this world."

After a pause, as if absorbed in the immensity of
the subject, the holy man continued his sublime
theme. Looking back to the earliest annals of time,
he showed how constantly every relapse of the human
race into idolatry has been followed by some manifestation of divine power, chastening the strong and
proud by punishment, and winning back the humble
by love. It was to preserve, he said, unextinguished
upon earth, that great and vital truth,—the Creation
of the world by one Supreme Being,—that God chose,
from among the nations, an humble and enslaved
race,—that he brought them out of their captivity
"on eagles' wings," and, surrounding every step of
their course with miracles, has placed them before the

eyes of all succeeding generations, as the depositaries of his will, and the ever-during memorials of his power.

Passing, then, in review the long train of inspired interpreters, whose pens and whose tongues were made the echoes of the Divine voice, he traced,* throughout the events of successive ages, the gradual unfolding of the dark scheme of Providence—darkness without, but all light and glory within. The glimpses of a coming redemption, visible even through the wrath of Heaven;—the long series of prophecy through which this hope runs, burning and alive, like a spark along a chain;—the slow and merciful preparation of the hearts of mankind for the great trial of their faith and obedience that was at hand, not only by miracles that appealed to the living, but by prophecies launched into the future to carry conviction to the yet unborn;—"through all these glorious and beneficent gradations we may track," said he, "the manifest footsteps of a Creator, advancing to his grand, ultimate end, the salvation of his creatures."

After some hours devoted to these holy instructions, we returned to the ravine, and Melanius left me at my cave; praying, as he parted from me,—with a benevolence which I but ill, alas! deserved,—that my soul might, under these lessons, be "as a watered garden," and, ere long, "bear fruit unto life eternal."

* In the original, the discourses of the Hermit are given much more at length.

Next morning, I was again at my study, and even more eager in the awakening task than before. With the commentary of the Hermit freshly in my memory, I again read through, with attention, the Book of the Law. But in vain did I seek the promise of immortality in its pages. "It tells me," said I, "of a God coming down to earth, but of the ascent of Man to heaven it speaks not. The rewards, the punishments it announces, lie all on this side of the grave; nor did even the Omnipotent offer to his own chosen servants a hope beyond the impassable limits of this world. Where, then, is the salvation of which the Christian spoke? or, if Death be at the root of the faith, can Life spring out of it?"

Again, in the bitterness of disappointment, did I mock at my own willing self-delusion,—again rail at the arts of that traitress, Fancy, ever ready, like the Delilah of this wondrous book, to steal upon the slumbers of Reason, and deliver him up, shorn and powerless, to his foes. If deception—thought I, with a sigh—be necessary, at least let me not practise it on myself;—in the desperate alternative before me let me rather be even hypocrite than dupe.

These self-accusing reflections, cheerless as they rendered my task, did not abate, for a single moment, my industry in pursuing it. I read on and on, with a sort of sullen apathy, neither charmed by style, nor transported by imagery,—that fatal blight in my heart having communicated itself to my imagination and taste. The curses and the blessings, the glory and the ruin, which the historian recorded and the prophet had predicted, seemed all of this world,—all temporal and earthly. That mortality, of which the fountain-head had tasted, tinged the whole stream ; and when I read the words, "all are of the dust, and all turn to dust again," a feeling like the wind of the desert came witheringly over me. Love, Beauty, Glory, everything most bright and worshipped upon earth, appeared sinking before my eyes, under this dreadful doom, into one general mass of corruption and silence.

Possessed by the image of desolation I had thus called up, I laid my head upon the book, in a paroxysm of despair. Death, in all its most ghastly varieties, passed before me ; and I had continued thus for some time, as under the influence of a fearful vision, when the touch of a hand upon my shoulder roused me. Looking up, I saw the Anchoret standing by my side ;—his countenance beaming with that sublime tranquillity, which a hope beyond this earth alone can bestow. How I did envy him !

We again took our way to the seat upon the mountain,—the gloom within my own mind making every thing around me more gloomy. Forgetting my hypocrisy in my feelings, I proceeded to make, at once, an avowal to him of all the doubts and fears which my study of the morning had awakened.

"Thou art yet, my son," he answered, "but on the threshold of our faith. Thou hast seen but the first rudiments of the Divine plan ;—its full and consummate perfection hath not yet opened upon thy mind. However glorious that manifestation of Divinity on Mount Sinai, it was but the forerunner of another, still more glorious, which, in the fulness of time, was to burst upon the world ; when all, that had seemed dim and incomplete, was to be perfected, and the promises, shadowed out by the 'spirit of prophecy,' realized ;—when the silence, that lay, as a seal, on the future, was to be broken, and the glad tidings of life and immortality proclaimed to the world ! "

Observing my features brighten at these words, the pious man continued. Anticipating some of the holy knowledge that was in store for me, he traced, through all its wonders and mercies, the great work of Redemption, dwelling in detail upon every miraculous circumstance connected with it,—the exalted nature of the Being by whose ministry it was accomplished, the noblest and first created of the Sons of God, inferior only to the one, self-existent Father ; — the mysterious incarnation of this heavenly messenger ;— the miracles that authenticated His divine mission ;— the example of obedience to God and love to man, which He set, as a shining light, before the world for ever ;—and, lastly and chiefly, His death and resurrection, by which the covenant of mercy was sealed, and "life and immortality brought to light."

" Such," continued the Hermit, " was the Mediator, promised through all time, to ' make reconciliation for iniquity,' to change death into life, and bring 'healing on his wings' to a darkened world. Such was the last crowning dispensation of that God of benevolence, in whose hands sin and death are but instruments of everlasting good, and who, through apparent evil and temporary retribution, bringing all things 'out of darkness into His marvellous light,' proceeds watchfully and unchangingly to the great, final object of His providence,—the restoration of the whole human race to purity and happiness!"

With a mind astonished, if not touched, by these discourses, I returned to my cave, and found the lamp, as before, ready lighted to receive me. The volume which I had been hitherto studying, was replaced by another, which lay open upon the table, with a branch of fresh palm between its leaves. Though I could not doubt to whose gentle and guardian hand I was indebted for this invisible watchfulness over my studies, there was yet a something in it, so like spiritual interposition, that it struck me with awe ;—and never more than at this moment, when, on approaching the volume, I saw, as the light glistened over its silver letters, that it was the very Book of Life of which the Hermit had spoken !

The midnight hymn of the Christians had sounded through the valley, before I had yet raised my eyes from that sacred volume ; and the second hour of the sun found me again over its pages.

## CHAPTER XVIII.

In this mode of existence I had now passed some days;—my mornings devoted to reading, my nights to listening, under the wide canopy of heaven, to the holy eloquence of Melanius. The perseverance with which I inquired, and the quickness with which I learned soon succeeded in deceiving my benevolent instructor, who mistook curiosity for zeal, and knowledge for belief. Alas! cold, and barren, and earthly was that knowledge,—the word without the spirit, the shape without the life. Even when, as a relief from hypocrisy, I persuaded myself that I believed, it was but a brief delusion, a faith whose hope crumbled at the touch,—like the fruit of the desert-shrub, shining and empty!

But, though my soul was still dark, the good Hermit saw not into its depths. The very facility of my belief, which might have suggested some doubt of its sincerity, was but regarded, by his innocent zeal, as a more signal triumph of the truth. His own ingenuousness led him to a ready trust in others; and the

examples of such conversion as that of the philosopher, Justin, who during a walk by the sea-shore
received the light into his soul, had prepared him for
illumination of the spirit, even more rapid than mine.

During all this time, I neither saw nor heard of
Alethe ; — nor could my patience have endured
through so long a privation, had not those mute
vestiges of her presence, that welcomed me every
night on my return, made me feel that I was still
living under her gentle influence, and that her sympathy hung round every step of my progress.  Once,
too, when I ventured to speak her name to Melanius,
though he answered not my inquiry, there was a
smile, I thought, of promise upon his countenance,
which love, far more alive than faith, was ready to
interpret as it desired.

At length,—it was on the sixth or seventh evening
of my solitude, when I lay resting at the door of my
cave, after the study of the day,—I was startled by
hearing my name called loudly from the opposite
rocks ; and looking up, saw, upon the cliff near the
deserted grottos, Melanius and—oh ! I *could not* doubt
—my Alethe by his side !

Though I had never, since the first night of my
return from the desert, ceased to flatter myself
with the fancy that I was still living in her presence,
the actual sight of her again made me feel for what a
long age we had been separated.  She was clothed
all in white, and, as she stood in the last remains of

the sunshine, appeared to my too prophetic fancy like a parting spirit, whose last footsteps on earth that pure glory encircled.

With a delight only to be imagined, I saw them descend the rocks, and, placing themselves in the boat, proceed directly towards my cave.  To disguise from Melanius the mutual delight with which we again met was impossible ;—nor did Alethe even attempt to make a secret of her joy.  Though blushing at her own happiness, as little could her frank nature conceal it as the clear waters of Ethiopia can hide their gold.  Every look, every word, bespoke a fulness of affection, to which, doubtful as I was of our tenure of happiness, I knew not how to respond.

I was not long, however, left ignorant of the bright fate that awaited me; but, as we wandered or rested among the rocks, learned everything that had been arranged since our parting.  She had made the Hermit, I found, acquainted with all that had passed between us; had told him, without reserve, every incident of our voyage,—the avowals, the demonstrations of affection on one side, and the deep sentiment that gratitude had awakened on the other.  Too wise to regard affections so natural, with severity,—knowing that they were of heaven, and but made evil by man,—the good Hermit had heard of our attachment with pleasure ; and, fully satisfied as to the honour and purity of my views, by the fidelity with which I had delivered up my trust into his hands, saw, in my affection for the young orphan, but a providential resource against that friendless solitude in which his death must soon leave her.

As, listening eagerly, I collected these particulars from their discourse, I could hardly trust my ears. It seemed a happiness too great to be true, to be real; nor can words convey any idea of the joy, the shame, the wonder with which I listened, while the holy man himself declared that he awaited but the moment, when he should find me worthy of becoming a member of the Christian Church, to give me also the hand of Alethe in that sacred union which alone sanctifies love, and makes the faith, which it pledges, holy. It was but yesterday, he added, that his young charge herself, after a preparation of prayer and repentance, such as even her pure spirit required, had been admitted, by the sacred ordinance of baptism, into the bosom of the faith;—and the white garment she wore, and the ring of gold on her finger, "were symbols," he added, " of that New Life into which she had been initiated."

I raised my eyes to hers as he spoke, but withdrew them again, dazzled and confused. Even her beauty, to my imagination, seemed to have undergone some brightening change ; and the contrast between that open and happy countenance, and the unblest brow of the infidel that stood before her, abashed me into a sense of unworthiness, and almost checked my rapture.

To that night, however, I look back, as an epoch in

my existence. It proved that sorrow is not the only
awakener of devotion, but that joy may sometimes
call the holy spark into life. Returning to my cave,
with a heart full, even to oppression, of its happiness,
I could find no other relief to my overcharged feelings than that of throwing myself on my knees, and,
for the first time in my life, uttering a prayer, that if,
indeed, there were a Being who watched over mankind, he would send down one ray of his truth into
my darkened soul, and make it worthy of the blessings, both here and hereafter, proffered to it!

My days now rolled on in a perfect dream of happiness. Every hour of the morning was welcomed as
bringing nearer and nearer the blest time of sunset,
when the Hermit and Alethe never failed to visit
my now charmed cave, where her smile left, at each
parting, a light that lasted till her return. Then, our
rambles together, by starlight, over the mountain ;—
our pauses, from time to time, to contemplate the
wonders of the bright heaven above us ; our repose
by the cistern of the rock, and our silent listening,
through hours that appeared minutes, to the holy
eloquence of our teacher ;—all, all was happiness of
the most heartfelt kind, and such as even the doubts,
the cold, lingering doubts, that still hung, like a mist,
around my heart, could neither cloud nor chill.

As soon as the moonlight nights returned, we used
to venture into the desert ; and those sands, which
had looked but lately so desolate in my eyes, now

assumed even a cheerful and smiling aspect. To the light, innocent heart of Alethe, everything was a source of enjoyment. For her, even the desert had its jewels and flowers; and, sometimes, her delight was to search among the sands for those beautiful pebbles of jasper that abound in them;—sometimes her eyes sparkled on finding, perhaps, a stunted marigold, or one of those bitter, scarlet flowers, that lend their dry mockery of ornament to the desert. In all these pursuits and pleasures the good Hermit took a share,—mingling with them occasionally the reflections of a benevolent piety, that lent its own cheerful hue to all the works of creation, and saw the consoling truth, "God is Love," written legibly everywhere.

Such was, for a few weeks, my blissful life. Oh, mornings of hopes, oh, nights of happiness, with what melancholy pleasure do I retrace your flight, and how reluctantly pass to the sad events that followed!

During this time, in compliance with the wishes of Melanius, who seemed unwilling that I should become wholly estranged from the world, I used occasionally to pay a visit to the neighbouring city, Antinoë, which, as the capital of the Thebaïd, is the centre of all the luxury of Upper Egypt. But here, so changed was my every feeling by the all-absorbing passion which now possessed me, that I sauntered, uninterested and unamused by either the scenes or the people that surrounded me, and, sighing for that

o

rocky solitude where Alethe breathed, felt *this* to be the wilderness, and *that* the world.

Even the thoughts of my own native Athens, that were called up, at every step, by the light Grecian architecture of this imperial city, did not awaken one single regret in my heart—one wish to exchange even an hour of my desert for the best luxuries and honours that awaited me in the Garden. I saw the arches of triumph ;—I walked under the superb portico, which encircles the whole city with its marble shade ;—I stood in the Circus of the Sun, by whose rose-coloured pillars the mysterious movements of the Nile are measured ;—on all these bright ornaments of glory and art, as well as on the gay multitude that enlivened them, I looked with an unheeding eye. If they awakened in me any thought, it was the mournful idea, that, one day, like Thebes and Heliopolis, this pageant would pass away, leaving nothing behind but a few mouldering ruins,—like the sea-shells found where the ocean has been,—to tell that the great tide of Life was once there !

But, though indifferent thus to all that had formerly attracted me, there were subjects, once alien to my heart, on which it was now most tremblingly alive ; and some rumours which had reached me, in one of my visits to the city, of an expected change in the policy of the Emperor towards the Christians, filled my mind with apprehensions as new as they were dreadful to me.

The peace and even favour which the Christians enjoyed, during the first four years of the reign of Valerian, had removed from them all fear of a renewal of those horrors which they had experienced under the rule of his predecessor, Decius. Of late, however, some less friendly dispositions had manifested themselves. The bigots of the court, taking alarm at the spread of the new faith, had succeeded in filling the mind of the monarch with that religious jealousy which is the ever-ready parent of cruelty and injustice. Among these counsellors of evil was Macrianus, the Prætorian Prefect, who was, by birth, an Egyptian, and had long made himself notorious, — so akin is superstition to intolerance,—by his addiction to the dark practices of demon-worship and magic.

From this minister, who was now high in the favour of Valerian, the new measures of severity against the Christians were expected to emanate. All tongues, in all quarters, were busy with the news. In the streets, in the public gardens, on the steps of the temples, I saw, everywhere, groups of inquirers collected, and heard the name of Macrianus upon every tongue. It was dreadful, too, to observe, in the countenances of those who spoke, the variety of feeling with which the rumour was discussed, according as they desired or dreaded its truth, — according as they were likely to be among the torturers or the victims.

Alarmed, though still ignorant of the whole extent of the danger, I hurried back to the ravine, and, going at once to the grotto of Melanius, detailed to him every particular of the intelligence I had collected. He listened to me with a composure which I mistook, alas! for confidence in his own security; and, naming the hour for our evening walk, retired into his grotto.

At the accustomed time, accompanied by Alethe, he came to my cave. It was evident that he had not communicated to her the intelligence which I had brought, for never did brow wear such happiness as that which now played around hers:—it was, alas! *not* of this earth. Melanius himself, though composed, was thoughtful; and the solemnity, almost approaching to melancholy, with which he placed the hand of Alethe in mine—in the performance, too, of a ceremony that *ought* to have filled my heart with joy— saddened and alarmed me. This ceremony was our betrothment, the act of plighting our faith to each other, which we now solemnized on the rock before the door of my cave, in the face of that calm, sunset heaven, whose one star stood as our witness. After a blessing from the Hermit upon our spousal pledge, I placed the ring—the earnest of our future union— on her finger; and, in the blush, with which she surrendered to me her whole heart at that instant, forgot every thing but my happiness, and felt secure even against fate!

We took our accustomed walk over the rocks and on the desert. So bright was the moon—more like the day-light, indeed, of other climes,—that we could see plainly the tracks of the wild antelopes in the sand ; and it was not without a slight tremble of feeling in his voice, as if some melancholy analogy occurred to him as he spoke, that the good Hermit said, " I have observed in the course of my walks, that wherever the track of that gentle animal appears, there is, almost always, the foot-print of a beast of prey near it." He regained, however, his usual cheerfulness before we parted, and fixed the following evening for an excursion, on the other side of the ravine, to a point looking, he said, " towards that northern region of the desert, where the hosts of the Lord encamped in their departure out of bondage."

Though, when Alethe was present, all my fears, even for herself, were forgotten in that perpetual element of happiness which encircled her like the air that she breathed, no sooner was I alone than vague terrors and bodings crowded upon me. In vain did I try to reason myself out of my fears, by dwelling only on the most cheering circumstances,—on the reverence with which Melanius was regarded, even by the Pagans, and the inviolate security with which he had lived through the most perilous periods, not only safe himself, but affording sanctuary in the depths of his grottos to others. Though somewhat calmed by these considerations, yet when I at length sunk off to sleep, dark, horrible dreams took possession of my mind. Scenes of death and of torment passed confusedly before me ; and when I awoke it was with the fearful impression that all these horrors were real.

## CHAPTER XIX.

AT length, the day dawned,—that dreadful day. Impatient to be relieved from my suspense, I threw myself into my boat,—the same in which we had performed our happy voyage,—and, as fast as oars could speed me, hurried away to the city. I found the suburbs silent and solitary, but, as I approached the Forum, loud yells, like those of barbarians in combat, struck on my ear, and, when I entered it,— great God, what a spectacle presented itself! The imperial edict against the Christians had arrived during the night, and already the wild fury of bigotry was let loose.

Under a canopy, in the middle of the Forum, was the tribunal of the Governor. Two statues,—one of Apollo, the other of Osiris,—stood at the bottom of the steps that led up to his judgment-seat. Before these idols were shrines, to which the devoted Christians were dragged from all quarters by the soldiers and mob, and there compelled to recant, by throwing incense into the flame. or. on their refusal. hurried

away to torture and death.   It was an appalling
scene ;—the consternation, the cries of some of the
victims,—the pale, silent resolution of others ;—the
fierce shouts of laughter that broke from the multitude, when the dropping of the frankincense on the
altar, proclaimed some denier of Christ; and the
fiend-like triumph with which the courageous Con-
fessors, who avowed their faith, were led away to
the flames ;—never could I have conceived such an
assemblage of horrors !

Though I gazed but for a few minutes, in those
minutes I felt and fancied enough for years.  Already
did the form of Alethe appear to flit before me
through that tumult;—I heard them shout her name;
her shriek fell on my ear ; and the very thought so
palsied me with terror, that I stood fixed and statue-
like on the spot.

Recollecting, however, the fearful preciousness of
every moment, and that—perhaps, at this very instant
—some emissaries of blood might be on their way
to the Grottos, I rushed wildly out of the Forum, and
made my way to the quay.

The streets were now crowded; but I ran headlong
through the multitude, and was already under the
portico leading down to the river,—already saw the
boat that was to bear me to Alethe,—when a Cen-
turion stood sternly in my path, and I was surrounded
and arrested by soldiers !   It was in vain that I implored, that I struggled with them as for life, assuring

them that I was a stranger,—that I was an Athenian,
—that I was—*not* a Christian. The precipitation of
my flight was sufficient evidence against me, and
unrelentingly, and by force, they bore me away to the
quarters of their Chief.

It was enough to drive me at once to madness!
Two hours, two frightful hours, was I kept waiting
the arrival of the Tribune of their Legion,*—my
brain burning with a thousand fears and imaginations,
which every passing minute made but more likely to
be realized. All I could collect, too, from the con-
versations of those around me but added to the
agonizing apprehensions with which I was racked.
Troops, it was said, had been sent in all directions
through the neighbourhood, to bring in the rebellious
Christians, and to make them bow before the Gods of
the Empire. With horror, too, I heard of Orcus,—
Orcus, the High Priest of Memphis,—as one of the
principal instigators of this sanguinary edict, and as
here present in Antinoë, animating and directing its
execution.

In this state of torture I remained till the arrival
of the Tribune. Absorbed in my own thoughts, I
had not perceived his entrance;—till, hearing a voice,
in a tone of friendly surprise, exclaim, " Alciphron ! "
I looked up, and in this legionary Chief recognised a
young Roman of rank, who had held a military command, the year before, at Athens, and was one of the

* A rank, resembling that of Colonel.

most distinguished visitors of the Garden. It was
no time, however, for courtesies ;—he was proceeding
with all cordiality to greet me, but having heard him
order my instant release, I could wait for no more.
Acknowledging his kindness but by a grasp of the
hand, I flew off, like one frantic, through the streets,
and, in a few minutes, was on the river.

My sole hope had been to reach the Grottos before
any of the detached parties should arrive, and, by a
timely flight across the desert, rescue, at least, Alethe
from their fury. The ill-fated delay that had occurred
rendered this hope almost desperate ; but the tranquillity I found everywhere as I proceeded down the
river, and my fond confidence in the sacredness of
the Hermit's retreat, kept my heart from sinking
altogether under its terrors.

Between the current and my oars, the boat flew,
with the speed of wind, along the waters ; and I was
already near the rocks of the ravine, when I saw,
turning out of the canal into the river, a barge
crowded with people, and glittering with arms ! How
did I ever survive the shock of that sight ? The
oars dropped, as if struck out of my hands, into the
water, and I sat, helplessly gazing, as that terrific
vision approached.   In a few minutes, the current
brought us together ;—and I saw, on the deck of the
barge, Alethe herself and the Hermit surrounded
by soldiers !

We were already passing each other when, with a

desperate effort, I sprang from my boat and lighted upon the edge of their vessel. I knew not what I did, for despair was my only prompter. Snatching at the sword of one of the soldiers, as I stood tottering on the edge, I had succeeded in wresting it out of his hands, when, at the same moment, I received a thrust of a lance from one of his comrades, and fell backward into the river. I can just remember rising again and making a grasp at the side of the vessel ;— but the shock, and the faintness from my wound, deprived me of all consciousness, and a shriek from Alethe, as I sunk, is all I can recollect of what followed.

Would I had then died !—Yet, no, Almighty Being ! —I should have died in darkness, and I have lived to know Thee !

On returning to my senses, I found myself reclined on a couch, in a splendid apartment, the whole appearance of which being Grecian, I for a moment, forgot all that had passed, and imagined myself in my own home at Athens. But too soon the whole dreadful certainty flashed upon me ; and, starting wildly—disabled as I was—from my couch, I called loudly, and with the shriek of a maniac, upon Alethe.

I was in the house, I then found, of my friend and disciple, the young Tribune, who had made the Governor acquainted with my name and condition, and had received me under his roof, when brought, bleeding and insensible, to Antinoë. From him I now learned at once,—for I could not wait for details, —the sum of all that had happened in that dreadful interval. Melanius was no more,—Alethe, still alive, but in prison!

"Take me to her,"—I had but time to say,—"take me to her instantly, and let me die by her side,"— when, nature again failing under such shocks, I re- lapsed into insensibility. In this state I continued for near an hour, and, on recovering, found the Tribune by my side. The horrors, he said, of the Forum were, for that day, over,—but what the morrow might bring, he shuddered to contemplate. His nature, it was plain, revolted from the inhuman duties in which he was engaged. Touched by the agonies he saw me suffer, he, in some degree, relieved them, by promising that I should, at nightfall, be conveyed to the prison, and, if possible through his influence, gain access to Alethe. She might yet, he added, be saved, could I succeed in persuading her to comply with the terms of the edict, and make sacrifice to the Gods.— "Otherwise," said he, "there is no hope;—the vindictive Orcus, who has resisted even this short respite of mercy, will, to-morrow, inexorably demand his prey."

He then related to me, at my own request,—though every word was torture,—all the harrowing details of the proceeding before the Tribunal. "I have seen courage," said he, "in its noblest forms, in the field; but the calm intrepidity with which that aged Hermit endured torments—which it was hardly less torment to witness—surpassed all that I could have conceived of human fortitude ! "

My poor Alethe, too,—in describing to me her conduct, the brave man wept like a child. Overwhelmed, he said, at first by her apprehensions for my safety, she had given way to a full burst of womanly weakness. But no sooner was she brought before the Tribunal, and the declaration of her faith was demanded of her, than a spirit almost supernatural seemed to animate her whole form. " She raised her eyes," said he, " calmly, but with fervour, to heaven, while a blush was the only sign of mortal feeling on her features ;—and the clear, sweet, and untrembling voice, with which she pronounced her own doom in the words, ' I am a Christian ! ' sent a thrill of admiration and pity throughout the multitude. Her youth, her loveliness, affected all hearts, and a cry of ' Save the young maiden ! ' was heard in all directions."

The implacable Orcus, however, would not hear of mercy. Resenting, as it appeared, with all his deadliest rancour, not only her own escape from his toils, but the aid with which she had, so fatally to his views, assisted mine, he demanded loudly and in the name of the insulted sanctuary of Isis, her instant death. It was but by the firm intervention of the Governor, who shared the general sympathy in her fate, that the delay of another day was granted to give a chance to the young maiden of yet recalling her confession, and thus affording some pretext for saving her.

Even in yielding, with evident reluctance, to this respite, the inhuman Priest would yet accompany it with some mark of his vengeance. Whether for the pleasure (observed the Tribune) of mingling mockery with his cruelty, or as a warning to her of the doom she must ultimately expect, he gave orders that there should be tied round her brow one of those chaplets of coral,* with which it is the custom of young Christian maidens to array themselves on the day of their martyrdom ;—" and, thus fearfully adorned," said he, "she was led away, amidst the gaze of the pitying multitude, to prison."

With these harrowing details the short interval till nightfall,—every minute of which seemed an age,—was occupied. As soon as it grew dark, I was placed upon a litter,—my wound, though not dangerous, requiring such a conveyance,—and, under the guidance of my friend, I was conducted to the prison. Through his interest with the guard, we were without difficulty admitted, and I was borne into the chamber where the maiden lay immured. Even the veteran guardian of the place seemed touched with compassion for his prisoner, and supposing her to be asleep, had the litter placed gently near her.

* Une "de ces couronnes de grain de corail, dont les vierges martyres ornoient leurs cheveux en allant à la mort."—*Les Martyrs*.

*The Chaplet*

She was half reclining, with her face hid in her hands, upon a couch,—at the foot of which stood an idol, over whose hideous features a lamp of naphtha that hung from the ceiling, shed, a wild and ghastly glare. On a table before the image stood a censer, with a small vessel of incense beside it,—one grain of which, thrown voluntarily into the flame, would, even now, save that precious life. So strange, so fearful was the whole scene, that I almost doubted its reality. Alethe! my own, happy Alethe! *can* it, I thought, be thou that I look upon?

She now, slowly, and with difficulty, raised her head from the couch, on observing which, the kind Tribune withdrew, and we were left alone. There was a paleness, as of death, over her features; and those eyes, which when last I saw them, were but too bright, too happy for this world, looked dim and sunken. In raising herself up, she put her hand, as if from pain, to her forehead, whose marble hue but appeared more death-like from those red bands that lay so awfully across it.

After wandering vaguely for a minute, her eyes rested upon me,—and, with a shriek, half terror, half joy, she sprung from the couch, and sunk upon her knees by my side. She had believed me dead; and, even now, scarcely trusted her senses. "My husband! my love!" she exclaimed; "oh, if thou comest to call me from this world, behold I am ready!" In saying thus, she pointed wildly to that ominous wreath, and then dropped her head down upon my knee, as if an arrow had pierced it.

"Alethe!" I cried,—terrified to the very soul by that mysterious pang,—and, as if the sound of my voice had re-animated her, she looked up, with a faint smile, in my face. Her thoughts, which had evidently been wandering, became collected; and in her joy at my safety, her sorrow at my suffering, she forgot entirely the fate that impended over herself. Love, innocent love, alone occupied all her thoughts; and the warmth, the affection, the devotedness, with which she spoke,—how, at any other moment, I would have blessed—have lingered upon every word!

But the time flew fast—that dreadful morrow was approaching. Already I saw her writhing in the hands of the torturer,—the flames, the racks, the wheels were before my eyes! Half frantic with the fear that her resolution was fixed, I flung myself from the litter in an agony of weeping, and supplicated her, by the love she bore me, by the happiness that awaited us, by her own merciful God, who was too good to require such a sacrifice—by all that the most passionate anxiety could dictate, I implored that she would avert from us the doom that was coming, and—but for once—comply with the vain ceremony demanded of her.

Shrinking from me, as I spoke,—but with a look more of sorrow than reproach,—"What, thou, too!" she said mournfully,—"thou, into whose spirit I had fondly hoped the same light had entered as into my own! No, never be thou leagued with them who would tempt me to 'make shipwreck of my faith!' Thou, who couldst alone bind me to life, use not, I entreat thee, thy power; but let me die, as He I serve hath commanded,—die for the Truth. Remember the holy lessons we heard together on those nights, those happy nights, when both the present and future smiled upon us—when even the gift of eternal life came more welcome to my soul, from the blessed conviction that thou wert to be a sharer in it;—shall I forfeit now that divine privilege? shall I deny the true God, whom we then learned to love?

"No, my own betrothed," she continued,—pointing to the two rings on her finger,—"behold these pledges,—they are both sacred. I should have been as true to thee as I am now to heaven,—nor in that life to which I am hastening shall our love be forgotten. Should the baptism of fire, through which I shall pass to-morrow, make me worthy to be heard before the throne of Grace, I will intercede for thy soul—I will pray that it may yet share with mine that 'inheritance, immortal and undefiled,' which Mercy offers, and that thou,—and my dear mother,—and I——"

She here dropped her voice; the momentary animation, with which devotion and affection had inspired her, vanished;—and there came a darkness

P

over all her features, a livid darkness,—like the
approach of death,—that made me shudder through
every limb. Seizing my hand convulsively, and
looking at me with a fearful eagerness, as if anxious
to hear some consoling assurance from my own lips,—
"Believe me," she continued, "not all the torments
they are preparing for me,—not even this deep,
burning pain in my brow, to which they will hardly
find an equal,—could be half so dreadful to me, as
the thought that I leave thee without—— "

Here, her voice again failed; her head sunk upon
my arm, and—merciful God, let me forget what I
then felt,—I saw that she was dying! Whether I
uttered any cry, I know not; but the Tribune came
rushing into my chamber, and, looking on the maiden
said with a face full of horror, "It is but too
true!"

He then told me in a low voice, what he had just
learned from the guardian of the prison, that the
band round the young Christian's brow was—oh,
horrible cruelty!—a compound of the most deadly
poison,—the hellish invention of Orcus, to satiate
his vengeance, and make the fate of his poor victim
secure. My first movement was to untie that fatal
wreath,—but it would not come away—it would not
come away!

Roused by the pain, she again looked in my face;
but, unable to speak, took hastily from her bosom
the small silver cross which she had brought with

her from my cave. Having pressed it to her own lips, she held it anxiously to mine, and seeing me kiss the holy symbol with fervour, looked happy and smiled. The agony of death seemed to have passed away ;—there came suddenly over her features a heavenly light, some share of which I felt descending into my own soul, and, in a few minutes more, she expired in my arms.

*Here ends the Manuscript ; but, on the outer cover there is, in the handwriting of a much later period, the following Notice, extracted, as it appears, from some Egyptian martyrology :—*

" Alciphron,—an Epicurean philosopher, converted to Christianity A.D. 257, by a young Egyptian maiden, who suffered martyrdom in that year. Immediately upon her death he betook himself to the desert, and lived a life, it is said, of much holiness and penitence. During the persecution under Dioclesian, his sufferings for the faith were most exemplary ; and being at length, at an advanced age, condemned to hard labour, for refusing to comply with an Imperial edict, he died at the Brass Mines of Palestine, A.D. 297.

" As Alciphron held the opinions maintained since by Arius, his memory has not been spared by Athanasian writers, who, among other charges, accuse him of having been addicted to the superstitions of Egypt. For this calumny, however, there appears to be no better foundation than a circumstance, recorded by one of his brother monks, that there was found, after his death, a small metal mirror, like those used in the ceremonies of Isis, suspended around his neck."

# NOTES.

Page 11.—For the importance attached to dreams by the ancients, see *Jortin*, Remarks on Ecclesiastical History, vol. i. p. 90.

Page 17.—"*The Pillar of Pillars*"—more properly, perhaps, "the Column of the Pillars," v. *Abdallatif*, Relation de l'Egypte, and the notes of *M. de Sacy*. The great portico round this column (formerly designated Pompey's, but now known to have been erected in honour of Dioclesian) was still standing, M. de Sacy says, in the time of Saladin. v. *Lord Valentia's Travels*.

Page 18.—Ammianus thus speaks of the state of Alexandria in his time, which was, I believe, as late as the end of the fourth century :— Ne nunc quidem in eadem urbe Doctrinæ variæ silent, non apud nos exaruit Musica nec Harmonia conticuit." Lib. 22.

Page 19.—From the character of the features of the Sphinx, and a passage in Herodotus, describing the Egyptians as μελαγχροες και ουλοτρικες, Volney, Bruce, and a few others, have concluded that the ancient inhabitants of Egypt were negroes. But this opinion is contradicted by a host of authorities. See *Castera's* notes upon *Browne's Travels*, for the result of Blumenbach's dissection of a variety of mummies. Denon, speaking of the character of the heads represented in the ancient sculpture and painting of Egypt says, "Celle des femmes ressemble encore à la figure des jolies femmes d'aujourd'hui : de la rondeur, de la volupté, le nez petit, les yeux longs, peu ouverts," etc.

etc. He could judge, too, he says, from the female mummies, "que leurs cheveux étoient longs et lisses, que le caractère de tête de la plupart tenoit du beau style."—"Je rapportai," he adds, "une tête de vieille femme qui étoit aussi belle que celles de Michel-Ange, et leur resembloit beaucoup."

In a *Description Générale de Thèbes*, by *Messrs. Jollois et Desvilliers*, they say, "Toutes les sculptures Egyptiennes, depuis les plus grands colosses de Thèbes jusqu'aux plus petites idoles, ne rappellent en aucune manière les traits de la figure des nègres ; outre que les têtes momies des catacombes de Thèbes présentent des profils droits." See also *M. Jomard's* "Description of Syene and the Cataracts," *Baron Larrey*, on the "conformation physique" of the Egyptians, etc. But the most satisfactory refutation of the opinion of Volney has been afforded within these few years, by *Doctor Granville*, who having been lucky enough to obtain possession of a perfect female mummy, has, by the dissection and admeasurement of its form, completely established the fact, that the ancient Egyptians were of the Caucasian race, not of the Ethiopian. See this gentleman's curious "*Essay on Egyptian Mummies,*" read before the Royal Society, April 14, 1825.

De Pauw, the great depreciator of everything Egyptian, has on the authority of a passage in Ælian, presumed to affix to the countrywomen of Cleopatra the stigma of complete and unredeemed ugliness. The following line of Euripides, however, is an answer to such charges ;—

Νειλου μεν αιδε καλλιπαρθενοι ροαι.

In addition to the celebrated instances of Cleopatra, Rhodope, etc., we are told, on the authority of Manetho (as given by Zoega from Georgius Syncellus), of a beautiful queen of Memphis, Nitocris, of the sixth dynasty, who in addition to other charms and perfections, was (rather inconsistently with the negro hypothesis) ξανθη την χροιαν.

See, for a tribute to the beauty of the Egyptian women, Montesquieu's Temple de Gnide.

Page 26.—"*Among beds of lotus-flowers.*"—v. *Strabo.*

Page 27.—"*Read those sublime words on the Temple of Neïtha.*"— Το δ' εν Σαει της Αθηνας, ην και Ισιν νομιζουσιν, εδος, επιγραφην εχει τοιαντην, Εγω ειμι παν το γεγονος, και ον και εσομενον, και τον εμονπεπλον ουδεις πω απεκαλυψεν. *Plutarch de Isid. et Osir.*

Page 27.—" *Wandered among the prostrate obelisks of Heliopolis.*"—De-là, en remontant toujours le Nil, on trouve à deux cent cinquante pas, ou environ de la Matarée, les traces de l'ancienne Héliopolis, ou Ville de Soleil, à qui ce lieu étoit particulièrement consacré. C'est pour cette raison qu'on l'appelloit encore l'Œil, ou la Fontaine du Soleil. *Maillet.*

Ib.—"*Isle of the Golden Venus.*"—"On trouve une île appelée Venus-Dorée, ou le champ d'or, avant de remonter jusqu'à Memphis." *Voyages de Pythagore.*

Page 29.—For an account of the Table of Emerald, v. *Lettres sur l'Origine des Dieux d'Egypte. De Pauw* supposes it to be a modern fiction of the Arabs. Many writers have fancied that the art of making gold was the great secret that lay hid under the forms of Egyptian theology. "La science Hermétique," says the Benedictine, Pernetz, "l'art sacerdotal, étoit la source de toutes les richesses des Rois d'Egypte, et l'objet de ces mystères si cachés sous le voile de leur prétendue Religion." *Fables Egyptiennes.* The hieroglyphs, that formerly covered the Pyramids, are supposed by some of these writers to relate to the same art. See *Mutus Liber, Rupellæ.*

Page 30.—" By reflecting the sun's rays," says *Clarke,* speaking of the Pyramids, "they appeared white as snow."

Page 31.—For Bubastis, the Diana of the Egyptians, v. *Jablonski,* lib. 3. cap. 4.

Page 33.—" *The light coracle,*" etc.—v. *Amailhon,* "*Histoire de la Navigation et du Commerce des Egyptiens sous les Ptolemées.*" See also, for a description of the various kinds of boats used on the Nile, *Maillet,* tom. i. p. 98.

Ib.—v. *Maurice,* Appendix to "Ruins of Babylon." Another reason, he says, for their worship of the Ibis, "founded on their love of geometry, was (according to Plutarch) that the space between its legs, when parted asunder, as it walks, together with its beak, forms a complete equilateral triangle." From the examination of the embalmed birds, found in the Catacombs of Saccara, there seems to be no doubt that the Ibis was the same kind of bird as that described by Bruce, under the Arabian name of Abou Hannes.

Page 34.—" *The golden blossoms of the bean-flower.*"—La fleur en est mille fois plus odoriférante que celles de nos fêves d'Europe, quoique leur parfum nous paroisse si agréable.  Comme on en sème beaucoup dans les terres voisines, du Caire, du côté de l'occident, c'est quelque chose de charmant que l'air embaumé que l'on respiré le soir sur les terrasses, quand le vent de l'ouest vient à souffler, et y apporte cette odeur admirable." *Maillet.*

Ib.—"*A sistrum,*" etc.—" Isis est genius," says *Servius,* " Ægypti, qui per sistri motum, quod gerit in dextra, Nili accessus recessusque significat."

Page 36.—" *The ivy that encircled it,*" etc.—The ivy was consecrated to Osiris. v. *Diodor. Sic.* 1. 10.

Ib.—" *The small mirror.*"—" Quelques unes," says *Dupuis,* describing the processions of Isis, " portoient des miroirs attachés à leurs épaules, afin de multiplier et de porter dans tous les sens les images de la Déesse." *Origine de Cultus,* tom. viii. p. 847.  A mirror, it appears, was also one of the emblems in the mysteries of Bacchus.

Page 37.—" *There lies to the north of Memphis,*" etc.—" Tout prouve que la territoire de Sakkarah étoit la Necropolis au sud de Memphis, et le faubourg opposé à celui-ci, où sont les pyramides de Gizeh, une autre Ville des Morts, qui terminoit Memphis au nord." *Denon.*

There is nothing known with certainty as to the site of Memphis, but it will be perceived that the description of its position given by the Epicurean corresponds, in almost every particular, with that which M. Maillet (the French consul, for many years, at Cairo) has, in his work on Egypt, left us.  It must be always borne in mind, too, that of the distances between the respective places here mentioned, we have no longer any accurate means of judging.

Ib.—" *Looking out with the same face and features.*"—" Par-là non seulement on conservoit les corps d'une famille entière, mais en descendant dans ces lieux soûterreins, où ils étoient déposés, on pouvoit se représenter en un instant tous ses ancêtres depuis plusieurs milliers d'années, tels a-peu-près qu'ils étoient de leur vivant." *Maillet.*

Page 38.—"*Pyramid beyond pyramid.*"—"Multas olim pyramidas fuisse e ruinis arguitur." *Zoega.*—*Vansleb*, who visited more than ten of the small pyramids, is of opinion that there must have originally been a hundred in this place.

See, on the subject of the lake to the northward of Memphis, *Shaw's Travels*, p. 302.

Page 43.—"*The Theban beetle.*"—"On voit en Egypte, après la retraite du Nil et la fécondation des terres, le limon couvert d'une multitude de scarabées. Un pareil phénomène a dû sembler aux Egyptiens le plus propre à peindre une nouvelle existence." *M. Jomard.*—Partly for the same reason, and partly for another, still more fanciful, the early Christians used to apply this emblem to Christ. "Bonus ille scarabæus meus," says St. Augustine, "non eâ tantum de causâ quod unigenitus, quod ipsemet sui auctor mortalium speciem induerit, sed quòd in hac nostrâ fæce sese volutaverit et ex hac ipsâ nasci voluerit."

Ib.—"*Enshrined within a case of crystal.*"—"Les Egyptiens ont fait aussi, pour conserver leurs morts, des caisses de verre." *De Pauw.* —He mentions, also, in another place, a sort of transparent substance, which the Ethiopians used for the same purpose, and which was frequently mistaken by the Greeks for glass.

Ib.—"*Among the emblems of death.*"—"Un prêtre, qui brise la tige d'une fleur, des oiseaux qui s'envolent, sont les emblèmes de la mort et de l'âme qui se sépare du corps." *Denon.*

Theseus employs the same image in the Phædra :—

Ορνις γαρ ὡς τις εκ χερων αφαντος ει
Πηδημ' ες ἁδου πικρον ὁρμησασα μοι.

Page 44.—"The singular appearance of a Cross so frequently recurring among the hieroglyphics of Egypt, had excited the curiosity of the Christians at a very early period of ecclesiastical history ; and as some of the Priests, who were acquainted with the meaning of the hieroglyphics, became converted to Christianity, the secret transpired. 'The converted heathens,' says Socrates Scholasticus, 'explained the symbol, and declared that it signified Life to Come.' " *Clarke.*

Lipsius, therefore, is mistaken in supposing the Cross to have been an emblem peculiar to the Christians. See, on this subject, *L'Histoire des Juifs*, liv. 6. c. 16.

It is singular enough that while the Cross was thus held sacred among the Egyptians, not only the custom of marking the forehead with the sign of the Cross, but Baptism and the consecration of the bread in the Eucharist were imitated in the mysterious ceremonies of Mithra. *Tertull. de Proscriptione Hereticorum.*

*Zoega* is of opinion that the Cross, said to have been for the first time found, on the destruction of the temple of Serapis, by the Christians, could not have been the crux ansata ; as nothing is more common than this emblem on all the Egyptian monuments.

Page 46.—"*Stood shadowless.*"—It was an idea entertained among the ancients that the Pyramids were so constructed ("mecanicâ con-structione," says *Ammianus Marcellinus*) as never to cast any shadow.

Page 47.—"*Rhodope.*"—From the story of Rhodope, *Zoega* thinks, "videntur Arabes ansam arripuisse ut in una ex pyramidibus, genii loco, habitare dicerent mulierem nudam insignis pulchritudinis quæ aspecto suo homines insanire faciat." *De Usu Obeliscorum.* See also *L'Egypte de Murtadi par Vattier.*

Page 48.—"*The Gates of Oblivion.*"—"Apud Memphim æneas quasdam portas, quæ Lethes et Cocyti (hoc est oblivionis et lamen-tationis) appellantur aperiri, gravem asperumque edentes sonum." *Zoega.*

Page 51.—"*A file of lifeless bodies.*"—See, for the custom of burying the dead upright ("post funus stantia busto corpora," as Statius describes it), Dr. Clarke's preface to the 2d section of his fifth volume. They used to insert precious stones in the place of the eyes. "Les yeux étoient formés d'émeraudes, de turquoises," *etc.*—v. *Masoudy,* quoted by *Quatremère.*

Page 53.—"*The din with which the gates clashed together.*"—The following verses of Claudian are supposed to have been meant as a description of those imitations of the noise of earthquake and thunder which by means of the Ceraunoscope, and other such contrivances, were practised in the shows of the Mysteries :—

> Jam mihi cernuntur trepidis delubra moveri
> Sedibus, et claram dispergere culmina lucem,
> Adventum testata Dei.  Jam magnus ab imis
> Auditur fremitus terris, templumque remugit
> Cecropium.                      *Rapt. Proserp.* lib. I.

Page 53. —"*It seemed as if every echo.*"—See, for the echoes in the pyramids, *Plutarch, de Placitis Philosoph.*

Page 55. —"*Pale phantom-like shapes.*"—"Ce moment heureux (de l'Autopsie) étoit preparé par des scènes effrayantes, par des alternatives de crainte et de joie, de lumière et de ténèbres, par la lueur des éclairs, par le bruit terrible de la foudre, qu'on imitoit, et par des apparitions de spectres, des illusions magiques, qui frappoient les yeux et les oreilles, tout ensemble." *Dupuis.*

Page 57. —"*Serpents of fire.*"—"Ces considérations me portent à penser pue, dans les mystères, ces phénomènes étoient beaucoup mieux exécutées, et sans comparaison plus terribles à l'aide de quelque composition pyrique qui est restée cachée, comme cele du feu Grégeois." *De Pauw.*

Ib. —"*The burning of those reed-beds of Ethiopia.*"—"Il n'y a point d'autre moyen que de porter le feu dans ces forêts de roseaux, qui répandent alors dans tout le païs une lumière aussi considérable que celle du jour même." *Maillet,* tom. I. p. 63.

Page 58. —"*The sound of torrents.*"—The Nile, *Pliny* tells us, was admitted into the Pyramid.

Page 59. —"*I had given myself up.*"—"On exerçoit," says *Dupuis,* "les recipiendaires, pendant plusieurs jours, à traverser, à la nage, une grande étendue d'eau.  On les y jettoit et ce n'étoit qu'avec peine qu'ils s'en retiroient.  On appliquoit le fer et le feu sur leurs membres.  On les faisoit passer à travers les flammes."

The aspirants were often in considerable danger, and Pythagoras, we are told, nearly lost his life in the trials.   v. *Recherches sur les Initiations, par Robin.*

Page 64.—"*The God of Silence and Light.*"—"Enfin Harpocrates représentoit aussi le Soleil.   Il est vrai que c'étoit aussi le Dieu du Silence ; il mettoit le doigt sur la bouche parcequ'on adoroit le Soleil avec un respectueux silence ; et c'est de là qu'est venu le Sigé des Basilidiens, qui tiroient leur origine de l'Europe . . . . . . Enfin Harpocrates étoit assis sur le lotus, qui est la plante du Soleil." *Hist. des Juifs.*

Page 65.—For the two cups used in the mysteries, see *L'Histoire des Juifs*, liv. 9. c. 16.

Ib.—"*Osiris.*"—Osiris, under the name of Serapis, was supposed to rule over the subterranean world ; and performed the office of Pluto, in the mythology of the Egyptians.   "They believed," says Dr. Pritchard, "that Serapis presided over the region of departed souls, during the period of their absence, when languishing without bodies, and that the dead were deposited in his palace." *Analysis of the Egyptian Mythology.*

Ib.—"*To cool the lips of the dead.*"—"Frigidam illam aquam post mortem, tanquam Hebes poculum, expetitam." *Zoega.*—The Lethe of the Egyptians was called Ameles.   See *Dupuis*, tom. 8. p. 651.

Page 66.—"*The young cup-bearer on the other side.*"—"Enfin on disoit qu'il y avoit deux coupes, l'une en haut et l'autre en bas.   Celui qui beuvoit de la coupe d'en bas, avoit toujours soif, ses désirs s'augmentoit au lieu de s'éteindre, mais celui qui beuvoit de la coupe en haut étoit rempli et content.   Cette première coupe étoit la connoissance de la nature, qui ne satisfait jamais pleinement ceux qui en sordent les mystéres ; et la seconde coupe, dans laquelle on devoit boire pour n'avoir jamais soif, étoit la connaissance des mystères du Ciel." *Hist. des Juifs*, liv. 9. chap. 16.

Ib. — "*She mingled a draught divine.*" — The της αθανασιας φαρμακον, which, according to Diodorus Siculus, Isis prepared for her son Orus.—Lib. 1.

Page 68.—" *Grasshopper, symbol of Initiation* "—*Hor. Apoll.*—The grasshopper was also consecrated to the sun as being musical.

Ib.—"*Isle of Gardens.*"—The isle Antirrhodus, near Alexandria. *Maillet.*

Ib.—" *Vineyard at Anthylla.*"—v. *Athen. Deipnos.*

Page 70.—" *We can see those stars.*"—"On voyoit en plein jour par ces ouvertures les étoiles, et même quelques planètes en leur plus grande latitude septentrionale ; et les prêtres avoient bientôt profité de ce phénomène, pour observer à diverses heures la passage des étoiles." *Séthos.*—*Strabo* mentions certain caves or pits, constructed for the purpose of astronomical observations, which lay in the Zelopolitan prefecture, beyond Heliopolis.

Page 71.—" *That dark Deity.*"—*Serapis*, Sol Inferus.—Athenodorus, scriptor vetustus, apud Clementem Alexandrinum in *Protreptico*, ait "simulacra Serapidis conspicue esse colore cœruleo et nigricante." Macrobius, in verbis descriptis, § 6. Docet, nos apùd Ægyptios "simulacra solis infera fingi colore cœruleo." *Jablonski.*

Ib.—"*A plantain.*"—This tree was dedicated to the Genii of the Shades, from its being an emblem of repose and cooling airs. "Cui imminet musæ falium, quod ab Iside infera genüsque ei addictis manu geri solitum, umbram requiemque et auras frigidas subindigitare videtur." *Zoega.*

Page 77.—" *He spoke of the pre-existence of the soul,*" etc.—For a full account of the doctrines which are here represented as having been taught to the initiated in the Egyptian mysteries, the reader may consult *Dupuis, Pritchard's Analysis of the Egyptian Mythology*, etc. |etc. "L'on découvroit l'origine de l'âme, sa chute sur la terre, à travers les sphères et les élémens, et son retour au lieu de son origine . . . . c'étoit ici la partie la plus métaphysique, et que ne pourroit guère entendre le commun des Initiés, mais dont on lui donnoit le spectacle par des figures et des spectres allégoriques." *Dupuis.*

Ib.—"*Those fields of radiance.*"—See *Beausobre*, lib. 3. c. 4, for the "terre bienheureuse et lumineuse," which the Manicheans supposed God to inhabit. Plato, too, speaks (in Phæd.) of a pure land lying in the pure sky (την γην καθαραν εν καθαρῳ κεισθαι ουρανῳ), the abode of divinity, of innocence, and of life."

Page 78.—"*As he spoke these words, a burst of pure, brilliant light.*" —The power of producing a sudden and dazzling effusion of light, which was one of the arts employed by the contrivers of the ancient Mysteries, is thus described in a few words by Apuleius, who was himself admitted to witness the Isiac ceremonies at Corinth:—"Nocte mediâ vidi solem candido coruscantem lumine."

Page 79.—"*Tracing it from the first moment of earthward desire.*"— In the original construction of this work, there was an episode introduced here (which I have since published in another form), illustrating the doctrine of the fall of the soul by the Oriental fable of the Loves of the Angels.

Page 80.—"*Restoring her lost wings.*"—*Damascius*, in his Life of Isidorus, says, "Ex antiquissimis Philosophis Pythagoram et Platonem Isidorus ut Deos coluit, et *eorum animas alatas esse* dixit quas in locum supercœlestem inque campum veritatis et pratum elevatas, divinis putavit ideis pasci." *Apud Phot. Bibliothec.*

Page 81.—"*A pale moonlike meteor.*"—*Apuleius*, in describing the miraculous appearances exhibited in the mysteries, says, "Nocte mediâ vidi solem candido coruscantem lumine." *Metamorphos.* lib. 11.

Ib.—"*So entirely did the illusion of the scene,*" etc.—In tracing the early connection of spectacles with the ceremonies of religion, *Voltaire* says, "Il y a bien plus ; les véritables grandes tragédies, les représentations imposantes et terribles, étoient les mystères sacrés, qu'on célébroit dans les plus vastes temples du monde, en présence des seuls Initiés ; c'étoit là que les habits, les décorations, les machines étoient propres au sujet ; et le sujet étoit la vie présente et la vie future." *Des divers changemens arrivés à l'art tragique.*

To these scenic representations in the Egyptian mysteries, there is evidently an allusion in the vision of Ezekiel, where the Spirit shows him the abominations which the Israelites learned in Egypt :—"Then said he unto me, 'Son of man, hast thou seen what the ancients of the house of Israel do in the dark, every man in *the chambers of his imagery?*'" Chap. 8.

Page 84.—" *The Seven Tables of stone.*"—" Bernard, Comte de la Marche Trévisane, instruit par la lecture des livres anciens, dit, qu'Hermes trouva sept tables dans la vallée d'Hebron, sur lesquelles étoient gravés les principes des arts libéraux." *Fables Egyptiennes.* See *Jablonski de stelis Herm.*

Page 85.—" *Beside the goat of Mendes.*"—For an account of the animal-worship of the Egyptians, see *De Pauw,* tom. 2.

Ib.—" *The crocodile with costly gems.*"—Herodotus (*Euterp.*) tells us that the people about Thebes and Lake Mœris kept a number of tame crocodiles, which they worshipped, and dressed them out with gems and golden ornaments in their ears.

Ib.—" *The Isiac serpents.*"—" On auguroit bien de serpens Isiaques, lorsqu'ils goûtoient l'offrande et se trainoient lentement autour de l'autel." *De Pauw.*

Page 86.—" *Hence, the festivals and hymns,*" etc.—For an account of the various festivals at the different periods of the sun's progress, in the spring, and in the autumn, see *Dupuis* and *Pritchard.*

Ib.—" *The Mysteries of the Night.*"—v. *Athenag. Leg. pro Christ.* p. 138.

Page 89.—" *A peal like that of thunder.*"—See, for some curious remarks on the mode of imitating thunder and lightning in the ancient mysteries, *De Pauw,* tom. 1. p. 323. The machine with which these effects were produced on the stage was called a ceraunoscope.

Page 93.—" *Windings capriciously intricate.*"—In addition to the accounts which the ancients have left us of the prodigious excavations in all parts of Egypt,—the fifteen hundred chambers under the labyrinth— the subterranean stables of the Thebaïd, containing a thousand horses —the crypts of Upper Egypt passing under the bed of the Nile, etc.— the stories and traditions current among the Arabs still preserve the memory of those wonderful substructions. " Un Arabe," says Paul

Lucas, "qui étoit avec nous, m'assura qu'étant entré autrefois dans le Labyrinthe, il avoit marché dans les chambres souterraines jusqu'en un lieu où il y avoit une grande place environnée de plusieurs niches qui ressembloit à de petites boutiques, d'où l'on entroit dans d'autres allées et dans chambres, sans pouvoir en trouver la fin." In speaking, too, of the arcades along the Nile, near Cosseir, "Ils me dirent même que ces souterrains étoient si profondes qu'il y en avoient qui alloient à trois journées de là, et qu'ils conduisoient dans un pays où l'on voyoit de beau jardins, qu'on y trouvoit de belles maisons," etc. etc.

See also in *M. Quatremère's Mémoires sur l'Egypte*, tom. 1. p. 142, an account of a subterranean reservoir, said to have been discovered at Kaïs, and of the expedition undertaken by a party of persons, in a long narrow boat, for the purpose of exploring it. "Leur voyage avoit été de six jours, dont les quatre premiers furent employés à pénétrer les bords ; les deux autres à revenir au lieu d'où ils étoient partis.. Pendant tout cet intervalle ils ne purent atteindre l'extrémité du bassin. L'émir Ala-eddin-Tamboga, gouverneur de Behnesa, écrivit ces détails au sultan, qui en fut extrêmement surpris."

Page 96.—"*The small island in the centre of Lake Mœris.*"—The position here given to Lake Mœris, in making it the immediate boundary of the city of Memphis to the south, corresponds exactly with the site assigned to it by Maillet :—"Memphis avoit encore à son midi un vaste reservoir, par où tout ce qui peut servir à la commodité et à l'agrément de la vie lui étoit voituré abondamment de toutes les parties de l'Egypte. Ce lac qui la terminoit de ce côté-la," etc. etc. Tom. 2. p. 7.

Ib.—"*Ruins rose blackly above the wave.*"—"On voit sur la rive orientale des antiquités qui sont presque entièrement sous les eaux." *Belzoni.*

Page 97.—"*Its thundering portals.*"—"Quorundam autem domorum (in Labyrintho) talis est situs, ut adaperientibus fores tonitruum intus terribile existat." *Pliny.*

Ib.—"*Leaves that serve as cups.*"—*Strabo.* According to the French translator of Strabo, it was the fruit of the *faba Ægyptiaca*, not the leaf, that was used for this purpose.   " Le κιβωριον," he says "devoit s'entendre de la capsule ou fruit de cette plante, dont les Egyptiens se servoient comme d'un vase, imaginant que l'eau du Nil y devenoit délicieuse."

Page 100.—" *The fish of these waters,*" etc.—*Ælian,* lib. 6. 32.

Page 101.—" *Pleasure-boats or yachts.*"—Called Thalameges, from the pavilion on the deck.  v. *Strabo.*

Page 102.—" *Covered with beds of those pale, sweet roses.*"—As April is the season for gathering these roses (see *Malte-Brun's Economical Calendar*), the Epicurean could not, of course, mean to say that he saw them actually in flower.

Page 103.—" *The lizards upon the bank.*"—" L'or et l'azur brillent en bandes longitudinales sur leur corps entier, et leur queue est du plus beau bleu céleste." *Sonnini.*

Page 104.—" *The canal through which we now sailed.*"—" Un Canal," says *Maillet,* "très profond et très large y voituroit les eaux du Nil."

Page 106.—" *For a draught of whose flood,*" etc.—" Anciennement on portoit les eaux du Nil jusqu'à des contrées fort éloignées, et surtout chez les princesses du sang des Ptolomées, mariées dans des familles étrangères." *De Pauw.*

The water thus conveyed to other lands was, as we may collect from Juvenal, chiefly intended for the use of the Temples of Isis, established in those countries.

> Si candida jusserit Io,
> Ibit ad Ægypti finem, calidaque petitas
> A Meroë portabit aquas, ut spargat in ædem
> Isidis, antiquo quæ proxima surgit ovili.
>
> *Sat.* vi.

Page 109.—" *Bearing each the name of its owner.*"—" Le nom du maître y étoit écrit, pendant la nuit, en lettres de feu." *Maillet.*

Page 109.—"*Cups of that frail crystal*,"—called Alassontes. For their brittleness *Martial* is an authority :—

> Tolle, puer, calices, tepidique toreumata Nili,
> Et mihi securâ pocula trade manu.

"Sans parler ici des coupes d'un verre porté jusqu'à la pureté du crystal, ni de celles qu'on appelloit Alassontes, et qu'on suppose avoir représenté des figures dont les couleurs changeoient suivant l'aspect sous lequel on les regardoit, à peu près comme ce qu'on nomme vulgairement *Gorge de pigeon*, etc." *De Pauw.*

Ib.—"*Bracelets of the black beans of Abyssinia.*"—The bean of the Glycyne, which is so beautiful as to be strung into necklaces and bracelets, is generally known by the name of the black bean of Abyssinia. *Niebuhr.*

Ib.—"*Sweet lotus-wood flute.*"—See *M. Villoteau on the musical instruments of the Egyptians.*

Page 110.—"*Shine like the brow of Mount Atlas at night.*"—*Solinus* speaks of the snowy summit of Mount Atlas glittering with flames at night. In the account of the Periplus of Hanno, as well as in that of Eudoxus we read that as those navigators were coasting this part of Africa torrents of light were seen to fall on the sea.

Page 111.—"*The tears of Isis.*"—"Per lacrymas, vero, Isidis intelligo effluvia quædam Lunæ, quibus tantam vim videntur tribuisse Ægypti." *Jablonski.*—He is of opinion that the superstition of the *Nucta*, or miraculous drop, is a relic of the veneration paid to the dews, as the tears of Isis.

Ib.—"*The rustling of the acacias,*" etc.—*Travels of Captain Mangles.*

Ib.—"*Supposed to rest in the Valley of the Moon.*"—*Plutarch. Dupuis*, tom. 10. The Manicheans held the same belief. See *Beausobre*, p. 565.

Page. 112.—"*Sothis, the fair Star of the Waters.*"—ὑδραγωγον is the epithet applied to this star by *Plutarch de Isid.*

Page 113.—"*Was its birth-star.*"—'Η Σωθεως ανατολη γενεσεως καταρχουσα της εις τον κοσμον. *Porphyr. de Antro Nymph.*

Page 118.—"*Golden Mountains.*"—v. *Wilford on Egypt and the Nile,* Asiatic Researches.

Ib.—"*Sweet-smelling wood.*"—"A l'époque de la crue le Nil Vert charie les planches d'un bois qui a une odeur semblable à celle de l'encens." *Quatremère.*

Ib.—"*Barges full of bees.*"—*Maillet.*

Page 119.—"*Such a profusion of the white flowers,*" etc.—"On les voit comme jadis cueiller dans les champs des tiges du lotus, signes du débordement et présages de l'abondance ; ils s'enveloppent les bras et le corps avec les longues tiges fleuries, et parcourent les rues," etc. *Description des Tombeaux des Rois, par M. Costaz.*

Page 122.—"*While composing his Commentary on the Scriptures.*"— It was during the composition of his great critical work, the Hexapla, that Origen employed these female scribes.

Page 124.—"*That rich tapestry,*" etc.

> Non ego prætulerim Babylonica picta superbè
> Texta, Semiramiâ quæ variantur acu.       *Martial.*

Page 126.—"*The duty of some of these young servitors.*"—De Pauw, who differs in opinion from those who supposed women to be eligible to the higher sacerdotal offices in Egypt, thus enumerates the tasks to which their superintendence was, as he thinks, confined :—"Les femmes n'ont pu tout au plus dans l'ordre secondaire, s'acquitter que de quelques emplois sans conséquence ; comme de nourrir des scarabées des musaraignes et d'autres petits animaux sacrés." Tom. 1. Sect. 2.

Page 139.—"*The Place of Weeping.*"—v. *Wilford, Asiatic Researches,* vol. 3, p. 340.

Page 146.—"*We had long since left this mountain behind.*"—The voyages on the Nile are under favourable circumstances performed with considerable rapidity. "En cinq ou six jours," says Maillet, "on pourroit aisément remonter de l'embouchure du Nil à ses cataractes, ou descendre des cataractes jusqu'à la mer." The great uncertainty of the navigation is proved by what *Belzoni* tells us :—"Nous ne mîmes cette fois que deux jours et demi pour faire le trajet du Caire à Melawi, auquel, dans notre second voyage, nous avions employés dix-huit jours."

Page 147.—"*Those mighty statues that fling their shadows.*"— "Elles ont près de vingt mètres (61 pieds) d'élévation ; et au lever du soleil, leurs ombres immenses s'étendent au loin sur la chaine Libyenne." *Description générale de Thèbes, par Messrs. Jollois et Desvilliers.*

Ib.—"*Those cool alcoves.*"—*Paul Lucas.*

Page 152.—"*Whose waters are half sweet, half bitter.*"—*Paul Lucas.*

Page 155.—"*Mountain of the Birds.*"—There has been much controversy among the Arabian writers with respect to the site of this mountain, for which see *Quatremère*, tom. I. art. *Amoun.*

Page 158.—"*The hand of labour had succeeded,*" etc.—The monks of Mount Sinai (*Shaw* says) have covered over near four acres of the naked rocks with fruitful gardens and orchards.

Page 160.—"*The image of a head.*"—There was usually, *Tertullian* tells us, the image of Christ on the communion cups.

Ib.—"*Kissed her forehead.*"—"We are rather disposed to infer," says the present *Bishop of Lincoln*, in his very sensible work on Tertullian, "that, at the conclusion of all their meetings for the purpose of devotion, the early Christians were accustomed to give the kiss of peace, in token of the brotherly love subsisting between them."

Page 161.—"*Came thus secretly before daybreak.*"—It was among the accusations of *Celsus* against the Christians, that they held their assemblies privately and contrary to law ; and one of the speakers in the curious work of *Minucius Felix* calls the Christians "latebrosa et lucifugax natio."

Page 164.—"*In the middle of the Seven Valleys.*"—See *Macrizy's* account of these valleys, given by *Quatremère*, tom 1. p. 450.

Ib.—"*Red lakes of Nitria.*"—For a striking description of this region, see "*Rameses,*" a work which, though in general too technical and elaborate, shows, in many passages, to what picturesque effects the scenery and mythology of Egypt may be made subservient.

Page 164.—"*In the neighbourhood of Antinoë.*"—From the position assigned to Antinoe in this work, we should conclude that it extended much farther to north than the few ruins of it that remain would seem to indicate,—so as to render the distance between the city and the Mountain of the Birds considerably less than what it appears to be at present.

Page 168.—"*When Isis, the pure star of lovers.*"—v. *Plutarch de Isid.*

Ib.—"*Ere she again embrace her bridegroom sun.*"—"Conjunctio solis cum luna, quod est veluti utriusque connubium." *Jablonski.*

Page 170.—"*Of his walks a lion is the companion.*"—*M. Chateaubriand* has introduced Paul and his lion into the "*Martyrs,*" liv. 11.

Page 177.—"*A swallow,*" etc.—"Je vis dans le désert des hirondelles d'un gris clair comme le sable sur lequel elles lent." *Denon.*

Ib.—"*The comet that once desolated this world.*"—In alluding to Whiston's idea of a comet having caused the deluge, *M. Girard*, having remarked that the word Typhon means a deluge, adds, "On ne peut entendre par le tems du règne de Typhon que celui pendant lequel le déluge inonda la terre, tems pendant lequel on dût observer la comète qui l'occasionna, et dont l'apparition fut, non seulement pour les peuples de l'Egypte, et de l'Ethiopie, mais encore pour tous les peuples le présage funeste de leur destruction presque totale." *Description de la Vallée de l'Egarement.*

Page 178.—"*In which the Spirit of my dream,*" etc.—"Many people," said *Origen*, "have been brought over to Christianity by the Spirit of God giving a sudden turn to their minds, and offering visions to them either by day or night." On this *Jortin* remarks :—"Why should it be thought improbable that Pagans of good dispositions, but not free from prejudices, should have been called by divine admonitions, by dreams or visions, which might be a support to Christianity in those days of distress ? "

Page 181.—"*One of those earthen cups.*"—*Palladius*, who lived some time in Egypt, describes the monk Ptolemæus, who inhabited the desert of Scete, as collecting in earthen cups the abundant dew from the rocks. *Bibliothec. Pat.* tom. 13.

Page 182.—"*It was to preserve, he said,*" etc.—The brief sketch here given of the Jewish dispensation agrees very much with the view taken of it by Dr. Sumner, in the first chapters of his eloquent work, the "Records of the Creation."

Page 184.—"*In vain did I seek the promise of immortality.*"—"It is impossible to deny," says Dr. Sumner, "that the sanctions of the Mosaic Law are altogether temporal . . . . . It is, indeed, one of the facts that can only be explained by acknowledging that he really acted under a divine commission, promulgating a temporary law for a peculiar purpose,"—a much more candid and sensible way of treating this very difficult point, than by either endeavouring, like Warburton, to escape from it into a paradox, or still worse, contriving, like Dr. Graves, to increase its difficulty by explanation. v. "*On the Pentateuch.*" See also *Horne's Introduction*, etc. vol. i. p. 226.

Page 185.—"*All are of the dust,*" etc.—While Voltaire, Volney, etc. refer to the Ecclesiastes, as abounding with tenets of materialism and Epicurism, Mr. Des Vœux and others find in it strong proofs of belief in a future state. The chief difficulty lies in the chapter from which this text is quoted ; and the mode of construction by which some writers attempt to get rid of it, namely, by putting these texts into the mouth of a foolish reasoner,—appears forced and gratuitous. v. *Dr. Hale's Analysis.*

Page 186.—"*The noblest and first-created*," *etc.*—This opinion of the Hermit may be supposed to have been derived from his master, Origen ; but it is not easy to ascertain the exact doctrine of Origen on this subject. In the Treatise on Prayer attributed to him, he asserts that God the Father alone should be invoked,—which, says Bayle, is to "enchérir sur les Hérésies des Sociniens." Notwithstanding this, however, and some other indications of, what was afterwards called, Arianism, (such as the opinion of the divinity being received by *communication*, which *Milner* asserts to have been held by this Father,) Origen was one of the authorities quoted by Athanasius in support of his high doctrines of co-eternity and co-essentiality. What Priestley says is, perhaps, the best solution of these inconsistencies :—"Origen, as well as Clemens Alexandrinus, has been thought to favour the Arian principles ; but he did it only in words, and not in ideas."—*Early Opinions, etc.* Whatever uncertainty, however, there may exist with respect to the opinion of Origen himself on this subject, there is no doubt that the doctrines of his immediate followers were, at least, Anti-Athanasian. "So many Bishops of Africa," says Priestley, "were, at this period (between the year 255 and 258), Unitarians, that Athanasius says, 'The Son of God '—meaning His divinity—' was scarcely any longer preached in the churches.' "

Page 187.—"*The restoration of the whole human race to purity and happiness.*"—This benevolent doctrine—which not only goes far to solve the great problem of moral any physical evil, but which would, if received more generally, tend to soften the spirit of uncharitableness, so fatally prevalent among Christian sects—was maintained by that great light of the early Church, Origen, and has not wanted supporters among more modern Theologians. That Tillotson was inclined to the opinion appears from his sermon preached before the Queen. Paley is supposed to have held the same amiable doctrine ; and Newton (the author of the work on the Prophecies) is also among the supporters of it. For a full account of the arguments in favour of this opinion, derived both from reason and the express language of Scripture, see *Dr. Southwood Smith's* very interesting work, " On the Divine Government." See also *Magee on Atonement*, where the doctrine of the advocates of Universal Restoration is thus briefly, and, I believe, fairly explained :—" Beginning with the existence of an infinitely powerful, wise, and good Being, as the first and fundamental principle of rational religion, they pronounce the essence of this Being to be love, and from this infer, as a demonstrable consequence, that none of the creatures formed by such a Being will ever be made eternally miserable . . . . . Since God (they say) would act unjustly in inflicting eternal misery for temporary crimes, the sufferings of the wicked can be but remedial, and will terminate in a complete purification from moral disorder, and in their ultimate restoration to virtue and happiness."

Page 187.—" *Glistened over its silver letters.*"  The Codex Cottonianus of the New Testament is written in silver letters on a purple ground. The Codex Cottonianus of the Spetuagint version of the Old Testament is supposed to be the identical copy that belonged to Origen.

Page 188.—" *Fruit of the desert-shrub.*"—v. *Hamilton's Ægyptiaca.*

Page 191.—" *The white garment she wore, and the ring of gold on her finger.*"—See, for the custom among the early Christians of wearing white for a few days after baptism, *Ambros. de Myst.*—With respect to the ring, the Bishop of Lincoln says, in his work on Tertullian, "The natural inference from these words (*Tertull. de Pudicitiâ*) appears to be, that a ring used to be given in baptism ; but I have found no other trace of such a custom."

Page 193.—" *Pebbles of jasper.*"—v. *Clarke.*

Ib.—" *Stunted marigold,*" etc.—" Les *Mesembryanthemum nodiflorum* et *Zygophyllum coccineum*, plantes grasses des déserts, rejetées à cause de leur âcreté par les chameaux, les chèvres, et les gazelles." *M. Delile upon the plants of Egypt.*

Ib.—" *Antinoë.*"—v. *Savary* and *Quatremère.*

Page 197.—" *I have observed in my walks.*"—" Je remarquai avec une réflexion triste, qu'un animal de proie accompagne presque toujours les pas de ce joli et frêle individu."

Page 200.—" *Some denier of Christ.*"—" Those Christians who sacrificed to idols to save themselves were called by various names, *Thurificati, Sacrificati, Mittentes, Negatores,* etc.  Baronius mentions a bishop of this period (253), Marcellinus, who, yielding to the threats of the Gentiles threw incense upon the altar. v. *Arnob. contra Gent.* lib. 7.

Page 205.—"*The clear voice with which,*" etc.—The merit of the confession "Christianus sum," or "Christiana sum," was considerably enhanced by the clearness and distinctness with which it was pronounced. *Eusebius* mentions the martyr Vetius as making it λαμπροτατη φωνη.

Page 210.—"*The band round the young Christian's brow.*"—We find poisonous crowns mentioned by *Pliny*, under the designation of "coronæ ferales." *Paschalius*, too, gives the following account of these "deadly garlands," as he calls them :—"Sed mirum est tam salutare inventum humanam nequitiam reperisse, quomodo ad nefarios usus traducent. Nempe, repertæ sunt nefandæ coronæ harum, quas dixi, tam salubrium per nomen quidem et speciem imitatrices, at re et effectu ferales, atque adeo capitis, cui imponuntur, interfectrices." *De Coronis.*

# ALCIPHRON

# ALCIPHRON.

## LETTER I.

FROM ALCIPHRON AT ALEXANDRIA TO CLEON AT ATHENS.

WELL may you wonder at my flight
   From those fair Gardens, in whose bowers
Lingers whate'er of wise and bright,
Of Beauty's smile or Wisdom's light,
   Is left to grace this world of ours.
Well may my comrades, as they roam,
   On evenings sweet as this, inquire
Why I have left that happy home
   Where all is found that all desire,
   And Time hath wings that never tire ;
Where bliss, in all the countless shapes
   That Fancy's self to bliss hath given,
Comes clustering round, like road-side grapes
   That woo the traveller's lip, at even ;
Where Wisdom flings not joy away,—
As Pallas in the stream, they say,

Once flung her flute,—but smiling owns
That woman's lip can send forth tones
Worth all the music of those spheres
So many dream of, but none hears ;
Where Virtue's self puts on so well
    Her sister Pleasure's smile that, loth
From either nymph apart to dwell,
    We finish by embracing both.


Yes, such the place of bliss, I own,
From all whose charms I just have flown ;
And ev'n while thus to thee I write,
    And by the Nile's dark flood recline,
Fondly, in thought, I wing my flight
Back to those groves and gardens bright,
And often think, by this sweet light,
    How lovelily they all must shine ;
Can see that graceful temple throw
    Down the green slope its lengthened shade
While, on the marble steps below,
    There sits some fair Athenian maid,
Over some favourite volume bending ;
    And, by her side, a youthful sage
Holds back the ringlets that, descending,
    Would else o'ershadow all the page.
But hence such thoughts !—nor let me grieve
O'er scenes of joy that I but leave,
As the bird quits awhile its nest
To come again with livelier zest.

And now to tell thee—what I fear
Thou'lt gravely smile at—*why* I'm here.
Though through my life's short, sunny dream,
   I've floated without pain or care,
Like a light leaf, down pleasure's stream,
   Caught in each sparkling eddy there ;
Though never Mirth awaked a strain
That my heart echoed not again ;
Yet have I felt, when ev'n most gay,
   Sad thoughts—I knew not whence or why—
   Suddenly o'er my spirit fly,
Like clouds, that, ere we've time to say
   " How bright the sky is ! " shade the sky.
Sometimes so vague, so undefined
Were these strange darkenings of my mind—
While nought but joy around me beam'd
  So causelessly they've come and flown,
That not of life or earth they seem'd,
  But shadows from some world unknown.
More oft, however, 'twas the thought
  How soon that scene, with all its play
  Of life and gladness must decay,—
Those lips I prest, the hands I caught—
Myself,—the crowd that mirth had brought
  Around me,—swept like weeds away !

This thought it was that came to shed
  O'er rapture's hour its worst alloys ;

R

And, close as shade with sunshine, wed
　　Its sadness with my happiest joys.
Oh, but for this disheart'ning voice
　　Stealing amid our mirth to say
That all, in which we most rejoice,
　　Ere night may be the earth-worm's prey
*But* for this bitter—only this—
Full as the world is brimm'd with bliss,
And capable as feels my soul
Of draining to its dregs the whole,
I should turn earth to heav'n, and be,
If bliss made Gods, a Deity!

Thou know'st that night—the very last
That with my Garden friends I pass'd—
When the School held its feast of mirth
To celebrate our founder's birth,
And all that He in dreams but saw
When he set Pleasure on the throne
Of this bright world, and wrote her law
　　In human hearts, was felt and known—
*Not* in unreal dreams, but true,
Substantial joy as pulse e'er knew,—
By hearts and bosoms, that each felt
*Itself* the realm where Pleasure dwelt.

That night, when all our mirth was o'er,
　　The minstrels silent, and the feet
Of the young maidens heard no more—
　　So stilly was the time, so sweet,

And such a calm came o'er that scene,
Where life and revel late had been—
Lone as the quiet of some bay,
From which the sea hath ebb'd away—
That still I linger'd, lost in thought,
  Gazing upon the stars of night,
Sad and intent, as if I sought
  Some mournful secret in their light ;
And ask'd them, mid that silence, why
Man, glorious man, alone must die,
While they, less wonderful than he,
Shine on through all eternity.

That night—thou haply may'st forget
  Its loveliness—but 'twas a night
To make earth's meanest slave regret
  Leaving a world so soft and bright.
On one side, in the dark blue sky,
Lonely and radiant was the eye
Of Jove himself, while, on the other,
  'Mong stars that came out one by one,
The young moon—like the Roman mother
  Among her living jewels—shone.
" Oh that from yonder orbs," I thought,
  " Pure and eternal as they are,
There could to earth some power be brought,
Some charm, with their own essence fraught,
  To make man deathless as a star.

And open to his vast desires
 A course, as boundless and sublime
As lies before those comet-fires,
 That roam and burn throughout all time!

While thoughts like these absorb'd my mind
 That weariness which earthly bliss,
However sweet, still leaves behind,
 As if to show how earthly 'tis,
Came lulling o'er me, and I laid
 My limbs at that fair statue's base—
That miracle, which Art hath made
 Of all the choice of Nature's grace—
To which so oft I've knelt and sworn,
 That, could a living maid like her
Unto this wondering world be born,
 I would, myself, turn worshipper.

Sleep came then o'er me,—and I seem'd
 To be transported far away
To a bleak desert plain, where gleam'd
 One single, melancholy ray,
Throughout that darkness dimly shed
 From a small taper in the hand
Of one, who, pale as are the dead,
 Before me took his spectral stand,
And said, while, awfully a smile
 Came o'er the wanness of his cheek—

" Go, and, beside the sacred Nile,
    You'll find th' Eternal Life you seek."


Soon as he spoke these words, the hue
Of death upon his features grew—
Like the pale morning, when o'er night
She gains the victory—full of light ;
While the small torch he held became
A glory in his hand, whose flame
Brighten'd the desert suddenly,
    Ev'n to the far horizon's line—
Along whose level I could see
    Gardens and groves, that seem'd to shine,
As if then freshly o'er them play'd
A vernal rainbow's rich cascade.
While music was heard everywhere,
Breathing, as 'twere itself the air,
And spirits, on whose wings the hue
Of heav'n still linger'd, round me flew,
Till from all sides such splendours broke,
That with the excess of light, I woke !


Such was my dream ;—and, I confess,
    Though none of all our creedless school
Hath e'er believed, or reverenced less
    The fables of the priest-led fool,
Who tells us of a soul, a mind,
Separate and pure, within us shrined,

Which is to live—ah hope too bright !—
For ever in yon fields of light ;—
Who fondly thinks the guardian eyes
    Of Gods are on him,—as if, blest
And blooming in their own blue skies,
Th' eternal Gods were not too wise
    To let weak man disturb their rest !—
Though thinking of such creeds as thou
    And all our Garden sages think,
Yet is there something, I allow,
    In dreams like this—a sort of link
With worlds unseen, which, from the hour
    I first could lisp my thoughts till now,
Hath master'd me with spell-like power.

And who can tell, as we're combined
Of various atoms,—some refined,
Like those that scintillate and play
In the fix'd stars,—some, gross as they
That frown in clouds or sleep in clay,—
Who can be sure, but 'tis the best
    And brightest atoms of our frame,
    Those most akin to stellar flame,
That shine out thus, when we're at rest ;—
Ev'n as their kindred stars, whose light
Comes out but in the silent night.
Or is it that there lurks, indeed,
Some truth in Man's prevailing creed,

And that our Guardians, from on high,
    Come, in that pause from toil and sin,
To put the senses' curtain by,
    And on the wakeful soul look in!


Vain thought!—but yet, howe'er it be,
Dreams, more than once, have proved to me
Oracles, truer far than Oak,
Or Dove, or Tripod ever spoke.
And 'twas the words—thou'lt hear and smile—
    The words that phantom seem'd to speak—
" Go, and beside the sacred Nile
    You'll find the Eternal Life you seek,—"
That, haunting me by night, by day,
    At length, as with the unseen hand
Of Fate itself, urged me away
    From Athens to this Holy Land ;
Where, 'mong the secrets, still untaught,
    The myst'ries that, as yet, nor sun
Nor eye hath reach'd—oh blessed thought!—
    May sleep this everlasting one.


Farewell!—when to our Garden friends
Thou talk'st of the wild dream that sends
The gayest of their School thus far,
Wandering beneath Canopus' star,
Tell them that, wander where he will,
    Or, howsoe'er they now condemn

His vague and vain pursuit, he still
   Is worthy of the School and them ;—
Still, all their own,—nor e'er forgets,
   Ev'n while his heart and soul pursue
Th' Eternal Light which never sets,
   The many meteor joys that *do*,
But seeks them, hails them with delight
Where'er they meet his longing sight.
And, if his life must wane away,
Like other lives, at least the day,
The hour it lasts shall, like a fire
With incense fed, in sweets expire.

## LETTER II.

FROM THE SAME TO THE SAME.

Memphis.

'TIS true, alas—the mysteries and the lore
I came to study on this wondrous shore,
Are all forgotten in the new delights,
The strange, wild joys that fill my days and nights.
Instead of dark, dull oracles that speak
From subterranean temples, those *I* seek
Come from the breathing shrines, where Beauty lives,
And Love, her priest, the soft responses gives.
Instead of honouring Isis in those rites
At Coptos held, I hail her, when she lights
Her first young crescent on the holy stream—
When wandering youths and maidens watch her beam
And number o'er the nights she hath to run,
Ere she again embrace her bridegroom sun.
While o'er some mystic leaf, that dimly lends
A clue into past times, the student bends,
And by its glimmering guidance learns to tread
Back through the shadowy knowledge of the dead,—

The only skill, alas, *I* yet can claim
Lies in deciphering some new loved-one's name—
Some gentle missive, hinting time and place,
In language, soft as Memphian reed can trace.

And where, oh where's the heart that could withstand
Th' unnumbered witcheries of this sun-born land,
Where first young Pleasure's banner was unfurl'd,
And Love hath temples ancient as the world!
Where mystery, like the veil by Beauty worn,
Hides but to heighten, shades but to adorn;
And that luxurious melancholy, born
Of passion and of genius, sheds a gloom
Making joy holy;—where the bower and tomb
Stand side by side, and Pleasure learns from Death
The instant value of each moment's breath.
Couldst thou but see how like a poet's dream
This lovely land now looks!—the glorious stream,
That late, between its banks, was seen to glide
'Mong shrines and marble cities, on each side
Glittering like jewels strung along a chain,
Hath now sent forth its waters, and o'er plain
And valley, like a giant from his bed
Rising with outstretch'd limbs, hath grandly spread.
While far as sight can reach, beneath as clear
And blue a heav'n as ever bless'd our sphere,
Gardens, and pillar'd streets, and porphyry domes,
And high-built temples, fit to be the homes
Of mighty Gods, and pyramids, whose hour
Outlasts all time, above the waters tower!

Then, too, the scenes of pomp and joy, that make
One theatre of this vast, peopled lake,
Where all that Love, Religion, Commerce gives
Of life and motion, ever moves and lives.
Here, up the steps of temples from the wave
Ascending, in procession slow and grave,
Priests in white garments go, with sacred wands
And silver cymbals gleaming in their hands ;
While there, rich barks—fresh from those sunny tracts
Far off, beyond the sounding cataracts—
Glide, with their precious lading to the sea :
Plumes of bright birds, rhinoceros ivory,
Gems from the isle of Meroe, and those grains
Of gold, wash'd down by Abyssinian rains.
Here, where the waters wind into a bay
Shadowy and cool, some pilgrims, on their way
To Sais or Bubastus, among beds
Of lotus flowers, that close above their heads,
Push their light barks, and there, as in a bower,
Sing, talk, or sleep away the sultry hour—
Oft dipping in the Nile, when faint with heat,
That leaf, from which its waters drink most sweet.
While haply, not far off, beneath a bank
Of blossoming acacias, many a prank
Is played in the cool current by a train
Of laughing nymphs, lovely as she,* whose chain
Around two conquerors of the world was cast
But, for a third too feeble, broke at last.

* Cleopatra.

For oh, believe not them, who dare to brand,
As poor in charms, the women of this land.
Though darken'd by that sun, whose spirit flows
Through every vein, and tinges as it goes,
'Tis but th' embrowning of the fruit that tells
How rich within the soul of ripeness dwells,—
The hue their own dark sanctuaries wear,
Announcing heav'n in half-caught glimpses there.
And never yet did tell-tale looks set free
The secret of young hearts more tenderly.
Such eyes!—long, shadowy, with that languid fall
Of the fringed lids, which may be seen in all
Who live beneath the sun's too ardent rays—
Lending such looks as, on their marriage days,
Young maids cast down before a bridegroom's gaze!
Then for their grace—mark but the nymph-like shapes
Of the young village girls, when carrying grapes
From green Anthylla, or light urns of flowers—
Not our own Sculpture, in her happiest hours,
E'er imaged forth, even at the touch of him *
Whose touch was life, more luxury of limb!
Then, canst thou wonder if, mid scenes like these,
I should forget all graver mysteries,
All lore but Love's, all secrets but that best
In heav'n or earth, the art of being blest?

Yet are there times,—though brief, I own, their stay,
Like summer-clouds that shine themselves away,—

* Apelles.

Moments of gloom, when ev'n these pleasures pall
Upon my sadd'ning heart, and I recall
That Garden dream—that promise of a power,
Oh were there such!—to lengthen out life's hour
On, on, as through a vista, far away
Opening before us into endless day!
And chiefly o'er my spirit did this thought
Come on that evening—bright as ever brought
Light's golden farewell to the world—when first
The eternal pyramids of Memphis burst
Awfully on my sight—standing sublime
'Twixt earth and heav'n, the watch-towers of Time,
From whose lone summit, when his reign hath past
From earth for ever, he will look his last!

There hung a calm and solemn sunshine round
Those mighty monuments, a hushing sound
In the still air that circled them, which stole
Like music of past times into my soul.
I thought what myriads of the wise and brave
And beautiful had sunk into the grave,
Since earth first saw these wonders—and I said,
"Are things eternal only for the Dead?
Is there for Man no hope—but this, which dooms
His only lasting trophies to be tombs!
But *'tis* not so—earth, heaven, all nature shows
He *may* become immortal,—*may* unclose
The wings within him rapt, and proudly rise
Redeem'd from earth, a creature of the skies!

And who can say, among the written spells
From Hermes' hand, that, in these shrines and cells
Have, from the Flood, lay hid, there may not be
Some secret clue to immortality,
Some amulet, whose spell can keep life's fire
Awake within us, never to expire!
'Tis known that, on the Emerald Table,* hid
For ages in yon loftiest pyramid,
The Thrice-Great † did himself, engrave, of old,
The chymic mystery that gives endless gold.
And why may not this mightier secret dwell
Within the same dark chambers? who can tell
But that those kings, who, by the written skill
Of th' Emerald Table, call'd forth gold at will,
And quarries upon quarries heap'd and hurl'd,
To build them domes that might outstand the world –
Who knows but that the heavenlier art, which shares
The life of Gods with man, was also theirs—
That they themselves, triumphant o'er the power
Of fate and death, are living at this hour;
And these, the giant homes they still possess,
Not tombs, but everlasting palaces,
Within whose depths, hid from the world above,
Even now they wander, with the few they love,
Through subterranean gardens, by a light
Unknown on earth, which hath nor dawn nor night!
Else, why those deathless structures? why the grand
And hidden halls, that undermine this land?

* See Notes on the Epicurean. † The Hermes Trismegistus.

Why else hath none of earth o'er dared to go
Through the dark windings of that realm below,
Nor aught from heav'n itself, except the God
Of Silence, through those endless labyrinths trod ? "

Thus did I dream—wild, wandering dreams, I own,
But such as haunt me ever, if alone,
Or in that pause 'twixt joy and joy I be,
Like a ship hush'd between two waves at sea.
Then do these spirit whisperings, like the sound
Of the Dark Future, come appalling round ;
Nor can I break the trance that holds me then,
Till high o'er Pleasure's surge I mount again !

Ev'n now for new adventure, new delight,
My heart is on the wing—this very night,
The Temple on that island, half-way o'er
From Memphis' gardens to the eastern shore,
Sends up its annual rite * to her, whose beams
Bring the sweet time of night-flowers and dreams ;
The nymph, who dips her urn in silent lakes,
And turns to silvery dew each drop it takes ;—
Oh, not our Dian of the North, who chains
In vestal ice the current of young veins,
But she who haunts the gay Bubastian † grove,
And owns she sees, from her bright heav'n above,
Nothing on earth to match that heav'n but Love.

* The great Festival of the Moon.
† Bubastis, or Isis, was the Diana of the Egyptian mythology.

Thinks then, what bliss will be abroad to-night !
Beside, that host of nymphs, who meet the sight
Day after day, familiar as the sun,
Coy buds of beauty, yet unbreathed upon,
And all the hidden loveliness, that lies,
Shut up, as are the beams of sleeping eyes,
Within these twilight shrines—to-night will be,
Soon as the Moon's white bark in heav'n we see,
Let loose, like birds, for this festivity !

And mark, 'tis nigh ; already the sun bids
His evening farewell to the Pyramids,
As he hath done, age after age, till they
Alone on earth seem ancient as his ray ;
While their great shadows, stretching from the light
Look like the first colossal steps of Night,
Stretching across the valley, to invade
The distant hills of porphyry with their shade.
Around, as signals of the setting beam,
Gay, gilded flags on every house-top gleam :
While, hark !—from all the temples a rich swell
Of music to the Moon—farewell—farewell !

## LETTER III.

FROM THE SAME TO THE SAME.

Memphis.

THERE is some star—or it may be
   That moon we saw so near last night—
Which comes athwart my destiny
   For ever, with misleading light.
If for a moment, pure and wise
   And calm I feel, there quick doth fall
A spark from some disturbing eyes,
That through my heart, soul, being flies,
   And makes a wildfire of it all.
I've seen—oh, Cleon, that this earth
Should e'er have giv'n such beauty birth!—
That man—but, hold—hear all that pass'd
Since yester-night, from first to last.

The rising of the Moon, calm, slow,
   And beautiful, as if she came
Fresh from the Elysian bowers below,
   Was, with a loud and sweet acclaim

S

Welcomed from every breezy height,
Where crowds stood waiting for her light.
And well might they who view'd the scene
    Then lit up all around them, say,
That never yet had Nature been
    Caught sleeping in a lovelier ray,
Or rivall'd her own noon-tide face,
With purer show of moonlight grace.

Memphis,—still grand, though not the same
    Unrivall'd Memphis, that could seize
From ancient Thebes the crown of Fame,
    And wear it bright through centuries—
Now, in the moonshine, that came down
    Like a last smile upon that crown,
Memphis, still grand, among her lakes,
    Her pyramids and shrines of fire,
Rose, like a vision, that half breaks
On one who, dreaming still, awakes
    To music from some midnight choir :
While to the west, where gradual sinks
    In the red sands, from Libya roll'd,
Some mighty column, or fair sphynx,
    That stood in kingly courts, of old,
It seem'd as, mid the pomps that shone
Thus gaily round him, Time look'd on,
Waiting till all, now bright and blest,
Should fall beneath him like the rest.

No sooner had the setting sun
Proclaim'd the festal rite begun,
And, mid their idol's fullest beams,
　The Egyptian world was all afloat,
Than I, who live upon these streams,
　Like a young Nile-bird, turn'd my boat
To the fair island, on whose shores,
Through leafy palms and sycamores,
Already shone the moving lights
Of pilgrims, hastening to the rites.
While, far around, like ruby sparks
Upon the water, lighted barks,
Of every form and kind—from those
　That down Syene's cataract shoots,
To the grand, gilded barge, that rows
　To sound of tambours and of flutes,
And wears at night, in words of flame,
On the rich prow, its master's name ;—
All were alive and made this sea
　Of cities busy as a hill
Of summer ants, caught suddenly
　In the overflowing of a rill.

Landed upon the isle, I soon
　Through marble alleys and small groves
　Of that mysterious palm she loves,
Reach'd the fair Temple of the Moon ;
And there—as slowly through the last
Dim-lighted vestibule I pass'd—

Between the porphyry pillars, twined
   With palm and ivy, I could see
A band of youthful maidens wind,
   In measured walk, half dancingly,
Round a small shrine, on which was placed
   That bird,* whose plumes of black and white
Wear in their hue, by Nature traced,
   A type of the moon's shadow'd light.

In drapery, like woven snow,
These nymphs were clad, and each, below
The rounded bosom, loosely wore
   A dark blue zone, or bandelet,
With little silver stars all o'er,
   As are the skies at midnight set.
While in their tresses, braided through,
   Sparkled the flower of Egypt's lakes,
The silvery lotus, in whose hue
   As much delight the young Moon takes,
As doth the Day-God to behold
   The lofty bean-flower's buds of gold.
And, as they gracefully went round
   The worshipp'd bird, some to the beat
Of castanets, some to the sound
   Of the shrill sistrum timed their feet ;
While others, at each step they took,
A tinkling chain of silver shook.

* The Ibis.

They seem'd all fair—but there was one
On whom the light had not yet shone,
Or shone but partly—so downcast
She held her brow, as slow she pass'd.
And yet to me, there seem'd to dwell
 A charm about that unseen face—
A something, in the shade that fell
 Over that brow's imagined grace,
Which took me more than all the best
Outshining beauties of the rest.
And her alone my eyes could see,
Enchain'd by this sweet mystery ;
And her alone I watch'd as round
She glided o'er that marble ground,
Stirring not more th' unconscious air
Than if a Spirit had moved there.
Till suddenly, wide open flew
The Temple's folding gates, and threw
A splendour from within, a flood
Of glory where these maidens stood.
While, with that light,—as if the same
Rich source gave birth to both,—there came
A swell of harmony, as grand
As e'er was born of voice and hand,
Filling the gorgeous aisles around
With that mix'd burst of light and sound.

Then was it, by the flash that blazed
 Full o'er her features—oh 'twas then.

As startingly her eyes she raised,
  But quick let fall their lids again,
I saw—not Psyche's self, when first
  Upon the threshold of the skies
She paused, while heaven's glory burst
  Newly upon her downcast eyes,
Could look more beautiful or blush
  With holier shame than did this maid,
Whom now I saw, in all that gush
  Of splendour from the aisles, display'd.
Never—tho' well thou know'st how much
  I've felt the sway of Beauty's star—
Never did her bright influence touch
  My soul into its depths so far ;
And had that vision linger'd there
  One minute more, I should have flown,
Forgetful *who* I was and where,
  And, at her feet in worship thrown,
  Proffer'd my soul through life her own.

But, scarcely had that burst of light
And music broke on ear and sight,
Than up the aisle the bird took wing,
  As if on heavenly mission sent,
While after him, with graceful spring,
  Like some unearthly creatures, meant
  To live in that mix'd element
  Of light and song, the young maids went

And she, who in my heart had thrown
A spark to burn for life, was flown.

In vain I tried to follow ;—bands
    Of reverend chanters fill'd the aisle :
Where'er I sought to pass, their wands
    Motion'd me back, while many a file
Of sacred nymphs—but ah, not they
Whom my eyes look'd for—throng'd the way.
Perplex'd, impatient, mid this crowd
Of faces, lights—the o'erwhelming cloud
Of incense round me, and my blood
Full of its new-born fire,—I stood,
Nor moved, nor breathed, but when I caught
    A glimpse of some blue, spangled zone,
Or wreath of lotus, which, I thought,
    Like those she wore at distance shone.

But no, 'twas vain—hour after hour,
    Till my heart's throbbing turn'd to pain,
And my strain'd eyesight lost its power,
    I sought her thus, but all in vain.
At length, hot—wilder'd,—in despair,
I rush'd into the cool night-air,
And hurrying (though with many a look
Back to the busy Temple) took
My way along the moonlight shore,
And sprung into my boat once more.

There is a Lake, that to the north
Of Memphis stretches grandly forth,
Upon whose silent shore the Dead
   Have a proud City of their own,*
With shrines and pyramids o'erspread,—
Where many an ancient kingly head
   Slumbers, immortalized in stone ;
And where, through marble grots beneath,
   The lifeless, ranged like sacred things,
Nor wanting aught of life but breath,
   Lie in their painted coverings,
And on each new successive race,
   That visit their dim haunts below,
Look with the same unwithering face,
They wore three thousand years ago.
There, Silence, thoughtful God, who loves
The neighbourhood of death, in groves
Of asphodel lies hid, and weaves
His hushing spell among the leaves,—
Nor ever noise disturbs the air,
   Save the low, humming, mournful sound
Of priests, within their shrines, at prayer
   For the fresh Dead entomb'd around.

'Twas toward this place of death—in mood
   Made up of thoughts, half bright, half dark—
I now across the shining flood
   Unconscious turn'd my light-wing'd bark.

* Necropolis, or the City of the Dead, to the south of Memphis.

The form of that young maid, in all
   Its beauty, was before me still ;
And oft I thought, if thus to call
   Her image to my mind at will,
If but the memory of that one
Bright looks of hers, for ever gone,
Was to my heart worth all the rest
Of woman-kind, beheld, possest—
What would it be, if wholly mine,
Within these arms, as in a shrine,
Hallow'd by Love, I saw her shine,
An idol worshipp'd by the light
Of her own beauties, day and night—
If 'twas a blessing but to see
And lose again, what would *this* be ?

In thoughts like these—but often crost
By darker threads—my mind was lost,
Till, near that City of the Dead,
Waked from my trance, I saw o'erhead—
As if by some enchanter bid
   Suddenly from the wave to rise—
Pyramid over pyramid
   Tower in succession to the skies ;
While one, aspiring, as if soon
   'Twould touch the heavens, rose o'er all ;
And, on its summit, the white moon
   Rested, as on a pedestal !

The silence of the lonely tombs
   And temples round, where nought was heard
But the high palm-tree's tufted plumes,
   Shaken, at times, by breeze or bird,
Form'd a deep contrast to the scene
Of revel, where I late had been ;
To those gay sounds, that still came o'er,
Faintly, from many a distant shore,
And th' unnumber'd lights, that shone
Far o'er the flood, from Memphis on
To the Moon's Isle and Babylon.

My oars were lifted, and my boat
   Lay rock'd upon the rippling stream ;
While my vague thoughts, alike afloat,
   Drifted through many an idle dream,
With all of which, wild and unfix'd
As was their aim, that vision mix'd,
That bright nymph of the Temple—now,
With the same innocence of brow
She wore within the lighted fane,—
Now kindling, through each pulse and vein
With passion of such deep-felt fire
As Gods might glory to inspire ;—
And now—oh Darkness of the tomb,
   That must eclipse ev'n light like hers !
Cold, dead, and blackening mid the gloom
   Of those eternal sepulchres.

Scarce had I turn'd my eyes away
   From that dark death-place, at the thought,
When by the sound of dashing spray
   From a light oar my ear was caught,
While past me, through the moonlight, sail'd
   A little gilded bark, that bore
Two female figures, closely veil'd
   And mantled, towards that funeral shore.
They landed—and the boat again
Put off across the watery plain.

Shall I confess—to *thee* I may—
   That never yet hath come the chance
Of a new music, a new ray
   From woman's voice, from woman's glance,
Which—let it find me how it might,
   In joy or grief—I did not bless,
And wander after, as a light
   Leading to undreamt happiness.
And chiefly now, when hopes so vain
Were stirring in my heart and brain,
When Fancy had allured my soul
   Into a chase, as vague and far
As would be his, who fix'd his goal
   In the horizon, or some star—
*Any* bewilderment, that brought
More near to earth my high-flown thought—
The faintest glimpse of joy, less pure,
Less high and heavenly, but more sure,

Came welcome—and was then to me
What the first flowery isle must be
To vagrant birds, blown out to sea.

Quick to the shore I urged my bark,
    And, by the bursts of moonlight shed,
Between the lofty tombs, could mark
    Those figures, as with hasty tread
They glided on—till in the shade
    Of a small pyramid, which through
Some boughs of palm its peak display'd,
    They vanish'd instant from my view.
I hurried to the spot—no trace
Of life was in that lonely place ;
    And, had the creed I hold by taught
Of other worlds, I might have thought
Some mocking spirits had from thence
Come in this guise to cheat my sense.

At length, exploring darkly round
The Pyramid's smooth sides, I found
An iron portal,—opening high
    'Twixt peak and base—and, with a pray'r
To the bliss-loving moon, whose eye
    Alone beheld me, sprung in there.
Downward the narrow stairway led
Through many a duct obscure and dread,
    A labyrinth for mystery made,

With wanderings onward, backward, round,
And gathering still, where'er it wound,
　　But deeper density of shade.

Scarce had I ask'd myself, "Can aught
　　That man delights in sojourn here?"—
When, suddenly, far off, I caught
　　A glimpse of light, remote, but clear,—
Whose welcome glimmer seem'd to pour
　　From some alcove or cell, that ended
The long, steep, marble corridor,
　　Through which I now, all hope, descended.
Never did Spartan to his bride
With warier foot at midnight glide.
It seem'd as echo's self were dead
In this dark place, so mute my tread.
Reaching, at length, that light, I saw—
　　Oh listen to the scene, now raised
Before my eyes—then guess the awe,
　　The still, rapt awe with which I gazed.
'Twas a small chapel, lined around
With the fair, spangling marble, found
In many a ruin'd shrine that stands
Half seen above the Libyan sands.
The walls were richly sculptured o'er,
And character'd with that dark lore
Of times before the Flood, whose key
Was lost in th' 'Universal Sea.'—

While on the roof was pictured bright
   The Theban beetle, as he shines,
   When the Nile's mighty flow declines,
And forth the creature springs to light,
With life regenerate in his wings :—
Emblem of vain imaginings !
Of a new world, when this is gone,
In which the spirit still lives on !

Direct beneath this type, relined
   On a black granite altar, lay
A female form, in crystal shrined,
   And looking fresh as if the ray
   Of soul had fled but yesterday.
While in relief, of silvery hue,
   Graved on the altar's front were seen
A branch of lotus, brok'n in two,
   As that fair creature's life had been,
And a small bird that from its spray
Was winging, like her soul, away.

But brief the glimpse I now could spare
   To the wild, mystic wonders round ;
For there was yet *one* wonder there,
   That held me as by witchery bound.
The lamp, that through the chamber shed
Its vivid beam, was at the head
Of her who on that altar slept ;
   And near it stood. when first I came.—

Bending her brow, as if she kept
   Sad watch upon its silent flame—
A female form, as yet so placed
   Between the lamp's strong glow and me,
That I but saw, in outline traced,
   The shadow of her symmetry.
Yet did my heart—I scarce knew why—
Ev'n at that shadow'd shape beat high.
Nor long was it, ere full in sight
The figure turn'd ; and, by the light
That touch'd her features, as she bent
Over the crystal monument,
I saw 'twas she—the same—the same—
   That lately stood before me—bright'ning
The holy spot, where she but came
   And went again, like summer lightning!

Upon the crystal, o'er the breast
Of her who took that silent rest,
There was a cross of silver lying—
   Another type of that blest home,
Which hope, and pride, and fear of dying
   Build for us in a world to come :—
This silver cross the maiden raised
To her pure lips :—then, having gazed
Some minutes on that tranquil face,
Sieeping in all death's mournful grace,
Upward she turn'd her brow serene,
   As if, intent on heaven, those eyes

Saw then nor roof nor cloud between
 Their own pure orbits and the skies ;
And, though her lips no motion made,
 And that fix'd look was all her speech,
I saw that the rapt spirit pray'd
 Deeper within than words could reach.
Strange pow'r of Innocence, to turn
 To its own hue whate'er comes near ;
And make even vagrant Passion burn
 With purer warmth within its sphere !
She who, but one short hour before,
Had come, like sudden wild-fire o'er
My heart and brain,—whom gladly, ever
 From that bright Temple, in the face
Of those proud ministers of heaven,
 I would have borne, in wild embrace,
And risk'd all punishment, divine
And human, but to make her mine ;—
That maid was now before me, thrown
 By fate itself into my arms—
There standing, beautiful, alone,
 With nought to guard her but her charms.
Yet did I—oh did ev'n a breath
 From my parch'd lips, too parch'd to move
Disturb a scene where thus, beneath
 Earth's silent covering, Youth and Death
 Held converse through undying love ?
No—smile and taunt me as thou wilt—
 Though but to gaze thus was delight,

Yet seem'd it like a wrong, a guilt,
　To win by stealth so pure a sight :
And rather than a look profane
　Should then have met those thoughtful eyes,
Or voice, or whisper broke the chain
　That link'd her spirit with the skies,
I would have gladly, in that place,
From which I watch'd her heavenward face,
Let my heart break, without one beat
That could disturb a prayer so sweet.

Gently, as if on every tread,
　My life, my more than life depended,
Back through the corridor that led
　To this blest scene I now ascended,
And with slow seeking, and some pain,
And many a winding tried in vain,
Emerged to upper air again.

The sun had freshly ris'n, and down
　The marble hills of Araby,
Scatter'd, as from a conqueror's crown,
　His beams into that living sea.
There seem'd a glory in his light,
　Newly put on—as if for pride
Of the high homage paid this night
　To his own Isis, his young bride,
Now fading feminine away
In her proud Lord's superior ray.

T

My mind's first impulse was to fly
  At once from this entangling net—
New scenes to range, new loves to try,
Or, in mirth, wine, and luxury
  Of every sense, that night forget.
But vain the effort—spell-bound still,
I linger'd, without power or will
  To turn my eyes from that dark door
Which now enclosed her 'mong the dead ;
  Oft fancying, through the boughs, that o'er
  The sunny pile their flickering shed,
'Twas her light form again I saw
  Starting to earth—still pure and bright,
But wakening, as I hoped, less awe,
  Thus seen by morning's natural light,
  Than in that strange, dim cell at night.

But no, alas,—she ne'er return'd :
  Nor yet—tho' still I watch—nor yet,
Though the red sun for hours hath burn'd,
  And now, in his mid course, hath met
The peak of that eternal pile
  He pauses still at noon to bless,
Standing beneath his downward smile,
  Like a great Spirit, shadowless !—
Nor yet she comes—while here, alone,
  Saunt'ring through this death-peopled place
Where no heart beats except my own,
Or 'neath a palm-tree's shelter thrown,
  By turns I watch, and rest, and trace

These lines, that are to waft to thee
My last night's wondrous history.

Dost thou remember, in that Isle
   Of our own Sea, where thou and I
Linger'd so long, so happy a while,
   Till all the summer flowers went by—
How gay it was, when sunset brought
   To the cool Well our favourite maids—
Some we had won, and some we sought—
   To dance within the fragrant shades,
And, till the stars went down, attune
Their Fountain Hymns * to the young moon?

That time, too—oh, 'tis like a dream—
   When from Scamander's holy tide
I sprung, as Genius of the Stream,
   And bore away that blooming bride,
Who thither came, to yield her charms
   (As Phrygian maids are wont, ere wed)
Into the cold Scamander's arms,
   But met, and welcomed mine, instead—
Wondering, as on my neck she fell,
How river-gods could love so well!
Who would have thought that he, who roved
   Like the first bees of summer then,
Rifling each sweet, nor ever loved
   But the free hearts, that loved again,

* These Songs of the Well, as they were called by the ancients, are
still common in the Greek isles.

Readily as the reed replies
To the least breath that round it sighs—
Is the same dreamer who, last night,
Stood awed and breathless at the sight
Of one Egyptian girl; and now
Wanders among these tombs, with brow
Pale, watchful, sad, as tho' he just,
Himself, had risen from out their dust!

Yet, so it is—and the same thirst
　For something high and pure, above
This withering world, which, from the first
　Made me drink deep of woman's love,—
As the one joy, to heav'n most near
Of all our hearts can meet with here,—
Still burns me up, still keeps awake
A fever nought but death can slake.

Farewell; whatever may befall,—
Or bright, or dark—thou'lt know it all.

## LETTER IV.

**FROM THE SAME TO THE SAME.**

WONDERS on wonders ; sights that lie
   Where never sun gave flow'ret birth ;
Bright marvels, hid from th' upper sky,
And myst'ries that are born and die
   Deep in the very heart of earth !—
All that the ancient Orpheus, led
   By courage that Love only gives,
Dared for a matchless idol, dead,
   I've seen and dared for one who lives.

Again the moon was up, and found
The echoes of my feet still round
The monuments of this lone place ;—
   Or saw me, if awhile my lid
Yielded to sleep, stretch'd at the base
   Of that now precious Pyramid,
In slumber that the gentlest stir,
The stillest, air-like step of her,

Whom ev'n in sleep I watch'd, could chase.
And then, such various forms she seem'd
To wear before me, as I dream'd !—
Now, like Neïtha, on her throne
At Saïs, all reveal'd she shone,
With that dread veil thrown off her brow,
Which mortal never raised till now ; *
Then quickly changed, methought 'twas she
    Of whom the Memphian boatman tells
Such wondrous tales—fair Rhodope,
    The subterranean nymph, that dwells
Mid sunless gems and glories hid,
The Lady of the Pyramid !

At length, from one of these short dreams
Starting—as if the subtile beams,
Then playing o'er my brow, had brought
Some sudden light into my thought—
Down for my boat-lamp to the shore,
    Where still it palely burn'd, I went ;
Resolved that night to try once more
    The mystery of this monument.

Thus arm'd, I scarce had reach'd the gate,
    When a loud screaming—like the cry
Of some wild creature to its mate—
    Came startling from the palm-grove nigh ;—

* See, for the veil of Neïtha, the inscription upon her temple as given by Plutarch, de Is. et Osir.

Or, whether haply 'twas the creak
  Of those Lethæan portals,\* said
To give us out a mournful shriek,
  When oped at midnight for the dead.
Whate'er it was, the sound came o'er
  My heart like ice, as through the door
Of the small Pyramid I went,
And down the same abrupt descent,
And through long windings, as before,
Reach'd the steep marble corridor.

Trembling I stole along—the light
  In the lone chapel still burn'd on ;
But she, for whom my soul and sight
  Look'd with a thirst so keen, was gone,—
By some invisible path had fled
Into that gloom, leaving the Dead
To its own solitary rest,
Of all lone things the loneliest.

As still the cross, which she had kist,
  Was lying on the crystal shrine,
I took it up, nor could resist
  (Though the dead eyes, I thought, met mine)
Kissing it too, while, half ashamed
Of that mute presence, I exclaim'd :

---

\* The brazen portals at Memphis, mentioned by Zoega, called the
Gates of Oblivion.

"Oh Life to Come, if in thy sphere
Love, Woman's love, our heav'n could be,
Who would not ev'n forego it here,
    To taste it there eternally?"
Hopeless, yet with unwilling pace,
Leaving the spot, I turn'd to trace
My pathway back, when, to the right,
I could perceive, by my lamp's light,
That the long corridor which, view'd
    Through distance dim, had seem'd to end
Abruptly here, still on pursued
    Its sinuous course, with snake-like bend
Mocking the eye, as down it wound
Still deeper through that dark profound.

Again, my hopes were raised, and, fast
    As the dim lamp-light would allow,
Along that new-found path I pass'd,
    Through countless turns; descending now
By narrow ducts, now, up again,
Mid columns, in whose date the chain
Of time is lost; and thence along
Cold halls, in which a sapless throng
Of Dead stood up, with glassy eye
Meeting my gaze, as I went by;
Till, lost among these winding ways,
    Coil'd round and round, like serpents' folds
I thought myself in that dim maze
    Down under Mœris' Lake. which holds

The hidden wealth of the Twelve Kings,
Safe from all human visitings.
At length, the path closed suddenly :
    And, by my lamp, whose glimmering fell
Now faint and fainter, I could see
    Nought but the mouth of a huge well,
Gaping athwart my onward track,—
A reservoir of darkness, black
As witches' cauldrons are, when fill'd
With moon-drugs in th' eclipse distill'd.
Leaning to look if foot might pass
Down through that chasm, I saw, beneath,
    As far as vision could explore,
The jetty sides all smooth as glass,
    Looking as if just varnish'd o'er
With that dark pitch the Sea of Death
    Throws out upon its slimy shore.

Doubting awhile, yet loth to leave
    Aught unexplored, the chasm I tried
With nearer search ; and could perceive
    An iron step that from the side
Stood dimly out ; while, lower still,
Another ranged, less visible,
But aptly placed, as if to aid
Th' adventurous foot, that dared the shade.
Though hardly I could deem that e'er
Weak woman's foot had ventured there.

Yet, urged along by the wild heat
That can do all things but retreat,
I placed my lamp,—which for such task
Was aptly shaped, like cap or casque
To fit the brow,—firm on my head,
 And down into the darkness went ;
Still finding for my cautious tread
 New foot-hold in that deep descent,
Which seem'd as tho' 'twould thus descend
In depth and darkness without end.
At length, this step-way ceased ; in vain
I sought some hold, that would sustain
My down-stretch'd foot—the polish'd side,
Slippery and hard, all help denied :
Till, as I bow'd my lamp around,
 To let its now faint glimmer fall
On every side, with joy I found
 Just near me, in the shining wall,
A window (which had 'scap'd my view
In that half shadow) and sprung through.

'Twas downward still, but far less rude—
 By stairs that through the live rock wound
 In narrow spiral round and round,
Whose giddy sweep my foot pursued
Till, lo, before a gate I stood,
Which oped, I saw, into the same
Deep well, from whence but now I came.
The doors were iron, yet gave way

Lightly before me, as the spray
Of a young lime-tree, that receives
Some wandering bird among its leaves.
But, soon as I had pass'd, the din,
    Th' o'erwhelming din, with which again
They clash'd their folds, and closed me in,
    Was such as seldom sky or main,
Or heaving earth, or all, when met
In angriest strife, e'er equall'd yet.
It seem'd as if the ponderous sound
    Was by a thousand echoes hurl'd
From one to th' other, through the round
    Of this great subterranean world,
Till, far as from the catacombs
Of Alexandria to the tombs
In ancient Thebes's Valley of Kings,
Rung its tremendous thunderings.

Yet could not ev'n this rude surprise,
    Which well might move far bolder men,
One instant turn my charmèd eyes
    From the blest scene that hail'd them then.
As I had rightly deem'd, the place
Where now I stood was the well's base,
The bottom of the chasm ; and bright
    Before me, through the massy bars
Of a huge gate, there came a light
    Soft, warm, and welcome, as the stars
Of his own South are to the sight

Of one, who, from his sunny home,
To the chill North had dared to roam.

And oh the scene, now opening through
   Those bars that all but sight denied!—
A long, fair alley, far as view
   Could reach away, along whose side
Went, lessening to the end, a row
   Of rich arcades, that, from between
Their glistening pillars, sent a glow
   Of countless lamps, burning unseen,
And that still air, as from a spring
Of hidden light, illumining.
While—soon as the wild echoes roused
From their deep haunts again were housed,—
I heard a strain of holy song
   Breathing from out the bright arcades
Into that silence—where, among
   The high sweet voices of young maids,
Which, like the small and heavenward spire
Of Christian temples, crown'd the choir,
I fancied, (such the fancy's sway)
   Though never yet my ear had caught
Sound from her lips—yet, in that lay
   So worthy of her looks, methought
That maiden's voice I heard, o'er all
   Most high and heavenly,—to my ear
Sounding distinctly, like the call
   Of a far spirit from its sphere.

But vain the call—that stubborn gate,
　　Like destiny, all force defied.
Anxious I look'd around—and, straight,
　　An opening to the left descried,
Which, though like hell's own mouth it seem'd,
Yet led, as by its course I deem'd,
Parallel with those lighted ways
That 'cross the alley pour'd their blaze.
Eager I stoop'd, this path to tread,
When, suddenly, the wall o'erhead
Grew with a fitful lustre bright,
Which, settling gradual on the sight
Into clear characters of light,
These words on its dark ground I read :—

　　　" You, who would try
　　　　This terrible track,
　　To live, or to die,
　　　　But ne'er to look back ;

　　　" You, who aspire
　　　　To be purified there
　　By the terrors of Fire
　　　　And Water and Air ;

　　" If danger and pain
　　　　And death you despise—
　　On—for again
　　　　Into light you may rise,—

" Rise into light
        With that Secret Divine
Now shrouded from sight
        By the Veils of the Shrine !


        " But if ———— "


                The words here dimm'd away
Till, lost in darkness, vague and dread,
    Their very silence seem'd to say
Awfuller things than words e'er said.


" Am I then in the path," I cried,
    " To the Great Mystery ?   Shall I see,
And touch,—perhaps, ev'n draw aside
Those venerable veils, which hide
    The secret of Eternity !"
This thought at once revived the zeal,
    The thirst for Egypt's hidden lore
Which I had almost ceased to feel,
    In the new dreams that won me o'er.
For now—oh happiness !—it seem'd
As if *both* hopes before me beam'd—
As if that spirit-nymph, whose tread
    I traced down hither from above,
To more than one sweet treasure led—
Lighting me to the fountain-head
    Of Knowledge by the star of Love.

Instant I enter'd—though the ray
    Of my spent lamp was near its last,—
And quick through many a channel-way,
    Ev'n ruder than the former, pass'd ;
Till, just as sunk the farewell spark,
I spied before me, through the dark,
A paly fire, that moment raised,
Which still as I approached it, blazed
With stronger light,—till, as I came
More near, I saw my pathway led
Between two hedges of live flame,—
    Trees all on fire, whose branches shed
A glow that, without noise or smoke,
    Yet strong as from a furnace, broke ;
While o'er the glaring ground between,
Where my sole, onward path was seen,
Hot iron bars, red as with ire,
    Transversely lay—such as, they tell,
Compose that trellis-work of fire.
    Through which the Doom'd look out in hell.

To linger there was to be lost—
    More and still more the burning trees
Closed o'er the path ; and as I crost—
    With tremour both in heart and knees—
Fixing my foot where'er a space
'Twixt the red bars gave resting-place,
Above me, each quick burning tree,
Tamarind, Balm of Araby,

And Egypt's Thorn combined to spread
A roof of fir above my head.
Yet safe—or with but harmless scorch—
 I trod the flaming ordeal through ;
And promptly seizing, as a torch
 To light me on to dangers new,
A fallen bough that kindling lay
 Across the path, pursued my way.

Nor went I far before the sound
 Of downward torrents struck my ear ;
And, by my torch's gleam, I found
That the dark space, which yawn'd around
 Was a wide cavern, far and near
Fill'd with dark waters, that went by
Turbid and quick, as if from high
They late had dash'd down furiously ;
Or, awfuller, had yet that doom
Before them, in the untried gloom.
No pass appear'd on either side ;
 And tho' my torch too feebly shone
To show what scowl'd beyond the tide,
 I saw but *one* way left me—on !
So, plunging in, with my right hand
 The current's rush I scarce withstood,
While, in my left, the failing brand
 Shook its last glimmer o'er the flood.
'Twas a long struggle—oft I thought,
That, in that whirl of waters caught,

I must have gone, too weak for strife,
　Down headlong, at the cataract's will—
Sad fate for one, with heart and life,
And all youth's sunshine round him still !
But, ere my torch was wholly spent,
　I saw,—outstretching from the shade
Into those waters, as if meant
　To lend the drowning struggler aid—
　A slender, double balustrade,
With snow-white steps between, ascending
　From the grim surface of the stream,
Far up as eye could reach, and ending
　In darkness there, like a lost dream.
That glimpse—for 'twas no longer—gave
　New spirit to my strength ; and now,
With both arms combating the wave,
　I rush'd on blindly, till my brow
Struck on that rail-way's lowest stair ;
When, gathering courage from despair,
I made one bold and fearful bound,
And on the step firm footing found.

But short that hope—for, as I flew
Breathlessly up, the stair-way grew
Tremulous under me, while each
Frail step, ere scarce my foot could reach
The frailer yet I next must trust,
Crumbled behind me into dust ;

Leaving me, as it crush'd beneath,
  Like shipwreck'd wretch who, in dismay,
Sees but one plank 'twixt him and death,
  And shuddering feels that one give way!
And still I upward went—with nought
  Beneath me but that depth of shade,
And the dark flood, from whence I caught
  Each sound the falling fragments made.
Was it not fearful ?—still more frail
  At every step crash'd the light stair,
While, as I mounted, ev'n the rail
  That up into that murky air
Was my sole guide, began to fail !—
When, stretching forth an anxious hand,
Just as, beneath my tottering stand,
Steps, rail-way, all, together went,
  I touch'd a massy iron ring,
That there—by what kind genius sent
I know not—in the darkness hung ;
  And grasping it, as drowners cling
To the last hold, so firm I clung,
And through the void suspended swung.

Sudden, as if that mighty ring
  Were link'd with all the winds in heaven
And, like the touching of a spring,
  My eager grasp had instant given
Loose to all blasts that ever spread
The shore or sea with wrecks and dead—

Around me, gusts, gales, whirlwinds rang
Tumultuous, and I seem'd to hang
Amidst an elemental war,
    In which wing'd tempests—of all kinds
And strengths that winter's stormy star
    Lights through the Temple of the Winds
In our own Athens—battled round,
Deafening me with chaotic sound.
Nor this the worst—for, holding still
    With hands unmov'd, though shrinking oft,
I found myself, at the wild will
    Of countless whirlwinds, caught aloft,
And round and round, with fearful swing,
Swept, like a stone-shot in a sling!
Till breathless, mazed, I had begun,—
    So ceaselessly I thus was whirled,—
To think my limbs were chained upon
    That wheel of the Infernal World,
To turn which, day and night, are blowing
    Hot, withering winds that never slumber;
And whose sad rounds, still going, going,
    Eternity alone can number!
And yet, ev'n then—while worse than Fear
    Hath ever dreamt seem'd hovering near
Had voice but ask'd me, "Is not this
    "A price too dear for aught below?"
I should have said, "For knowledge, yes—
    "But for bright, glorious Woman—no."

At last, that whirl, when all my strength
 Had nearly fled, came to an end ;
And, through that viewless void, at length
 I felt the still-grasp'd ring descend
Rapidly with me, till my feet—
Oh, ne'er was touch of land so sweet
To the long sea-worn exile—found
A resting-place on the firm ground.
At the same instant o'er me broke
 A glimmer through that gloom so chill,
Like daylight, when beneath the yoke
 Of tyrant darkness struggling still—
And by th' imperfect gleam it shed,
I saw before me a rude bed,
Where poppies, strew'd upon a heap
Of wither'd lotus, wooed to sleep.
Blessing that couch—as I would bless,
 Ay, ev'n the absent tiger's lair,
For rest in such stark weariness,—
 I crawl'd to it and sunk down there.

How long I slept, or by what means
 Was wafted thence, I cannot say ;
But, when I woke—oh the bright scenes,
 The glories that around me lay—
If ever yet a vision shone
On waking mortal, *this* was one !
But how describe it ? vain, as yet,
 While the first dazzle dims my eyes,

All vain the attempt—I must forget
  The flush, the newness, the surprise,
The vague bewilderment, that whelms,
  Ev'n now, my every sense and thought,
Ere I can paint these sunless realms,
  And their hid glories, as I ought.
While thou, if ev'n but *half* I tell,
Wilt that but *half* believe—farewell!

## LETTER V.

FROM ORCUS, HIGH PRIEST OF MEMPHIS, TO DECIUS, THE
PRÆTORIAN PREFECT.

REJOICE, my friend, rejoice :—the youthful Chief
Of that light Sect which mocks at all belief,
And, gay and godless, makes the present hour
Its only heaven, is now within our power.
Smooth, impious school !—not all the weapons aimed
At priestly creeds, since first a creed was framed,
E'er struck so deep as that sly dart they wield,
The Bacchant's pointed spear in laughing flowers
        conceal'd.
And oh, 'twere victory to this heart, as sweet
As any *thou* canst boast,—ev'n when the feet
Of thy proud war-steed wade through Christian blood,
To wrap this scoffer in Faith's blinding hood,
And bring him, tamed and prostrate, to implore
The vilest gods ev'n Egypt's saints adore.

What !—do these sages think, to *them* alone
The key of this world's happiness is known ?

That none but they, who make such proud parade
Of Pleasure's smiling favours, win the maid,
Or that Religion keeps no secret place,
No niche, in her dark fanes, for Love to grace?
Fools!—did they know how keen the zest that's given
To earthly joy, when seasoned well with heaven;
How Piety's grave mask improves the hue
Of Pleasure's laughing features, half seen through,
And how the Priest, set aptly within reach
Of two rich worlds, traffics for bliss with each,
Would they not, Decius,—thou, whom th' ancient tie
'Twixt Sword and Altar makes our best ally,—
Would they not change their creed, their craft, for
    ours?
Leave the gross daylight joys that, in their bowers,
Languish with too much sun, like o'er-blown flowers,
For the veil'd loves, the blisses undisplay'd
That slily lurk within the Temple's shade?
And, 'stead of haunting the trim Garden's school,—
Where cold Philosophy usurps a rule,
Like the pale moon's, o'er passion's heaving tide;
Where Pleasure, cramp'd and chill'd by wisdom's pride,
Counts her own pulse's regulated play,
And in dull dreams dissolves her life away,—
Be taught by *us*, quit shadows for the true,
Substantial joys we sager Priests pursue,—
Who, far too wise to theorize on bliss,
Or pleasure's substance for its shade to miss,
Preach *other* worlds, but live for only *this*:

Thanks to the well-paid Mystery round us flung,
Which, like its type, the golden cloud that hung
O'er Jupiter's love-couch its shade benign,
Round human frailty wraps a veil divine.

Still less should they presume, weak wits, that they
Alone despise the craft of us who pray ;—
Still less their creedless vanity deceive
With the fond thought, that we who pray believe.
Believe !—Apis forbid—forbid it, all
Ye monster Gods, before whose shrines we fall,—
Deities, framed in jest, as if to try
How far gross Man can vulgarize the sky ;
How far the same low fancy that combines
Into a drove of brutes yon zodiac's signs,
And turns that Heaven itself into a place
Of sainted sin and deified disgrace,
Can bring Olympus ev'n to shame more deep,
Stock it with things that earth itself holds cheap.
Fish, flesh, and fowl, the kitchen's sacred brood,
Which Egypt keeps for worship, not for food,—
All, worthy idols of a Faith that sees
In dogs, cats, owls, and apes, divinities !

Believe !—oh, Decius, thou, who hast no care
Of things divine, beyond the soldier's share,
Who takes on trust the faith for which he bleeds,
A good, fierce God to swear by, all he needs,—

Little canst thou, whose creed around thee hangs
Loose as thy summer war-cloak, guess the pangs
Of loathing and self-scorn with which a heart,
Stubborn as mine is, acts the zealot's part,—
The deep and dire disgust with which I wade
Through the foul juggling of this holy trade,—
This mud profound of mystery, where the feet,
At every step, sink deeper in deceit.
Oh ! many a time, when, mid the Temple's blaze,
O'er prostrate fools the sacred cist I raise,
Did I not keep still proudly in my mind
The power this priestcraft gives me o'er mankind,—
A lever, of more might, in skilful hand,
To move this world, than Archimede e'er plann'd,—
I should, in vengeance of the shame I feel
At my own mockery, crush the slaves that kneel
Besotted round ; and,—like that kindred breed
Of reverend, well-drest crocodiles they feed,
At famed Arsinoë,*—make my keepers bless,
With their last throb, my sharp-fang'd Holiness.

Say, *is* it to be born, that scoffers, vain
Of their own freedom from the altar's chain,
Should mock thus all that thou thy blood hast sold,
And I my truth, pride, freedom, to uphold ?
It must not be :—think'st thou that Christian sect,
Whose followers, quick as broken waves, erect

* For the trinkets with which the sacred Crocodiles were ornamented
see the Epicurean, chap. 10.

Their crests anew and swell into a tide,
That threats to sweep away our shrines of pride—
Think'st thou, with all their wondrous spells, ev'n they
Would triumph thus, had not the constant play
Of Wit's resistless archery clear'd their way ?—
That mocking spirit, worst of all the foes,
Our solemn fraud, our mystic mummery knows,
Whose wounding flash thus ever 'mong the signs
Of a fast-falling creed, prelusive shines,
Threatening such change as do the awful freaks
Of summer lightning, ere the tempest breaks.

But, to my point,—a youth of this vain school,
But one, whom Doubt itself hath failed to cool
Down to that freezing point, where Priests despair
Of any spark from th' altar catching there,—
Hath, some nights since,—it was, methinks, the night
That followed the full Moon's great annual rite,—
Through the dark, winding ducts, that downward stray
To there earth-hidden temples, track'd his way,
Just at that hour when, round the Shrine, and me,
The choir of blooming nymphs thou long'st to see,
Sing their last night-hymn in the Sanctuary.
The clangour of the marvellous Gate, that stands
At the Well's lowest depth,—which none but hands
Of new, untaught adventurers, from above,
Who know not the safe path, e'er dare to move,—
Gave signal that a foot profane was nigh :—
'Twas the Greek youth, who, by that morning's sky,

Had been observed, curiously wandering round
The mighty fanes of our sepulchral ground.

Instant, th' Initiate's Trials were prepared,—
The Fire, Air, Water ; all that Orpheus dared,
That Plato, that the bright-hair'd Samian * pass'd,
With trembling hope, to come to—*what*, at last ?
Go, ask the dupes of Myst'ry ; question him
Who, mid terrific sounds and spectres dim,
Walks at Eleusis ; ask of those, who brave
The dazzling miracles of Mithra's Cave,
With its seven starry gates ; ask all who keep
Those terrible night-myst'ries where they weep
And howl sad dirges to the answering breeze,
O'er their dead Gods, their mortal Deities,—
Amphibious, hybrid things, that died as men,
Drown'd, hang'd, impaled, to rise, as gods, again ;—
Ask *them*, what mighty secret lurks below
This sev'n-fold mystery—can they tell thee ? No ;
Gravely they keep that only secret, well
And fairly kept, that they have none to tell ;
And, duped themselves, console their humble pride
By duping thenceforth all mankind beside.

And such th' advance in fraud since Orpheus' time,—
That earliest master of our craft sublime,—
So many minor Mysteries, imps of fraud,
From the great Orphic Egg have wing'd abroad,

* Pythagoras.

That, still t' uphold our Temple's ancient boast,
And seem most holy, we must cheat the most ;
Work the best miracles, wrap nonsense round
In pomp and darkness, till it seems profound ;
Play on the hopes, the terrors of mankind,
With changeful skill ; and make the human mind
Like our own sanctuary, where no ray,
But by the Priest's permission, wins its way,—
Where, through the gloom as wave our wizard rods,
Monsters, at will, are conjured into Gods ;
While Reason, like a grave-faced mummy, stands,
With her arms swathed in hieroglyphic bands.

But chiefly in the skill with which we use
Man's wildest passions for Religion's views,
Yoking them to her car like fiery steeds,
Lies the main art in which our craft succeeds.
And oh be blest, ye men of yore, whose toil
Hath, for our use, scoop'd out of Egypt's soil
This hidden Paradise, this mine of fanes,
Gardens, and palaces, where Pleasure reigns
In a rich, sunless empire of her own,
With all earth's luxuries lighting up her throne ;—
A realm for mystery made, which undermines
The Nile itself and, 'neath the Twelve Great Shrines
That keep Initiation's holy rite,
Spreads its long labyrinths of unearthly light,
A light that knows no change,—its brooks that run
Too deep for day, its gardens without sun,

Where soul and sense, by turns, are charm'd, surprised,
And all that bard or prophet e'er devised
For man's Elysium, priests have realized.


Here, at this moment,—all his trials past,
And heart and nerve unshrinking to the last,—
The young Initiate roves,—as yet left free
To wander through this realm of mystery,
Feeding on such illusions as prepare
The soul, like mist o'er waterfalls, to wear
All shapes and hues, at Fancy's varying will,
Through every shifting aspect, vapour still ;—
Vague glimpses of the Future, vistas shown,
By scenic skill, into that world unknown,
Which saints and sinners claim alike their own ;
And all those other witching, wildering arts,
Illusions, terrors, that make human hearts,
Ay, ev'n the wisest and the hardiest, quail
To *any* goblin throned behind a veil.


Yes,—such the spells shall haunt his eye, his ear,
Mix with his night-dreams, form his atmosphere ;
Till, if our Sage be not tamed down, at length,
His wit, his wisdom, shorn of all their strength,
Like Phrygian priests, in honour of the shrine,—
If he become not absolutely mine,
Body and soul, and, like the tame decoy
Which wary hunters of wild doves employ,

Draw converts also, lure his brother wits
To the dark cage where his own spirit flits,
And give us, if not saints, good hypocrites,—
If I effect not this, then be it said
The ancient spirit of our craft hath fled,
Gone with that serpent-god the Cross hath chased
To hiss its soul out in the Theban waste.

THE END.